Praise for Catherine Mann

"Catherine Mann's military romances launch you into a world chock-full of simmering passion and heart-pounding action. Don't miss 'em!"

—*USA Today* bestselling author Merline Lovelace

"Exhilarating romantic suspense."

—*The Best Reviews*

"A great read."

—*Booklist*

"Terrific romantic suspense that never slows down . . . An action-packed story line."

—*Midwest Book Review*

"As gripping in its suspense as it is touching in ~~its~~ emotional pull."

—*Romance Junkies*

HOTSHOT

CATHERINE MANN

BERKLEY SENSATION, NEW YORK

THE BERKLEY PUBLISHING GROUP
Published by the Penguin Group
Penguin Group (USA) Inc.
375 Hudson Street, New York, New York 10014, USA
Penguin Group (Canada), 90 Eglinton Avenue East, Suite 700, Toronto, Ontario M4P 2Y3, Canada
(a division of Pearson Penguin Canada Inc.)
Penguin Books Ltd., 80 Strand, London WC2R 0RL, England
Penguin Group Ireland, 25 St. Stephen's Green, Dublin 2, Ireland (a division of Penguin Books Ltd.)
Penguin Group (Australia), 250 Camberwell Road, Camberwell, Victoria 3124, Australia
(a division of Pearson Australia Group Pty. Ltd.)
Penguin Books India Pvt. Ltd., 11 Community Centre, Panchsheel Park, New Delhi—110 017, India
Penguin Group (NZ), 67 Apollo Drive, Rosedale, North Shore 0632, New Zealand
(a division of Pearson New Zealand Ltd.)
Penguin Books (South Africa) (Pty.) Ltd., 24 Sturdee Avenue, Rosebank, Johannesburg 2196, South Africa

Penguin Books Ltd., Registered Offices: 80 Strand, London WC2R 0RL, England

This is a work of fiction. Names, characters, places, and incidents either are the product of the author's imagination or are used fictitiously, and any resemblance to actual persons, living or dead, business establishments, events, or locales is entirely coincidental. The publisher does not have any control over and does not assume any responsibility for author or third-party websites or their content.

HOTSHOT

A Berkley Sensation Book / published by arrangement with the author

PRINTING HISTORY
Berkley Sensation mass-market edition / May 2009

ISBN: 978-0-425-22833-3

BERKLEY® SENSATION
Berkley Sensation Books are published by The Berkley Publishing Group,
a division of Penguin Group (USA) Inc.,
375 Hudson Street, New York, New York 10014.
BERKLEY® SENSATION and the "B" design are trademarks of Penguin Group (USA) Inc.

PRINTED IN THE UNITED STATES OF AMERICA

10 9 8 7 6 5 4 3 2 1

Much love to my children Brice, Haley, Robbie, and Maggie. You have blessed my life with your gap-toothed smiles and boundless love.

ACKNOWLEDGMENTS

Parenthood brings untold joys—and fears. It seems every generation vows times are tougher for youths. Without question, I believe teens today face greater challenges, temptations, and dangers than I could have ever imagined during my high school tenure. Now as a mother of four, I spend my fair share of hours worrying, the worst nightmare scenarios expanding in my overactive writer's imagination. Granted, my kids haven't given me much grief so far. (Not that we parents need an excuse to worry!) However, in the darkest moments of concern I feel a kindred motherhood connection to those struggling to keep their children safe. From that, this book was born, along with the hope that the next generation will find the world a safer place for their kids.

Many thanks to all who helped me in the telling of this story: my genius editor, Wendy McCurdy; my savvy agent, Barbara Collins Rosenberg; critique mavens, Joanne Rock and Stephanie Newton; medical fact-checker extraordinaire, Karen Tucker, R.N.; my law-enforcement honorary son, Jasen Wells; motorcycle experts, Dianna Love and her husband, Karl Snell; and as always, a special thanks to my own flyboy hero and the love of my life, Rob.

ONE

Major Vince "Vapor" Deluca didn't need to ask if there were Harleys in heaven. For him, hogs and planes both transported him from this world to brush the edge of paradise.

Not to mention both had saved his hell-bound ass on more than one occasion. And right now, he needed some of that heavenly salvation—on wings rather than wheels—in a serious way if he expected to pull off this potentially explosive mission.

Flying his AC-130 gunship at twenty-five thousand feet, Vince peered into a monitor, watching the increasingly restless crowd below in the rural Honduran town. With the help of his twelve crew members, he monitored citizens pouring out of the hills to cast their votes in the special election, an election that could turn volatile in a heartbeat, the politics of this country precarious with warlords determined to stop the process. Local government officials had requested U.S. help with crowd control, using any means possible to keep the peace.

Vince cranked the yoke into a tight turn, flying over the voting place, a white wooden church. The sensors bristled along the side of the aircraft to scan the snaking crowd lining up. His sensors were so good the guys in back were able to study faces, gestures, and even guns worn like fashion accessories.

He knew too well how mob mentality could unleash an atomic *Lord of the Flies* destructive force.

His fists clenched around the yoke. "Okay, crew, eyeballs out. Let's score one for democracy."

"Vapor," the fire control officer, David "Ice" Berg, droned from the back, as cool and calm as his last name implied, "take a look at this dude in the camera. I think he's the ringleader."

Vince checked the screen, and yeah, that guy had whacko written all over him. "He seems like a hard-core cheerleader yelling and flapping his arms around."

Copilot Jimmy Gage thumbed his interphone. "Those gymnastics of his are working." Jimmy's fists clenched and unclenched as if ready to break up the brawl mano a mano. He'd earned his call sign Hotwire honestly. Vince's best bud, they'd often been dubbed in bars the Hotwire and the Hotshot. "The crowd's getting riled up down there. Hey, Berg, do things look any better from your bird's-eye view?"

"Give me a *C* for chaos," Berg answered, dry as ever.

Vince worked his combat boots over the rudders while keeping his eyes locked on the screen scrolling an up-close look at the ground. "Roger that. All Cheerleader Barbie needs is a ponytail and a pair of pom-poms instead of that big-ass gun slung over his shoulder." A riot seemed increasingly inevitable, which was not surprising, since human intel had already uncovered countless attempts to terrorize voters into staying home. "Barbie definitely bears watching, especially with those ankle biters around."

He monitored the group of children playing on swings nearby while adults waited to vote. Conventional crowd-control techniques could sometimes escalate the frenzy. This mission called for something different, something new. Something right up his alley as a member of the air force's elite dark ops testing unit. In emergency situations they were called upon to pull a trick or two from their developmental arsenal and pray it worked as advertised, since failure could spark an international incident or, worse yet, harm a kid.

Today, he and his dark ops crew were flying the latest brainchild of the nonlethal weapons crowd. A flat microwave antenna protruded from the side of the lumbering aircraft. The ADS—Active Denial System—had the power to scorch people without leaving marks. Testing showed that as it heated up the insides, people scattered like ants from a hill after a swift kick.

Uncomfortable, but preferable to a lethal bullet.

Jimmy made a notation in his flight log. "Careful with your bank there, Vapor. Getting a little shallow." Once his pencil slowed, he glanced over at Vince. "Barbie might be providing a distraction for someone else to make a move."

Valid point. He increased the bank and smoothed the action with a touch of rudder. "Good thing there are thirteen of us to scan the mob, because we're going to need all eyes out."

A string of acknowledgments echoed over Vince's headset just as Barbie grabbed the butt of his rifle and—slam—the past merged with the present.

A group of misfit teens festering with discontent. Four

hands hauling him from his Kawasaki rat bike. Screaming. Gunshots.

A girl in the way.

Sweat stinging his eyes now as well as then, Vince reached up to adjust his air vents for like the nine hundredth time since takeoff. How could they make this airplane so high-tech and not get the damn air-conditioning to work?

"Time's run out for Barbie." The rattling plane vibrated through his boots all the way up to his teeth. "Crank it, Berg."

"Concur," the fire control officer drawled from the back. "Let's light him up."

"I'm in parameters, aircraft stable, cleared to engage." Vince monitored as a crosshair tuned in on the infrared screen in front of him and centered on the troublemaker. He hoped this would work, prayed this guy was a low level troublemaker and not one of the area's ruthless mercenaries. He didn't relish the thought of the situation escalating into a need for the more conventional guns aft of the nonlethal ADS.

That wouldn't go well for the "get out the vote" effort.

"Ready," Berg called.

"Cleared to fire," answered Vapor.

"Firing . . ."

No special sounds or even so much as a vibration went through the craft. The only way to measure success was to watch and wait and . . .

Bingo.

Barbie started hopping around like he'd been stung by a swarm of bees. His AK-47 dropped from his hand onto the dusty ground. The crowd stilled at the dude's strange behavior, all heads turning toward him as if looking for an explanation.

Jimmy twitched in his seat. "I halfway wanna laugh at the poor bastard, except I know how bad the ADS stings."

"Amen, brother." Before integrating the ADS onto the airplane, they'd tested it on themselves. It was disorienting and unpleasant, to say the least, but not damaging.

He was willing to take that searing discomfort and more to power through developing this particular brainchild, a personal quest for him. He could have been on the side of the evil cheerleader today if not for one person: a half-crazy old war vet who took on screwed-up teens that most good citizens avoided on the street. Don Bassett had never asked for anything in return.

Until this morning.

Vince relegated that BlackBerry e-mail he'd received minutes before takeoff to the back of his mind. "No time to get complacent, everybody. Keep looking. I can't imagine our activist with the automatic weapon is alone."

The system had the capability to sweep the whole group with a broader band, but he hoped that wouldn't be necessary, as it would likely shut down voting altogether.

Badass Barbie shook his head quickly, looked around, then leapt toward his AK-47 lying in the dust.

Berg centered the crosshairs again. "I think he needs another taste."

Vapor replied, "Roger. Cleared to fire."

"Firing . . ."

The rabble-rouser again launched into some kind of erratic pep rally routine.

"Stay on him." Vince eyed the monitor, heart drumming in time with the roaring engines. "Run him away from the crowd."

Berg kept the crosshairs planted on the troublemaker as

he attempted to escape the heat. The wiry man sidled away. Faster. Faster again, until he gave up and broke into a sprint, disappearing around a corner of the building.

Hell, yeah.

Vince continued banking left over the village so the cameras could monitor the horde. As hoped, the crowd seemed to chat among themselves for a while, some looking up at the plane, discussing, then slowly re-forming a line to the church.

Cheers from the crew zipped through the headset for one full circle around the now-peaceful gathering. Things could still stir up in a heartbeat, but the pop from the ADS had definitely increased the odds for the good guys.

God, he loved it when a plan came together. "Crew, let's run an oxygen check and get back in the game."

His crew called in one by one in the same order as specified in the aircraft technical order, ending with him.

Vince monitored his oxygen panel. "Pilot check complete."

With luck, the rest of the election would go as smoothly, and they would be back in the good ole U.S. of A. tomorrow night.

Five peaceful hours later, Vince cranked the yoke, guiding the AC-130 into a roll, heading for the base, where he would debrief this mission and lay out plans for their return home.

And contact Don Bassett.

Vince finally let the message flood his mind. He couldn't simply ignore the note stored on his BlackBerry. The e-mail scrolled through his head faster than data on his control panel:

I need your help. My daughter's in danger.

That in and of itself wasn't a surprise. Bassett's only daughter had been flirting with death before she even got her braces off. Her parents kept bailing out Shay's ungrateful butt. What did surprise him, however, was Don asking for help. The dude was a giver, not a taker. It meant that, for whatever reason, he must be desperate.

Not that the reason even mattered. Whatever the old guy wanted, he could have. If not for Don Bassett's intervention seventeen years ago, Vince wouldn't need a motorcycle or airplane to transport him from his fucked-up world.

Because seventeen years ago, he'd led the riots.

Seventeen years ago, one of his fellow gang members had been gunned down by cops just doing their jobs.

Seventeen years ago, he could have been looking at twenty-five to life..

★ CLEVELAND, OHIO: TWO DAYS LATER

"Suicide hotline. This is Shay." Shay Bassett wheeled her office chair closer to her desk. Tucking the phone under her chin, she shoved aside the steaming cup of java she craved more than air.

"I need help," a husky voice whispered.

Shay snagged a pencil and began jotting notes about the person in crisis on the other end of the line:

Male.
Teen?

"I'm here to listen. Could you give me a name to call you by?" Something, anything to thread a personal connection through the phone line.

"John, I'm John, and I hurt so much. If I don't get relief soon, I'll kill myself."

His words clamped a corpse-cold fist around her heart. She understood the pain of these callers, too much so, until sometimes she struggled for objectivity.

Shay zoned out everything but the voice and her notes.

Voice stronger, deeper.
Older teen.
Background noise, soft music.
Bedroom or dorm?

She scribbled furiously, her elbow anchoring the community center notepad so the window fan wouldn't ruffle the pages. "John, have you done anything to harm yourself?"

"Not yet."

"I'm really glad to hear that." Still, she didn't relax back into the creaky old chair in spite of killer exhaustion from pulling a ten-hour shift at the community center's small health clinic on top of volunteering to man the hotline this evening. "Can you tell me what's wrong?"

His breathing grew heavier, faster. "The line for one nine hundred do-me-now is busy, and if I don't get some phone sex soon, I'm gonna explode." Laughter echoed in the background, no doubt a bunch of wasted frat boys listening in on speakerphone. "How about you give me some more of those husky tones, baby, so I can—"

"Good-bye, John." She thumbed the Off button.

What an ass. Not to mention a waste of her precious time and resources. She pitched her pencil onto a stack of HIV awareness brochures.

The small community center in downtown Cleveland

was already understaffed and underfunded, at the mercy of fickle government grants and the sporadic largesse of bene-factors. Different from bigger free clinics, they targeted their services toward teens. Doctors volunteered when they could, but the place operated primarily on the back of her skills as a nurse, along with social worker Angeline and youth activities director Eli.

Bouncing a basketball on the cracked tile, Eli spun his chair to face her, his blond dreadlocks fanning along his back. "Another call for a free pizza?"

"A request for phone sex." She pulled three sugar packs from her desk drawer.

"Ewww." Angeline leaned her hip against her desk, working a juggling act with her purse, files, and cane.

Only in her fifties, Angeline already suffered from ar-thritis aggravated by the bitter winters blowing in off Lake Erie. Of course, that was Cleveland for you, frigid in the winter and a furnace in the summer.

Forecast for today? Furnace season. The fan sucked muggy night air through the window.

"I apologize for my gender." Eli kept smacking the ball, the thumping as steady as a ticking clock.

"Who said it was a guy?" Shay tapped a sugar pack, then ripped it open.

Angeline jabbed her parrot-head cane toward Shay. "You called the person John."

"Busted." She poured the last of the three sugars into the coffee, her supper since she'd missed eating with her dad. No surprise. They canceled more plans than they kept.

Angeline hitched her bag the size of the Grand Canyon onto her shoulder. "Always testing the boundaries, aren't ya, kiddo?"

Not so much anymore. "Calls like that just piss me off.

What if someone in a serious crisis was trying to get through and had to be rerouted? That brief delay, any hint of a rejection, could be enough to push a person over the edge."

"You're preaching to the choir here." Angeline's cell phone sang with the bluesy tones of "Let's Get It On." "Shit. I forgot to call Carl back."

Eli tied back two dreads to secure the rest of the blond mass. "Apparently we're in the phone sex business after all."

"Don't be a smart-ass." Angeline stuffed another file into her bag that likely now weighed more than the wiry woman.

"Nice talk. Why don't I walk you to your car?" He slid the neon yellow purse from her shoulder and hooked it on his own.

"You can escort me out, but Carl'll kick your lily white ass if you hit on me."

"If I thought I stood a chance with you . . ."

Shaking her head, Angeline glanced back at Shay. "Make sure the guard walks you all the way to your car."

"Of course. I even have my trusty can of Mace."

And a handgun.

She wasn't an idiot. The crime rate in this corner of Cleveland upped daily. Places like L.A. or New York were still considered the primary seats of gang crime. Money and protection followed that paradigm, which sent emergent gangs looking for new—unexpected—feeding grounds. Like Cleveland.

Hopefully, her testimony at the congressional hearing next week would help bring about increased awareness, help, and most of all *funds*.

"Tell Carl I said hello." With a final wave, Shay turned her attention to the stack of medical charts of teenage girls who'd received HPV vaccines. At least she had all evening to catch up—a plus side to having no social life.

She sipped her now lukewarm coffee.

The phone jangled by her elbow, startling her.

She snagged the cordless receiver. "Suicide hotline. This is Shay."

"I'm scared."

Something in that young male voice made her sit up straighter, her fingers playing along the desk for her pencil.

Boy.
Local accent.
Definitely teen.
Frightened as hell.

Too many heartbreaking hours volunteering told her this kid didn't want phone sex or a pizza.

"I'm sorry you're afraid, but I'm glad you called." She waited for a heartbeat; not that long, given her jackhammer pulse rate, but enough for the boy to speak. When he didn't, she continued, "I want to help. Could you give me a name to call you by?"

"No name. I'm nobody."

His words echoed with a hollow finality.

"You called this line." She kept her voice even. "That's a good and brave thing you did."

"You're wrong. I'm not brave at all. I'm going to die, but I don't want it to hurt. That makes me a total pussy."

No pain?
No cutting or shooting.

"Have you taken anything?" Alcohol? Drugs? Poison? Last month, a pregnant caller swallowed drain cleaner.

"Just my meds for the day."

On medication.
Illness?
Physical or psych?

"So you have a regular doctor?"

"I don't want to talk about that."

She knew when to back off in order to keep the person chatting. "What would you like to discuss?"

"Nothing." His voice grew more agitated, angry even, as it cracked an octave. "This is stupid. I shouldn't have called."

She rushed to speak before he could hang up, "Why are you scared?"

Voice changing.
14–15 years old?

"I told you already. I'm scared of the pain. It hurts if I live, and it's gonna hurt to die. I'm fucked no matter what."

She tried to keep professional distance during these calls, but sometimes somebody said something that just reached back more than a decade to the old Shay. The new Shay, however, shuttled old Shay to the time-out corner of her brain.

"You called this number, so somewhere inside, you must believe there's a third option."

The phone echoed back at her with nothing more than labored breathing and the faint whine of a police siren.

"Who or what makes you hurt?"

Still no answer.

"Hello?"

"Good-bye."

The line went dead.

"No! No, no, no, damn it." She thumbed the Off button once. Twice. Three freaking frustrated times before slamming the phone against the battered gunmetal gray desk.

She sucked in humid hot-as-hell air to haul back her professionalism. She had to finish her notes in case the boy called again. Please, God, she hoped that he would call and that he wasn't already as dead as the phone line.

Shay glanced at her watch. A four-minute conversation. Would that kid be alive to see the next hour?

She scrubbed her hand over her gritty eyes until the folder holding the rough draft of her upcoming congressional report came back into focus. It was a good thing after all that her dinner plans fell through. She was in no shape to exchange trivial chitchat with her father, who she barely knew and who knew even less about her. The report would make for better company anyway.

Each cup of coffee bolstered her to keep plugging away on fine tuning her stats and wording. Maybe she really could find a ray of hope through political channels rather than picking away one shift at a time. She just had to hang on until next week for her congressional testimony at Case Western Reserve University.

The old Shay ditched the time-out corner to remind her that even one day was an eternity when every sixteen minutes someone succeeded in committing suicide. Thinking of how many people that could be by next week . . . The math made her nauseated.

Flipping to the next page, she spun her watch strap around and around over the faded scar on her wrist that still managed to throb with a phantom pain even after seventeen years.

Two

★ ──

Across the street from the free clinic, the teenage boy pitched the prepaid cell phone in the industrial trash can chained to a streetlight. The receiver rattled to rest beside soda cans and a used condom.

He ducked back into a shadowy alley beside the crappy corner market run by a snarky old bitch who stroked her Louisville Slugger anytime he walked through the door. He normally wouldn't come near this store at all anymore, but he could see the community center good from this spot.

He could see *her*. Shay.

The fan in her window swirled the light along the sidewalk. The pieces of her tall shadow were chopped up by the blades and spat outside along with the glow.

Was the skinny chick reckless or just plain stupid? Didn't she know how dangerous it was to sit like that with the window open? Anybody could climb through and pin her to the floor before she could even shout *rape*. And the center's old rent-a-cop couldn't find his ass with both shaking hands, much less handle the nightstick he carried.

Like the billy club would protect anybody against knives or guns anyway. Did she think she was safe just because she wasn't a big-boobed street corner skank? Most of the guys he hung with got their rocks off from slapping around somebody smaller.

The same kind of guy who'd "asked" him to get close to her. To watch her.

Fingers tracing the damp paint he'd sprayed over a rival gang's tag on the brick wall, he looked past the blades to Shay. The fan lifted her short brown hair as she hunched over her desk, writing. About him? He'd been watching her taking notes while he talked. She'd seemed upset when he hung up. Like she cared.

She hadn't even recognized his voice. Yeah, he'd changed it some. But still.

He couldn't let that matter. The clueless do-gooders around here only made things worse, interfering in a war they could never understand. Shay would have to look out for herself the same way he took care of himself.

Because while his life didn't matter, there were others' that did.

* * *

When Vince had agreed to hop a plane the minute he got back to the States and meet Don Bassett in Cleveland, he'd expected something along the lines of a discussion over a beer in a bar. He'd even been looking forward to that brewski, a drink he would no doubt need when talking about Shay and whatever trouble she'd landed in now.

Instead, Vince found himself driving with Don to a cut-rate hotel.

"Uh, Don, is Shay in there?" Vince stepped out of the sedan and looked at the older guy over the roof. "If so, I'm not sure what help—"

"She's at a local community center where she works." News to Vince, since they never talked about Shay. "Everything will make sense soon enough. Patience."

What was up with all this covert crap? Had Don Bassett gone off his rocker? Don strode away from the rental car, quick strides eating up the walkway.

Oh-kay. Still no details. He hadn't been able to pry jack shit from Don on the phone or on the way from the airport to the—he looked up—Lake Erie Inn.

A rusted security light flickered erratically over Don like an off-tempo disco ball. The old guy hadn't packed on the pounds like many did after leaving the military regimen. Still lanky—sorta like Richard Gere in a brown leather flight jacket and dress slacks—he had a distinguished distance to him that generated unwavering respect if not necessarily warm fuzzies.

And that respect kept Vince following along.

A second-story door swung open, hard-core jamming music swelling as three teenagers stumbled out. College students, he would wager.

"Gee, Don, don't I get dinner first? I feel so cheap."

"Good thing I know you're serious underneath that bullshit, boy." The older man didn't so much as crack a smile. Strange for a guy who'd always covered stress with a laugh.

Vince's neck itched with the funky feeling that had always warned him when something was off. It should have been tough getting leave the second he landed in the U.S. Vacation time was a distant memory to military personnel these days. Yet his request had sailed through faster than a Honda Gold Wing on a patch of oil.

He'd thought himself lucky. Now he wondered.

Itchy feeling in full-out burn mode, Vince kept pace past a soda machine, the red logo sun-faded to Pepto-Bismol pink. "I'm all for patience, but I think it's time to clue me in."

"Not much longer." Don waved him toward a first corner room. "Our contacts are waiting inside. We needed to pick a no-questions kind of place away from official channels. Somewhere we wouldn't run into an old acquaintance in the hall."

Not a problem, since there were no halls. Although this was exactly the sort of place he would expect to bump into someone from his old crowd. If they weren't all in jail.

"I sincerely hope your friends aren't wearing spiked collars and stilettos," Vince mumbled.

Don swiped the room card. "Unlikely."

Cool air gusted through the open door. He nodded to Don. "After you, sir."

He followed his old mentor into a suite of sorts with a kitchenette to go with the king-size bed. The bed was empty—thank you, patron saints of the road. The table, however, was packed with one man and two women, all wearing suits.

Don pushed the door closed quickly, sealing them inside with the other three people. Two Vince recognized, and one he didn't.

So . . . Starting with the familiar. Faces he'd seen on the news. A South Dakota congresswoman and a California congressman who definitely weren't toting leather whips or spiked doggy collars.

Don clapped Vince on the shoulder. "Have a seat, son. This is about to get interesting."

Do ya think? Vince pulled a chair from against the wall. "Good evening, everyone."

A meeting with Congress members in a hotel was usually cause for tabloid news and some racy photos. *This* appeared to be a different kind of gathering altogether.

He studied the second female, a redhead, probably in her early forties, who definitely wasn't Shay Bassett. He might not know this woman, but she had FBI written all over her dark suit, tight bun, and expressionless face. Well, damn. That oil slick greasing his leave papers traced all the way to FBI headquarters.

Okay, then. Consider him officially hooked. He took in details he'd missed at first glance. A computer hummed beside the Fed. A tangle of cords attached the laptop to a portable projector. A video screen filled a corner.

He normally wouldn't pass up the coffee and doughnuts laid out on the other counter, but he had the feeling this meeting required his undivided attention.

The Fed extended her hand. "Hello, Major Deluca. My name is Special Agent Paulina Wilson. You may already be familiar with Congresswoman Raintree and Congressman Mooney."

Vince nodded in greeting, exchanging quick pleasantries with both, more than ready to get down to business.

"Good, good," Wilson continued, not a hair out of place, her slash of red lipstick the only color breaking up her otherwise pale face. "You'll have to pardon our, uh, informal setting today, but what we're about to discuss is of the utmost secrecy. Sometimes the safest place is outside official walls."

Sure, he understood. Much of what he did in his dark ops job was top secret. He'd just never held the covert meetings in a cheap hotel before.

Special Agent Wilson clicked on the projector. The first

PowerPoint slide filled the screen with a photo of a sprawling university campus. "A bipartisan committee from Congress will be holding a hearing at Case Western Reserve University next week. Led by Congressman Mooney and Congresswoman Raintree, the committee will be speaking on antigang legislation under consideration."

Anybody who watched the news knew that was in the works. How did it play into Shay Bassett being in danger? And why would the FBI be interested in her?

Don leaned forward, fingers steepled on the table. "My daughter is one of the witnesses, presenting information gleaned from her experiences working at the Cleveland Community Center."

Now *that* was news to him.

Special Agent Wilson adjusted the focus. "As with functions of this nature, we've had our surveillance ears open for anything out of the ordinary. I don't have to tell you what a national uproar it would cause if anyone managed to infiltrate a congressional meeting of any sort, much less one receiving this much attention."

Vince looked at the two pale Congress members, then back at the agent. "I'm assuming you don't mean trouble with picket lines or pies in the face."

Both Congress members chuckled. The Fed, however, could have been one of the unflinching guards outside of Buckingham Palace.

Wilson pivoted on a clunky heel. "You're correct. This goes beyond expected concerns about protestors. We increased our wiretaps and cell phone monitoring in the area. During the course of one of those conversations, a local gang member's name was mentioned in connection with a well-known terrorist cell."

Whoa. Vince straightened in his seat. They'd gone from disruptions during a televised event to talk of terrorism. Joke time was officially over.

"We secured a search warrant for the gangbanger's apartment—or rather his parents' apartment. We found CDs for terrorist recruitment and training. We also found manuals for creating bombs packed with ball bearings and instructions for building improvised explosive devices out of remote control toys." She clicked through a series of photos from inside the apartment, zeroing in on the confiscated items. "We also discovered a map of the planned driving route to Case Western and a floor plan of the building where the hearing will take place."

A chill settled in his gut, and yet he could see in her eyes the agent wasn't anywhere near done with her surprises.

"We also found copies of the correspondence sent requesting this information, written on stationery from the Cleveland Community Center and signed by Shay Bassett."

Shay.

Just her name slammed him back in his seat, much less the possibility that she could be in the middle of some terrorist plot. He'd spent so many years trying not to think of Shay Bassett, and now thoughts of her roared in to fill the void.

Wilson clicked to the next image, a photo of Shay administering shots in an immunization line.

A brunette, lean, earthy beauty.

He could have been in a time warp.

She'd been trouble on smokin' hot legs from the first time she'd tried to seduce him just to piss off her old man. Trouble or not, then or now, surely she couldn't be a knowing participant in anything this appalling.

Wilson thumbed the remote, a split screen displaying a photo of a tattooed teen alongside the picture of Shay. "This is the young man we're investigating. We questioned him but didn't hold him. We're going to observe him—and Shay—instead. It's more critical to learn who's orchestrating this."

Vince tore his eyes off Shay. "How do I come into play, Agent Wilson?"

"Don Bassett recommended you."

And for that matter, what was Don doing here?

Don nudged aside his full cup of coffee. "I work for the agency now." The CIA. Holy crap. "Anything I do here is unofficial, since this is FBI territory. I also have an obvious conflict of interest because of Shay, but I had been keeping an ear to the ground on the presecurity because of her involvement. When this came up, I immediately thought of your, uh, skill set."

"My skill set? And what would you mean by that?" All signs indicated they already knew, but old habits died hard. Vince rolled out the pat answer he used with his mama, dates, and curious biker mechanics. "I just work in a military test unit."

Without identification patches. Developing military equipment no one knew about. Answerable only to the air force chief of staff.

Don smiled. "Exactly how I would have answered the question. As I said, your skill set could be valuable, particularly with the surveillance, to find out how widespread this problem may be. I presented the proposal to Special Agent Wilson, and she agreed. We contacted the air force, and here you are."

Vince stared at his former mentor with a whole new perspective. Don wasn't just sitting a desk job and stirring interest in CAP in his free time, as would have been his due right. The old guy had traded up.

Special Agent Wilson continued, "The boy has gone missing, and it's our belief if he's been recruited, there could be more. You will stay here in Cleveland under the guise of helping fuel interest in forming a Civil Air Patrol unit. Share your success story of how being recruited into the volunteer group saved you from a life of crime as a teen. Since you and Bassett have a connection from your younger years, showing up here to help out his daughter shouldn't raise any red flags."

Don smiled, but it didn't reach his eyes. "We've even pulled strings with the Joint Chiefs of Staff so your surveillance will blend into standard testing expenses. Beyond helping us here, you'll actually be able to write this off as a field test and move a project into the war arena faster. A fine economical blending of government resources, if I do say so myself."

Special Agent Wilson tapped her thumbnail against the slide changer in her fist. "It's a lot to absorb, but rest assured, we're taking care of details. We're in contact with your squadron commander. In fact, Lieutenant Colonel Scanlon is on standby waiting for your call after this meeting so you can be reassured that we're on the up-and-up. He seems to have the utmost confidence in your capabilities."

No small praise, that. Vince shifted in his chair uncomfortably.

"You're cleared for any form of surveillance. Your choice."

"I'll need a support team—"

"Of course, you'll have your pick of members from your

squadron," she responded without hesitation. "We'll leave the specifics of that up to you. Your commander will work out of D.C., coordinating any issues with Congress. Our Congress members here are flying back to D.C., but they're leaving behind their aides to prepare for the event. However, the aides don't have the clearance to know about our mission. Are there any questions so far?"

Like, was there someone else to do this, someone who wouldn't send Shay running and screaming for the hills? But he owed Don his life. Time to repay the debt. "No questions."

Wilson set down the slide changer. "I hope I don't need to impress upon you what chaos a hit on Congress could cause. We cannot allow another terrorist attack on our own soil."

She pinned him with a steely gaze. Was she wondering if he would cut Shay slack because of his loyalty to Don? Did Don think bringing him in would give an edge of leniency if it turned out Shay was involved?

Good God, there were freaking land mines all over everywhere in this mission, beyond just literal ones some terrorist might plant. Not that he could turn his back on Don and all he'd learned from the man about honor.

Even if that meant turning Don's daughter over to the Feds.

*　*　*

The boy had never called back.

Not that night or the next.

Shay had stayed well past the clinic's closing hours, willing the phone to ring. No one had called, a mixed blessing, since at least it meant nobody else was in crisis.

She glanced at her cherry red watch her mother had

given her as a birthday gift to add to her watch and bracelet collection. The psychology grad student who'd volunteered to pull the eleven o'clock night shift was a half hour late, and she'd had zero luck in reaching him. She would leave him a note and forward all calls to her cell. Plenty of nights passed with no phone-ins, so she should still be able to sleep.

She eyed the receiver one last time before hitching her small Vera Bradley backpack over one shoulder and turning off the window fan puffing in an unusually cool breeze for once.

As she pulled her lab coat off the coat tree, the back door creaked open. Finally. The grad student. She would even have time to brief Geoff about the caller before she fell asleep on her feet.

She started into the hall. And stopped short. A hooded figure slid from the corridor toward the main clinic. Tall, frighteningly so, but with an awkward thinness of either a teen or a junkie.

Shay stumbled, her chest tightening. If she could just make it back into her office before he—

Her Nike thudded against the trash can. *Shit. Shit. Shit!* She stooped to grab it before it clattered to the ground.

The hooded boy spun to face her, his face covered with a greasy bandanna. "Stop, bitch, or I'll slice off your face."

He swished a machete through the air.

She held up her hands and patted lightly in a universal calm-down gesture even as the glinting edge made her break out in a cold sweat.

A member of the Apocalypse gang.

She knew from the weapon.

God, how she wished he'd been carrying *anything* other than a blade. Even a dull butter knife freaked her out to this day with a phobia so strong she avoided them at the dinner table.

"Stay where you are." His hand shook, grease under his nails. Did he work in some kind of mechanic shop or garage? "No pressing some secret alarm or anything to bring the cops."

Where was the security guard? So far it seemed she was completely alone. She kept searching for clues, anything to give her an advantage in talking to him.

Anything to take her mind off the memory of the glide of steel across her skin.

"Your guard guy decided to take a nap in his truck," he said as if reading her mind. "So let's step this up before the old fart gets back."

"What do you want?" At least her voice didn't shake. She clutched her tiny backpack closer to her side.

"I wanted to walk in here without anybody seeing me, but you shot that to hell, bitch. Now open that cabinet where you keep the drugs. And don't bother telling me you haven't got a key. I've seen you lock it up before."

He must be one of the clinic patients. That narrowed the field down to about a thousand.

Her eyes snagged on the tattoos along the tops of his fingers, tiny rattlesnakes. Recognition flooded through her. She'd treated him last week when he came in wanting drugs for "back pain." More like he wanted some cash from selling the pills on the street the minute he left.

Should she let him know she recognized him? Would that seal her very painful death warrant?

Something prompted her otherwise, a sense from her brief meeting with him that told her he respected strength. And, of course, she did have a protective edge he knew nothing about.

"You really need to go into another line of work." She crossed her arms, one hand subtly dipping into her backpack. "All of those tattoos make you too readily identifiable to the police, *Kevin*."

His chin wavered even as his jaw jutted. "If you're so smart, you shoulda kept your mouth shut." He tugged down his bandanna to reveal a pale face barely sporting peach fuzz. "What makes you think I won't kill you now to keep you from IDing me later?"

She slid her hand out of her backpack and leveled her small but accurate pistol at him. "What makes you think I won't *shoot* you first?"

His eyes went wide. Good. And thank heavens her risk paid off in mentioning his tats, since he'd been distracted long enough for her to find her own weapon without fumbling. She owed her dad a big fat thank-you for giving her the Khar PM9 when she took this job.

The angry blade steadied in Kevin's fist. "You're not gonna use it, 'cause you're not a killer."

"And neither are you." She hoped.

"You're crazy."

Like she hadn't heard that before. "Which makes me a lot more likely to shoot you." She leveled the barrel. "Just because I'm not a murderer doesn't mean I won't blow off your kneecap. Now put that blade on the floor and get out of here."

She would call the police on him the second he cleared the door, a much safer option than trying to subdue him herself. She wanted him and his machete out of her face.

A rumble sounded outside, growing louder. The *growl, growl, growl* of a motorcycle approaching vibrated the windows. She could have sworn she felt it in her toes.

Help?

Please, not backup for Kevin.

"Fuck," the teen spat out.

The front doorknob rattled. Then creaked.

The hooded teenager twisted and made a break for the back exit, the machete still firmly in his fist. What was wrong with all the locks around here? She bolted them tight, and still people waltzed right in.

Her heart rate stuttered. She eyed the back exit and the front entrance. She wasn't trusting that Geoff would come striding in with his Case Western student backpack this time.

Shay gripped her gun and dashed back into her office. Fishing frantically through her backpack, she searched for her cell phone. She grabbed the receiver just as a hulking man in motorcycle garb filled her office doorway.

Definitely not Geoff or Eli.

Her mouth went dry. Broad shoulders made larger by black leathers nearly touched either side of the frame. His neck was almost as big as his totally shaved head.

This guy wouldn't need a machete. He could snap her in two with his ham-fisted grip.

Her hands started shaking. Her thumb searched for 911.

"Stand back." She raised her gun and her phone. She wasn't taking her sights off the hulk for even a second.

His eyes were so dark that from a distance she could only just see the thin ring of blue at the outer edges of his wide pupils. His whole badass look was enough to make a woman pull out her Mace in the middle of the afternoon.

For the first time she truly questioned the wisdom of carrying the small 9 mm, because her feet were frozen and her finger was twitchy. "The clinic closed six hours ago. My gun's loaded, and I'm not afraid to use it."

"Shay, put your weapon and phone down." He raised his

hands to chest level. "I just missed catching the kid when he ran out the back door, and I've already called the cops."

Something in his gravelly voice reached into her brain, probing around for a place to take hold. She could have sworn she'd never heard those deep tones before. She searched his face, trying to remember where she might have met him.

When.

Her trembling hands went still. She wasn't even sure her heart still worked because of the roaring in her ears. He might not look or sound the same as the dark-haired thug who'd turned her life upside down seventeen years ago, but somehow she knew.

Vince Deluca was back.

THREE

Vince watched Shay cradle her cell phone in one hand and her tiny chick gun in the other, all the while studying him as if he were the same gutter scum he'd been seventeen years ago.

Was she the same volatile train wreck? Or had she shifted into darker agendas? She definitely still didn't give a shit about her life, if the past ninety seconds were anything to judge by.

Vince pressed deeper into the room, biker boots thudding against scarred wood floors in this crumbling dump they called a teen center. "What the hell are you doing hanging around this neighborhood after dark, in an unlocked building?"

Shay rested her tiny weapon on the corner of the desk with exaggerated care while tucking the phone into her jeans pocket. Faded jeans molded to lean legs with a granola girl appeal.

"Nice to see you again, too, Vince."

"Not so nice to see you're still in the middle of a mess."

He brushed past her to check outside the window, above the fan. A car took a token pause at the red light before roaring through. A kid smoked dope beside a grocery market—a teen shorter than the hooded guy here earlier.

"As charming as ever."

"I'm sorta preoccupied with making sure you don't get hacked to pieces." He weighed the option of running after the kid over the risk of leaving her here alone. No contest. "The cops should arrive any second now. It's best if we both stay put."

"I agree, in case you were interested in my opinion." She hitched a slim hip on the edge of her desk, right beside the gun, as if she didn't trust him much more than the coked-up teen who'd bolted out the back door before Vince could stop him. "You're the last person I expected to show up. Why are you here?"

He stalked closer, having learned long ago it wasn't wise to take his eyes off Shay Bassett. "I'm on R & R for the next few weeks and decided to visit your father while he's in town. Do you have any idea why that kid broke in?"

"Drugs." Her golden brown eyes flickered with the first signs of something other than irritation. "Is there some other reason for this R & R? Are you all right?"

"Just overworked. But who isn't these days?" He scanned the stark office with its old metal desks in three corners, filing cabinets in the fourth, and a huge window with crappy locks. Locks that apparently didn't get used, because the fan kept the window propped open. "Your father was worried when you didn't show up at the restaurant."

She gave him a one-shoulder shrug, a bead of sweat on her brow the only sign of what she'd been through. "He cancels on me. I cancel on him. It's a thing we do. Make appointments. Pretend we want to see each other but find an excuse at the last minute." She straightened, her thumb fidgeting with the butt of the gun. "Were you at the restaurant with him?"

"We waited for an hour before we started looking for you." He pivoted back out into the hall toward the rear entrance. He twisted the dead bolt right below a Crime Stoppers placard bolted down at eye level.

"Don wanted us to meet up?" Shay called from a few steps behind. "That old man is crazier than I thought."

"He told me you're interested in starting up a Civil Air Patrol squadron for teens here." Vince turned around and shouldered past her on his way to the front door, assessing the place for the best way to stage surveillance.

The walls were lined with pen and ink sketches and watercolor paintings, obviously by the teens, framed and mounted by the staff in some kind of attempt to re-create a mom's refrigerator door. As if that would be enough to make them think someone cared.

Shay reached past to flick both bolts. "You can tell Don I did lock up and set the alarm system."

So she still didn't call Don "Dad." He'd never understood that. He would have killed to have a father like Don Bassett. "The kid probably picked it open with a fourth grade magician's set."

"Vince, you're new here. We do the best we can with what we have."

"You should have called your dad to meet you here. Any man would have been over in a heartbeat." He pulled out his phone. "As a matter of fact, I should text him now."

"Why don't you do that on your way back to your car?" She smiled for the first time.

"Motorcycle." He glanced down at his cell phone and away from how pretty she looked when she ditched the scowl. "Your dad hooked me up with a killer loaner while I'm on leave." He thumbed the rest of his text message to Don. "It's not often a guy on a government salary gets to drive a 1098R Ducati."

"Of course he did. He would do anything for you."

He glanced up from his phone. "Aren't you kinda old for jealousy?"

She blinked her expression blank, the tiny gold studs in her ears the only visible glint. Even her lips were free of so much as lip gloss. "Thank you for coming in when you did. The police will be here any minute."

"I'll stick around while you wait. They'll want my statement, too." Vince stood his ground. The clock ticked through another two minutes.

She sighed. "Well, Vince, your hairdo—or lack thereof—is different, but you're obviously still you."

He scrubbed his palm over his shaved bald scalp. "Cuts down on morning grooming."

Her eyes followed his hand so intently he could almost swear he felt her touch replacing his on his bare skull. A touch he'd wanted once upon a teenage fantasy, except nothing, but *nothing* could have made him betray Don Bassett's trust. Even thoughts of getting naked with Shay in those days had left him with a guilt so heavy he'd rediscovered his path to the confessional.

He pivoted away from her, the air too thick with the scent of soap. Soap, for God's sake. "Where the hell are the police?"

"Probably busy with a dozen other bigger problems. I expect it'll be a while before they get around to taking my statement." She crossed to the window and turned on the box fan. "Thank you for putting yourself in harm's way to help. I really do mean that."

"Is that gun loaded?"

Silently, she emptied the bullets on the desktop, each one thudding against her desk calendar.

Images of her alone with that kid sent his biceps twitching. "Cokeheads have a strength even bullets can't always stop. What if he'd taken the gun away from you?"

"He didn't, and if he'd inched even one step toward me, I would have shot him in the kneecap. Everyone around here knows I don't back down. He wouldn't have come in at all if he knew I was still around."

"Part of me applauds your bravado, and another part wonders if you still have a death wish."

Her head jerked up. Her face paled so white, her freckles stood out in darker contrast.

Why the surprise? Everyone had known how reckless she was back in the day.

Only for her father would he put himself through the mind game torture of dealing with this woman.

★ ★ ★

Don Bassett rammed his Beemer into fourth gear, plowing down side streets, still a couple of miles away from the Cleveland Community Center. Vince's text message had come through just as he was checking out Shay's empty apartment.

He'd been annoyed that she wouldn't pick up her cell phone, but she frequently ignored it when the suicide hotline was busy. Or if she was indulging in one of her two-hour-long hydro soaks in a bubble bath.

And just that fast, the past backhanded him.

The metallic taste of blood filled his mouth. Only a

memory, but one seared in his brain until it blocked out the soothing smell of well-oiled leather seats. He'd bitten a chunk out of the side of his tongue when he'd found teenage Shay in the bath, arm draped over the side, slashed wrist bleeding all over the floor. A horror they'd kept from everyone except Shay's doctors.

He steadied his breathing until the cool blasts from the air conditioner snaked through. God, he preferred staying busy and numb. He refused to believe his daughter was involved with terrorists. Even so, somehow she'd still landed in *their* crosshairs.

Changing from lane to lane around slower drivers cruising a club strip, he thumbed the four on his cell phone, speed dialing to . . .

"Special Agent Wilson." Her voice clipped through the airwaves.

"Bassett here," he answered even though she had to know it was him from the caller ID.

Rustling sounded in the background, like sheets tangled around legs. "I'm assuming you have a good reason for waking me up."

"My daughter didn't show for dinner and wasn't answering her cell. Given current circumstances, we got worried." He blew through a red light. "Deluca just found her at the clinic."

"She works there, so that's no surprise," she answered, her voice still raspy from sleep.

"Shay was in the middle of a break-in." He roared past a string of half-crumbling old factories. "It appeared to be a drug-seeking teen."

"Appeared?" Her voice cleared, all business.

"I don't have much in the way of details. I'm on my way over, but the police will probably get there first."

"I'll look into it."

She'd damn well better. "The sooner the better."

"I should have answers by the time you return to D.C. You're taking the red-eye flight back, right?"

"That's the plan." His jaw unclenched as he felt more in control of his world again, enough so he could allow himself the pleasure of envisioning Special Agent Wilson with her auburn hair flowing unbound to her naked waist. "I appreciate this, Paulina. Will you be at the airport, or should I take a cab?"

"Oh, I'll be there, all right." Her voice went from professional to husky as fast as his pants throbbed. "Pink will be the color of the day."

Nothing turned him on more than plucking free the pins from her severe bun and watching her hair tumble over her breasts plumped upward in a merry widow.

A beep sounded. Call waiting. "Sorry, babe, but I've got someone on the other line. See you tomorrow."

He checked the LCD panel and flinched. His erection deflated. Fast.

Cheeks puffing, he switched over. "Yeah, Jayne? What's up?"

Conversations with his ex-wife were best kept short and to the point.

"Hello, Don." Ice froze the phone lines. "You're late with your alimony payment."

And she waited until nearly midnight to tell him this?

Of course their communication skills had never been top-notch, even in the beginning when they'd been in love with each other and the wild monkey sex. Eventually their marriage had ended up as yet another casualty of the military way of life.

Too long apart.

Too much stress.

Not enough of everything else.

"Jayne . . ." He didn't bother hiding the irritation in his voice anymore. "You know my bank sends it automatically. If there's a screwup, it's on their end."

"And it's your responsibility to fix it," she said as if patiently explaining two plus two to one of the first graders she taught. Of course she always had been a Wonder Woman do it all—without the sequined bra and Teflon wristbands. "I don't want a penny of your money for me. I never have. But Sean's tuition payment is due."

Sean. Of course. He should have known that would be the only reason for a call from Jayne.

How many years was that mama's boy moocher going to stay in college? He should have had two degrees and a six-figure job by now. Weren't adult children supposed to have suburban lives and give him grandkids? Not his.

He considered telling her about Shay and the break-in for all of three seconds before deciding to wait for more information. "Can we talk about this later? I'm tied up right now."

"Of course you are. Try to take care of it by the end of the week, please."

The line went dead abruptly.

Don slowed his Beemer at the yellow light by the corner grocery, even though the street was pretty much deserted, then accelerated toward the clinic. A fence surrounded the side lot, empty but for Shay's old Ford, a car on blocks, and a motorcycle, the 1098R Ducati he'd lined up for Vince.

No security lights or guards surrounded the forty thousand dollar machine. Vince must have been gunning for bear to have left the machine so vulnerable in this kind of neighborhood.

Where the hell were the police? They couldn't have already arrived and taken statements that fast.

He tried the front door. Locked. Thank God. He circled around to the back.

The light burned dimly, either from a dying bulb or one so smeared with grease it diluted the glow. Motion sensors would be nice. But then Shay had told him often enough they barely had the extra funds to replace the basketball net, much less money to spruce up the place.

As of tomorrow, he would buy motion sensor lights himself and donate the blasted things. He and Shay had never enjoyed much of a father-daughter relationship, but she wouldn't say no to anything for the center.

Don sidestepped a Dumpster reeking of rotten food and a hint of marijuana smoke. One stride past in the dark, and he tripped. What the fuck?

He grabbed the edge of the rusty trash bin to regain his balance and looked down.

At a dead body.

Lying beside a second body, equally dead.

His heart rate thundered so loudly he almost reached for his nitro tablets. Instead, he grabbed for his phone while searching for details in the dim light without disturbing the scene. Praying he wouldn't see the face of his daughter or Vince. While dialing, he studied the corpses, the smell of the Dumpster, pot, and death nearly gagging even a seasoned pro like him.

First, a college-age man wearing a Case Western backpack, his neck sliced so deep his spine notched through the coagulated blood.

Second, another male, head twisted at an awkward angle but the blood-smeared face still recognizable as the boy they'd been investigating. A machete pierced his hooded sweatshirt and into his bird-thin chest.

Don gripped the phone. His daughter wasn't dead. Vince hadn't been caught in the crossfire.

His pulse slowed enough that he figured he would live to see tomorrow. The ringing on the other end of the phone stopped.

"This is nine-one-one. What's your emergency?"

Four

Shay had worked in an emergency room for three years before transferring to the community center's small clinic. But no amount of trauma training would help the two lifeless bodies sprawled on the unforgiving cement. The murders—the violence and brutality—went beyond anything she'd seen.

She stood with Vince just outside the yellow crime scene tape surrounding the Dumpster. People in uniform ducked under the tape in a back-and-forth dance of the police, medical examiner, detectives.

The metallic smell of blood hung on the humid night air like heavy raindrops weeping for the dead. Someone had killed the college volunteer and the misguided kid who'd tried to rob her. She may have threatened to shoot Kevin during their standoff, but she hadn't wanted him dead. If she'd disabled him with a shot to the leg, might the noise have run off whoever had been lying in wait? Or would that person have killed her father instead?

A quick check reassured her that Don stood safe and alive beside his Beemer with a detective.

The security guard spoke with a local detective while standing next to a trash can in case he vomited again. She and Vince gave their statements to a cop from a gang violence task force.

The steely eyed cop cradled his PDA in his hand, his name tag reading Officer L. Jaworski, a newbie who tended to stroke his club like some kind of touchstone for good luck. "Which entrance did you use?"

Vince stepped closer to her. "I entered the front door, followed him as far as the back, then returned to make sure Shay was all right."

"Ma'am"—the policeman glanced up from typing notes into his PDA—"did you leave the doors unlocked?"

"No, I always lock all the doors the minute the center officially closes."

"You're certain?"

She struggled not to get defensive. These kids made fun of the young cop enough on their own without her showing even a hint of frustration with his bullish tactics. "Positive. Locks are like toys to these kids. Kevin could have easily jimmied the front door."

Her eyes traveled back to the dead teen. No one had pulled the ugly machete from his chest. It seemed obscene to leave it there just for evidence photos, even if he was long past feeling pain. "We've had at least a dozen break-ins."

The young cop nodded while notating. "He probably picked the front lock, then ran out of the back, which left that door unlocked as well. How well do you know the boy?"

She rubbed her hands up and down her arms, the late-night wind blowing in off Lake Erie for a chilly summer night. "I only met him once before—when he came in last week, asking for pain medication. Tonight he said he wanted drugs. His machete leads me to believe he must be a member of the Apocalypse gang."

Jaworski eyed Kevin's chest, the teen's hoodie gaping wide to expose the wound and his Grim Reaper tattoo sliced down the middle. She pressed a hand to her throat and held back a shiver. She was a nurse, damn it.

Vince shrugged out of his leather jacket and draped it over her shoulders before she could argue. And she would have argued. Already his scent wrapped around her as firmly as the coat.

"It's going to be okay, ma'am." The policeman spoke with that universal "calming" tone she'd often used on hysterical patients, except she wasn't anywhere near hysterical. "We can only speculate at this point, but if this boy was just after drugs, you're safe now."

She didn't particularly appreciate the condescension, but she held her peace. She and Jaworski had butted heads in the past. Rumor had it he'd once been put on unpaid leave for beating down a kid.

Vince stepped closer to the cop, edging his shoulder between the man and Shay. "She's not safe as long as she's working here with persistent break-ins. Whoever did this moved fast and professionally, because I didn't hear a thing go down, and believe me, I was listening."

Jaworski bucked up territorially. "Maybe we should sign you on to the force."

Vince smiled, even though negative vibes rolled off him in waves. "Never one of my top ten career choices as a teen."

Suddenly Vince's attitude became crystal clear. He'd had issues with authority back when she'd known him. He might look different, but perhaps he hadn't changed that much on the inside.

He'd been arrested, resisted arrest, taken a billy club to the knee once so hard it sent him to the ground. Back then, there weren't video cameras following cops around. There'd been fault on both sides. She should know. She'd been there.

Jaworski tapped in another note on his PDA before looking up. "I'm going to need everyone to come down to the station for fingerprinting to rule you out as suspects."

The rasp of a long zipper cut the air as they sealed away the first body. She swallowed back bile just before the second rasp. "Do we ride with you for these prints, or are we free to take our own vehicles?"

Tapping his baton, the police officer seemed to be weighing the option of cramming Vince into the back of the cop cruiser just for the hell of it.

Vince eyed the crowd mixed with people in bathrobes and teens decked out with attitude. "If it's just the same to you, we'd rather not leave the Beemer and the bike unattended in this neighborhood."

"Well, pal—"

"Excuse me, but for the record, that's Major."

She blinked back her surprise. She hadn't known he'd progressed so far up the ranks.

"Major, then." Jaworski hitched his hands on his belt, just beside his service revolver. "Quit busting my chops. We're doing the best we can with the manpower on hand. I would think you military types could understand what it's like to be understaffed for fighting a war. And make no mistake about it, we've got a war on our hands here."

Vince nodded curtly. The cop had been wise to speak Vince's language.

Her father shouldered in, slipping right back into his role of easing the way for the teens he'd mentored. "I'm sorry, Officer. We're all a little rattled here. Of course we're glad to comply with whatever you need from us to find out who's responsible for the death of these two young men."

"Good." The officer tucked his PDA inside his jacket. "You may drive your own vehicles, but we'll be behind you."

Jaworski eyed Vince a final time before loping away toward his patrol car.

Her father turned to Vince. "You've got Shay, right? I need to make some calls."

She should have been used to his brusque ways after all these years, and on most days, she managed to let it roll right off her, how he had more time for others than his own family. She stared at his retreating back, mad as hell.

"Hey, Dad, I'm a thirty-three-year-old woman, and there are police all around. I'm fine on my own." And she was just fine and dandy, thanks for asking, old man.

He pivoted on his loafers. "I'm glad you weren't hurt," he said with no emotion, no hug. "It's probably best you don't call your mother. I'll tell her what she needs to know so she won't be surprised if she reads something in the morning paper. Thanks, Vince, for looking after her."

Her father pulled out his cell phone, his mind obviously already miles away as he turned back toward his Beemer.

Shay tugged her keys out of her paisley backpack. "Wow, the warm fuzzies are so thick I'm all atwitter," she muttered, tugging off Vince's jacket and passing it back to him. "Thanks for the loaner. I really do appreciate it."

"*De nada.*" Nothing.

Not exactly nothing. Her dad had a jacket, too, and he hadn't noticed her teeth chattering as fast as the click of the crime scene photographer's camera. "It seems crazy to be cold in the summer. Must have been shock trying to grab hold of me."

"You're hanging in there better than the security guard."

She checked on the old man happily taking a ride from the cop. By morning, their only guard would likely be applying for a job as a Wal-Mart greeter.

Shay hitched her backpack in place and started toward her car. "Vince, why are you really here?"

"I told you already." He walked beside her, his face as unreadable as her father's had been. "To catch up with your dad while he's in town. He told me he would be here to offer input for you about starting up a Civil Air Patrol squadron."

Something about his arrival still bothered her. Wouldn't a guy taking some R & R from battle go on a real vacation to the beach or the mountains? A cruise, even.

Why was he hanging out at a run-down community center in Cleveland, Ohio? "I spend hours a week listening for nuances in people's voices. I'm darn near a walking lie detector. There's something going on between you and my dad."

"I can assure you we are both heterosexuals."

She ground her teeth. "That's not what I meant, and you know it."

Key chain rattling in her hand, she thumbed the Unlock button. He body blocked her and stepped ahead, checking the front and backseat. "Pop your trunk."

Even if he was helping, she still resented his steamroller attitude. "You're kidding, right?"

"Pop the damn trunk," he barked.

She startled back a step then braced. She wasn't a needy teen anymore, willing to take whatever anyone dished out. "Do not speak to me that way."

He scrubbed a hand over his face, then his bare head. "I apologize for my tone. It's been a long, crappy day. I'm torqued off because one of those overworked cops still should have gotten here faster. I'm even more upset that two people are dead for no apparent reason."

"Amen to that." She thumbed open the trunk on her rust bucket of a car. Salted snowy roads had taken their toll on the Ford compact, but she couldn't see spending money on something nicer when it could be jacked on any given day.

Vince clicked on a small flashlight on his key chain. He swept the beam through her trunk, illuminating her rolled-up sleeping bag, hiking boots and—her guilty pleasure—a sealed container of instant hot chocolate. A smile tugged at a corner of his mouth as his beam lingered on the cocoa.

Then, *snap*, he clicked the light off. "Get in your car. Lock the doors. And drive very, very carefully to the police station. I'll be behind you all the way."

* * *

Don spun the steering wheel on his way onto the highway, heading for the airport, listening to Paulina Wilson chew his hide over the cell phone. Lucky for him, years of combat time had rendered him an expert at numbing himself on command.

"Damn it, Don, you need to back down with all these orders. I'm already up to my ass in panicked calls from that California congressman, Mooney. You're CIA, so you get the international problems." Her husky tones went raspy with irritation. "I'm FBI, which makes this U.S.-based mess *my* jurisdiction."

He knew the best way to sidetrack her when she got her professional panties in a twist. "So if we were in Paris, I would get to be on top."

Silence vibrated through the airwaves while highway lamps strobed light through his windows. They both knew jockeying for top was one of their favorite sex games.

She cleared her throat. "Inappropriate, Don. Have you forgotten there were two dead people on your daughter's doorstep? We've lost an important link to a terrorist plot."

"Of course I haven't forgotten a thing." Another reason to appreciate that numbing habit he'd honed. "Like how my daughter is still walking around out there."

"I've added a higher security detail trailing her."

Not the answer he wanted. "Tell that to the dead kid. A lot can happen in a few days. Vince will be tied up with his team giving the telecomm briefing, and I'll be in D.C., which is a helluva long way to watch her back." He'd almost lost his daughter once, the only thing to ever break his control. "She needs to know to be extra careful."

"Even assuming she's completely innocent, she *needs* to act natural so as not to set off any alarms that would put her in more danger." Paulina spoke slowly but firmly. "Bottom line, Don, it's not your call. She's already getting special consideration because I pulled strings for you. Think like an agent, not her father. You'll only make things worse for her if you deviate from the path we both know is the safest."

He took his frustration down a notch. He didn't have any choice but to keep silent. Best to move past it and hope his daughter wouldn't hate him even more when she found out.

Three exhales later, he'd shifted gears in his mind as well as on the Beemer. His brain filled with thoughts of seeing Paulina at the airport. After work they would race to her apartment. There was no love between them, not even like, because that would entail getting to know each other. They enjoyed something more in line with mutual respect and sex.

And sex offered the perfect way out of this discussion. "What would you like as payback for all this special consideration you're giving me?"

She laughed, but with an edge that relayed clearly she hadn't forgotten a word of their argument. "I think it's more a matter of what else I can do for you, lover."

* * *

Motorcycle rumbling under him, Vince trailed Shay down the neighborhood road dense with trees. After their compulsory trip the police station, the feel of the first-rate bike should have soothed the beast at the end of a nightmare day.

Except he'd never had a day quite like this one.

Sure, he'd been confronted with dead bodies before, and he'd thought he could handle seeing Shay Bassett again. But no memory of her from the past could have prepared him for her in the present, standing down a coked-up kid carrying a fucking machete.

He wasn't naive enough to think the kid's murder would put an end to the threat. The timing didn't feel coincidental. Maybe the kid hadn't been hyped up, or maybe someone got him juiced and sent him in for her. But there was more to this than any of them knew.

He cleared the security gate and pulled into the complex of two-story brick town houses. He cruised to a stop in the spot next to hers. Shay swung her long legs out of the rusty sedan, tweaking his attention much the same way she'd done as a teen. She'd known how to use those gams to her best advantage back then in short skirts.

Somehow her current, less in-your-grill uniform of jeans

and cotton button-down with a community center logo still
packed a helluva punch.

She hip-bumped the car door closed. "I suppose you
want to check the place before I walk inside."

Hell yes, he wanted to do a walk-through, not that she
seemed happy about the prospect, and he certainly couldn't
brief her on the plan, not with her connection to the kid still
suspect.

For now though, he needed to secure Shay.

Good old reverse psychology used to work like a charm
on her. So if he wanted inside, the best way would be to
make her think otherwise. "Looks like a nice neighborhood
to me." He scanned the area. Security lighting illuminated a
neatly landscaped dog-walk park. "I figure you're safe."

Her brown eyes widened. "It is. I am."

"Well, good then, I'm outta here." He started to turn toward his bike again, slow, giving her a second, then glanced
back, and sure enough, she didn't look all that comfortable
about entering her apartment. "Is something wrong?"

"Dead bodies." She rubbed her hands along her arms
again just as she'd done outside the community center. "As
a nurse, I've seen them before, but tonight, this was . . ."

"Obscenely violent." He stepped closer to her, mind
games over for the night. "You had also just been held up
by someone with a machete."

"I know what to expect in my job, and I hate seeming
like a wimp."

"Especially in front of me, I'll bet."

"Nice to see your ego hasn't suffered over the past seventeen years." She shot him a schoolteacherish glance. "I
may have thrown myself at you a while back, but you can
be sure I haven't built a miniature altar with your picture
and pink heart candles."

He thumped his chest. "I'm crushed.

She jabbed a thumb toward her front door, covered with a wrought-iron gate. "Pop the damn trunk, so to speak. You're a lot scarier-looking than I am, anyway."

Scary? If she felt that way about him, she sure hid it well.

Once she unlocked the door, he angled past her as she tapped in the security code. "Hold tight to that chick gun until I call the all clear."

The apartment echoed with silence other than a trickle, trickle, trickle that he soon realized was a wall-mounted waterfall rather than a leaky faucet. He walked down the narrow hall, past the wall fountain made of stone, a blue glow emanating from the pool at the base.

He clicked on the switch, track lighting rippling to life in the—so far—empty apartment. He scanned the simple brown sofa, strewn with bright pillows, a blanket over the back.

And a dog curled in the middle staring back with wide eyes.

Vince scratched the mini mutt with wiry fur behind the ear. "You're a rotten watchdog."

The bristly pup lapped his tongue over Vince's wrist. With a final pat, he walked away, past the kitchenette with a decorative butter churn. "You okay there, Shay?"

"Still holding up the doorframe."

"Keep talking to me so I know you're all right. I'm heading back to your bedroom." He sidestepped an antique spinning wheel.

"Just ignore the trapeze and the garter belt hanging from the ceiling fan."

His pulse surged, even though sarcasm dripped from her words. "No dominatrix whip? How sad."

He flicked on her bedroom light. The ceiling fan circled to life without a piece of lingerie in sight. He strode past the old-fashioned wooden bed tightly made with a quilt. "Talk. I can't hear you."

"Vince, hands off my panties."

"Yeah, yeah." It was easy enough for her to joke when she didn't know the full extent of the danger. He resisted the urge to lock her in her apartment until he could share details. He ducked to check under the bed and found nothing but wicker baskets neatly aligned.

A trapeze definitely would have been a shocker in this Amish decor.

He scanned for anything linking her to the dead kid, any evidence of her participation in the gang-terrorist connection. He tugged open her bedside table and found a stash of community center stationery. Could be innocent enough.

His eyes roamed her CD collection in a spinning tower, searching for anything that looked like the cheap training footage the Feds had found in the dead kid's apartment.

Nothing suspicious, which meant she could either be innocent or careful.

"Shay? Is there a back door?"

"Nope, and if you take much longer, I'm going to grow roots here. I don't know about you, but I just want to go to bed and put this day behind me."

He really didn't need an image of her curling up in that bed wearing . . . Stopping that thought midflight, he checked the two bathrooms and computer/guest room until he was content everything was as it should be, all the way down to the doilies. "All's clear."

"Thank you. I appreciate the look around, but I think we can finally turn the page on this strange reunion." She stepped inside, giving him a wide berth.

"Rearm your security system and double-check those dead bolts. I don't believe you're going to get much protection from this yippy yard shark." He ruffled the mutt, maybe ten pounds of steel wool fur.

"Yard shark?" She parked herself by the small dining table, the farthest point from him.

"Dogs usually don't like motorcycles. A charging pooch can make maneuvering tricky."

"Then I guess my place is officially Vince-proofed to make up for Buster's guard doggy deficiencies."

"Where did you find this bruiser?" he asked, not ready to leave her alone just yet. Instincts counted for everything in a job, and right now his instincts told him this woman needed more than a little gun and a lazy puppy.

"Actually, he found me." She snapped her fingers, and the dog bounded from the sofa toward her. "I went hiking with friends and stumbled across this guy abandoned with no collar. Are you ready to go now?"

"What?" He looked up and found her eying the door pointedly. "I don't even get a drink of water?"

She scooped up her pet, stroking a springy thatch of bristle on top of Buster's head. "Do you *need* a glass of water?"

"Not really. Just wanted you to offer. So about those hiking friends, is there some guy in your life?" Some fella to whom he could pass over protection duty or at least split time with?

"Noneya."

"None of my business, huh?" He scanned her cluttered apartment. "I don't see cuddly couple pictures anywhere."

"They're all in my boudoir on a ruffled table with heart candles."

"Scented?" Why was he goading her? She'd been through

hell. Maybe that was it. He wanted to distract her. Yeah, he was gonna go with that. "I checked your bedroom, remember? Nice undies."

She set the dog down with an exasperated sigh. "What is wrong with you? We've seen dead bodies tonight. It's"—she glanced at her wristwatch—"three twenty-seven in the morning, and I have to be at work in less than four hours. You never even liked me, so I know you're not flirting."

"I flirt with everyone." True enough. Women understood he was never in one place long enough for any kind of deep relationship.

"And there your charm just lost what little shine it had." She patted her mouth in a big, exaggerated yawn, one mimicked by Buster.

"You're right. I should get going." He couldn't stay here and pick fights with her until the threat left. He would be better served catching a couple hours' shut eye so he didn't fall asleep in the middle of the telecomm.

"Yes, you should." She crowded his space and urged him toward the door.

He stopped dead in his tracks, forcing her to stop just short of bumping into him. There was one last detail he *could* take care of now. "You really should lighten up on your old man a bit."

"Uh"—she inched back a step—"what part of noneya do you not understand?"

"I've never been good at keeping my big nose out of other people's business." God, he hoped she was as innocent as she appeared.

"My dad and I don't have business for anyone to get into."

"He cares." Strange how the guy instilled so much loyalty in the teens he'd worked with but not an ounce of it carried over to his own daughter.

She looked around the apartment. "I'm really feeling the love from Don right now. You can barely tolerate me, and yet *you*'re here to make sure I'm okay."

"People have different ways of showing they care."

"With Don, it's kinda like that tree falling in a forest thing. Does it really count if you never get to hear it? Or see it? And oh my God, I can't believe I'm still talking to you. This is it." She spun him around, hands planted on his back. "Reunion officially over."

Her touch seared.

He paused in the doorway, glancing back over his shoulder. "No good-bye hug?"

Her lips pursed tight. "Thank you for your help. Take care of yourself, and I'll see you in another seventeen years."

He fished his keys from his pocket. *Seventeen years? Think again.*

FIVE

★

Don watched his back.

A CIA guy in FBI headquarters in D.C. couldn't be too careful, after all. Rivalry between the agencies didn't disappear, even with better communication. Of course, communication had never been his strong suit. Just ask Jayne, who was still chewing his ass via e-mail.

Between Jayne and Paulina, he couldn't catch a break.

At least he had one major thing to be grateful for. Paulina's handwriting experts had determined that Shay's signature on the letters found in young Kevin's apartment had been a forgery. The Feds no longer suspected she was involved.

She was just sitting in the middle of a bull's-eye.

Striding into the FBI briefing room, Don walked alongside Lieutenant Colonel Rex Scanlon, the commander of Vince Deluca's dark ops test squadron and a man in serious need of new glasses to replace his Buddy Holly frames.

Scanlon would stay in D.C. throughout the operation, acting as a liaison between Vince's team and the intelligence community here.

Within minutes, the briefing room would be filled with Congress members and NSA representatives. All were gathering for the telecomm with Vince Deluca and the team of crewmembers he'd put together in Cleveland.

A single table stretched down the middle of the room with a television suspended from the ceiling, the monitor filled with the image of a room similar to this one. The select team of aviators began to file into that faraway room.

Scanlon made a beeline toward the coffeepot like a man on a mission for java, the manna of any respectable workaholic. The commander kept his voice low as he gave Don a running commentary on the flyers filing in after Vince, starting with a lanky, athletic type. "That's Captain Jimmy Gage, a copilot who used to fly surveillance planes. Hotwire's the man to watch your back in a bar fight—if he hasn't started the brawl himself."

Don watched Jimmy Gage fold into a seat next to Vince. "Jimmy Gage's file says he's fearless, that he will try anything in a plane."

"And his file is right."

God, he missed the crew days. Mentoring kids was important to him, but it hadn't completely filled the void, and his CIA work tended to be solo or administrative. Fingering the nitro tablets in his pocket, he had to face reality.

Getting old stank.

Scanlon filled a cup with steaming java as the next aviator in a green flight suit streamed into the room on the television. "That's Tech Sergeant Mason 'Smooth' Randolph. He's all about finesse on the ground and in the air."

Don mentally scanned the files he'd read. The flight en-

gineer also pulled gunner and loadmaster duties. These
dark ops test aviators could fly anything, anywhere, even
swapping out positions without hesitation. Of course, working in the test world meant being able to fly a new aircraft
or an old one with cutting-edge modifications and write the
manual—if the aircraft didn't crash and burn first.

Scanlon gestured with his coffee cup toward the TV
screen. "Watch your women around Smooth. He uses that
same finesse with the ladies."

Don's eyes shot straight to Paulina, who was adjusting
the volume on the telecomm monitor. Damn, her ass looked
great in those pencil-thin skirts, and it appeared the young
sergeant had noticed, too, as she walked back out the door.
Don frowned as Scanlon continued.

"Lastly, Deluca brought in the expertise of Captain
David 'Ice' Berg. His analytical genius is invaluable in
synthesizing data."

"A navigator, right?"

"That's what he started out as, then later trained to be a
fire control officer. He and Deluca haven't worked together
often. He's stepping in for the nav Deluca usually flies
with, Chuck Tanaka." Scanlon's face went dark.

Don trod warily. Tanaka's hellish experience overseas
had rocked the CIA world. Two and a half months ago, Tanaka had been kidnapped in Eastern Europe by a group selling military secrets to the highest bidder. Vince's test unit
had been instrumental in breaking up the ring while locating
and rescuing Tanaka. But not before the man endured two
weeks of torture. "Tanaka's still in the hospital, correct?"

Scanlon topped off his coffee with an overly controlled
precision. "He's actually right up the road in Maryland at
Malcolm Grow Medical Center at Andrews Air Force Base.
Being here in D.C. gives me a chance to check in on him."

Tanaka had a long road ahead of him. No doubt he would spend some time on a shrink's couch. Don's hand dropped to his BlackBerry.

Why couldn't Jayne understand it was guys like Tanaka who suffered from PTSD, not him? So he'd flown combat missions. The stress had been intense at times, but he dealt with it fine on his own. He still was, damn it. She was just looking for ways to blame him for the past rather than owning up to her part.

Paulina returned, cutting his thought short as she escorted in Congresswoman Raintree, Congressman Mooney, and two representatives from the NSA. Don settled into his seat along with everyone else, careful to keep his eyes on Paulina's face and nothing else.

"Good afternoon, ladies and gentlemen. And welcome to our air force contingent in Cleveland. For those of you I haven't met yet, I'm Special Agent Paulina Wilson. Thank you, Colonel Scanlon, for sharing some of your people with us for this operation. We realize how undermanned units are these days and appreciate your help in getting to the root of this terrorist threat."

The T word always sucked the air right out of a room.

The commander wrapped his hands around the handheld device linked to the main computer with Vince's Power-Point presentation. "We go where we're needed."

She nodded.

Was that a hot pink bra peeking from her navy blue jacket when she adjusted her notes on the podium?

Don forced his attention back to her face—okay, her eyes rather than her Angelina Jolie pouty lips.

"I understand you've all read the briefings on our situation in Cleveland and understand the time crunch we're facing in making sure this hearing runs without incident.

We've taken every precaution to guard the congressional aides already in Cleveland, but we hope you understand they don't have the clearance to be brought into the loop yet."

Paulina took a step back. "Now I'll turn over the floor to Major Vince Deluca, so he can outline his plans."

Even on the small screen, Vince dwarfed the podium. "Thank you, Agent Wilson. My plan is threefold. We'll start with surveillance prior to the hearing in hopes that we can nip this in the bud, then follow-up observation and protection at Case Western the day of the hearing."

Everyone shifted their attention to the handheld devices in front of them as Vince clicked the first slide, an image of the restored old brick factory where Shay worked. "This smaller community center in Cleveland, Ohio, reaches out to area gang members. Given evidence collected from a murdered teen's apartment, we have reason to believe gang members from this area have connections to international terrorists. And that terrorists outside of the country are using these teens to carry out a plot to set off some kind of explosion during the upcoming congressional hearing."

Don studied the two Congress members heading the hearing. Both appeared stalwart, committed. Congresswoman Raintree had prior service in the army, working with young recruits. Congressman Mooney had a well-known history of incorporating reformed troubled teens into his staff. Kids who'd grown into adults like Vince—who was continuing his brief.

"That evidence shows the teen had a connection to Shay Bassett, the nurse on staff. Monitoring her is a logical place to start. We need better surveillance in and around the clinic, something my unit is able to provide. We're focusing on the youth group meetings held by the center's activities director and nurse. There's one scheduled for tonight."

The next slide appeared of Shay and Eli, overseeing an immunization line in a cinderblock room. He was proud of his daughter, even if they'd never had a particularly close relationship. The divorce from Jayne right after Shay graduated hadn't helped matters, but there wasn't much he could do to change that now.

Vince thumbed the image control. "For monitoring these meetings, we will employ nanotechnology."

Next slide, a small mechanical . . . insect?

"We use models that look like a bumblebee or spider, with a camera or listening device installed. We can fly it by remote from a control station, sending the bee or spider into a room. We'll have a lot of eyes watching the feed coming in. Our air force team will be on site checking, while also transmitting the images to the FBI and NSA representatives. Any questions so far?"

Vince waited through a string of "No," "Not so far," and "Not yet" before continuing. "If we're lucky enough to narrow our field of suspects, we'll move on to phase two. We employ a military tracker to check cell phone calls. We can do this from the ground, but it's more effective when used in flight. The radar is so precise that it can target a weapon. Civilian monitoring relays what tower the phone is pinging off of, which only offers up a twenty-mile radius. With our new equipment, we can determine exactly where the call is coming from."

Congresswoman Raintree raised a finger. "Why hasn't the military passed this along for police use?"

"Excellent question, ma'am. They know about the technology, but like anything that's new, it costs money, lots of money, making it prohibitively expensive for regular law enforcement. We're still in the testing stage but feel confident enough in its safety to use this opportunity for a field test."

Don willed down the frustration, the downright discontent over not being in the middle of what Vince and his fellow aviators created as a regular course of business.

Raintree nodded. "Funds are definitely a concern. It's reassuring to see all of you reaching across territorial issues to blend resources and work together."

"We will be using the PC-6 Pilatus," Vince continued, the slide displaying an inconspicuous small craft that could have been sitting on anyone's private runway. "It's a recent addition to the air force fleet. There's currently a squadron at Hurlburt Field, the home of Air Force Special Operations. We have allocated one from them. It's a single-engine turboprop, very unobtrusive, painted to look like a civilian plane. It can be flown by one pilot and one person to man the equipment. I'll be flying with Captain Jimmy Gage, while Captain Dave Berg and Sergeant Mason Randolph monitor data on the ground."

Paulina slid off her glasses and tapped the tip against her chin. "Tell me more about this plane and what makes it different from, say, a Cessna."

Vince gripped the podium. "Colonel Scanlon, would you like to answer that one?"

Scanlon took the floor. "The plane is designed for utility work, carries interesting sensors airborne, has good cargo space, and a sweet maneuverability for getting in and out of small spaces. The plane itself has already been used in Iraq. We're working from our end to improve the monitoring equipment." He waved for Vince to resume the briefing.

"That brings us to phase three, the actual congressional

hearing. As you know, Congress doesn't draw a lot of security, just their scaled-down version of the Secret Service. Traditionally, they only get Secret Service protection if one of them is running for president. We're also concerned for the safety of the congressional witness, Shay Bassett, given the recent deaths at her clinic."

Vince turned toward his navigator. "Berg, how about you explain more about the workings of the nanosensor monitoring capabilities."

Berg steepled his fingers, his low-spoken words the kind that carried far. "There's versatility. We can also park the aircraft and simply use the mounted controls for nanosensors in the plane if we're certain the target will stay stationary."

Congresswoman Raintree gestured with her silver pen. "So the pluses of this method—you'll be virtually undetectable."

"Exactly," Scanlon answered while the other guests listened raptly. "The plane doesn't look dangerous or threatening. It's one of the most innovative additions we've seen added to the inventory. It's cheap and easy to fly."

Paulina shifted in her seat, a hint of pink lace playing hide-and-seek in a way that had Don looking at her more often than he wanted. "And the downside? Because in my experience there's always a downside, Major Deluca."

"Nonexistent defenses."

Congressman Mooney scrubbed a hand along his tanned jaw. "Colonel, what happens, then, if you are detected?"

"Someday—hopefully soon—we'll have radar sensors. We're actively working to make that happen. But for now, the pilot's skills with evasive maneuvers would be the only defense."

Congresswoman Raintree rolled the Cross pen between

two fingers. "Do you trust Major Deluca to have those skills?"

"Without question, ma'am," Scanlon answered, no hesitation.

Congressman Mooney exchanged a look with Raintree before she, as the senior Congress member, continued, "We're pleased with what you have in place to protect our safety and the integrity of the congressional hearing. We appreciate the time and resources you're contributing on behalf of this very important piece of legislation."

Paulina stood, pink lace dipping out of sight. "Then we're a go. Major Deluca and his team will carry on in Cleveland and proceed with putting the first nanosensor in place at a teen function scheduled at the center tonight."

Don studied his old student filling the screen and hoped Vince was as good at his job as the squadron commander touted. Because God help them all if fiery Shay caught him planting that flying nanosensor bug on her home turf without her knowledge.

* * *

Shay swatted away a mosquito as she leaned into the trunk of her car to heft out another crate of soda bottles.

This gathering would be a simpler one, given what had happened to Kevin and the student. She pushed herself to move ahead, even when she wanted to shout of her frustration over the senseless deaths. Their murders drove her to bring some kind of peace to this area.

Starting today.

For the most part, the community center staff had found low key worked best for these get-togethers. The important element? Food. These kids poured out for food. Problem was, in the long run, hot dogs and pizza had a tough time competing with crack and X. For now, a buffet and a listening ear were about all she had at her disposal.

And, of course, the local police department came through with an extra car parked conspicuously out front. Anything that brought the East Side Mercenaries and Apocalypse into the same place at once warranted official observation. So far, the rival gangs had kept to a wary standoff throughout the four-hour events.

A huge, freaking accomplishment on the part of the center's staff.

Trying to balance the flat of two-liter colas, she reached to close the hood. A pair of thick, masculine arms came around from behind her and scooped up the drinks. She spun around to find . . .

"Vince?" Shay covered her confusion with bravado. "Holy crap, has it been seventeen years already?"

He secured his hold on the sodas, arms bulging in a form-fitting black T-shirt. He smelled of a fresh shower and a scent essentially *him*. "I'm on vacation. I leave when the wind moves me."

"Where's a good lake effect storm when you need one?"

His deep laugh caught her off guard. "I actually came by to see if you need help setting up. Quit being an ungrateful brat and grab that grocery sack of chips."

She tugged out the blessedly lighter bag, searching his face. What was his real agenda? Because he'd never, ever sought her company without an order from her father. "You actually *want* to spend more time with me?"

She set her inner lie detector on high sensitivity and waited.

"Like I said, I'm here to help." He looked left, then right, giving her a clear view of the dot on one of his earlobes where his piercing had closed. He used to wear a small silver hoop in the old days. "It doesn't appear you're in any position to turn down an extra set of hands."

He had her there. And when it came to these kids, she would do anything for them. Her lie detector didn't catch anything but truth, although no question, he'd only told her a fraction of the story.

"Okay then. Let's put those muscles to work. But I'm warning you, the air conditioner barely works, and those oversized fans are noisy."

She guided him past the outside basketball court where Eli was cursing as he climbed up the post to replace the broken chain net. "That's our activities director and resident basketball champ."

Vince eyed the guy with blond dreadlocks and a sunburn. "I never knew Lake Erie attracted surfers."

"His look appeals to the kids." Sure, she was babbling, but it beat awkward silences. Or talk about her lingerie. "I'm the caterer for these events, and our social worker, Angeline, parks herself inside at the welcome desk where she can rest her feet. Her husband helps, too, if you can call watching ball games on his portable TV chaperoning. Parent volunteers are tough to come by, but luckily we have a few diehards who are willing to pull shifts."

His footsteps echoed behind her, biker boots heavy on concrete. She rushed past the Dumpster toward the back entrance, working like crazy to block out the memory of finding the college volunteer's and Kevin's bodies sprawled and bloody.

Once she cleared the door, she could breathe well enough to speak again. "How did you know about these weekly shindigs?"

He pointed toward the billboard on the wall. "I saw your flyer posted when I was in here last time."

Music drifted down the corridor from the DJ running a sound check. "With everything going on—a robbery, two stabbings, and police statements—you can't possibly have had time to read over the clinic's calendar."

"I'm an observant guy who likes to do his civic duty. I wear a uniform, remember?"

Just like the one her dad used to wear.

Her arms clenched tighter around the chips. "Where are you stationed these days?"

"Nellis Air Force Base outside of Las Vegas."

"What happens in Vegas . . ." She forced her grip to slacken before she turned the snacks to crumbs. "Vince, let's quit with this polite chitchat. I've got enough on my mind with a murderer running around on the loose. Straight up, why are you really here?"

"Can't get anything past you, can I?" He turned sideways to make room for a janitor rolling a stack of chairs. "Your father is worried about you after the murders outside the clinic, so I volunteered to hang with you for a while, check things out, and do some good for the community at the same time."

Her father again?

More likely Vince was making excuses for her dad, based on how he'd defended Don back at her apartment. The men in uniform always did stick together.

And, oh joy, if Vince was half as committed to pleasing her father as he'd been before, she would have a full-time job prying his butt out of the center, a problem that would have to wait until after the gathering, since she had her hands full with the normal neighborhood problems. Like kids wanting to kill each other rather than share the same pizza.

She gestured to the line of tables covered in butcher paper. "You can put those over there."

"Shay?" he said, voice carrying even above the roar of the oversized fans.

"The faster we can get these unloaded, the sooner I can make sure nobody's slipping something in the drinks."

"Shay," he said again, more insistent this time.

She forced herself to meet his gaze steady on. "Yes?"

"I understand this is your job, but promise me you'll be extra careful."

The intensity of his stare unsettled her. The unrepentant flirt was easier to deal with. "I'm always careful." *Sort of.*

She busied herself placing the chips at the food station, her gaze skipping away and over to Angeline at the welcome table talking with three new teens.

Her stomach clenched.

The East Street Mercenaries had arrived.

Six

★ ──────────────────────────────────

Shay checked the pack of Apocalypse members already settled in across the room. They'd noticed the arrival of the three Mercenaries but made no overt moves. The oldest in the pack smirked and looked away. The rest followed suit.

She shifted her attention back to the Mercenaries checking in with Angeline, who was busy keeping track of attendance as best she could. A record of who was where would be important if things went badly here or later in the street.

Shay glanced back at Vince, large and burly as always. Any irritations she felt would have to take a backseat. She could use his muscle right now. She'd bet Vince knew a thing or two about crowd control.

He joined her at the food table. "Have you heard anything more about the murders?"

"The police aren't talking to me."

"I meant have you heard anything via the grapevine from the kids." He nodded toward Angeline pressing her hand to a pregnant girl's stomach while two boys shuffled their feet behind her. "When I was a teen, everyone knew where the lines were drawn, what went down where, and who pulled it off."

"I wasn't as in the know as you." Even though she'd sure tried her best to fit in with him and his friends. She strode toward the back entrance again.

Vince followed, his words drifting over her shoulder like rumbling thunder. "You were off-limits to all of us because of your old man."

Not all of them. She'd managed to snag Tommy's attention. Vince's best friend. Her payback. "What would you have thought of me if I'd been someone else's daughter?"

"I would have thought you were lucky, spoiled, and ungrateful."

Not a rousing endorsement. "You thought that anyway."

He just smiled.

She refused to care what he believed anymore.

Eli double-timed past, basketballs tucked under his arms. "Heads up. Both sides are starting to trickle in."

"Thanks, Eli, got an eye on it." She stole a quick check out into the parking lot before looking back at Vince. He seemed genuinely interested in her work here, in the whole layout of the place, and she couldn't help but be sucked in by that. "Eli is our activities director. Eli, this is Major Vince Deluca, an . . . old friend."

The two men assessed each other with a territorial manner before Eli moved on. Vince hefted out another tray of drinks. "We never had anything like this back then. The way your dad set up the Civil Air Patrol was revolutionary."

More praise for Pops. Sweat trickled down her neck. "I'm hoping to set up the same sort of thing here, but it's tougher to get recruits these days."

"These kids make everybody back in our day look positively Disney."

"I wouldn't go that far, but yeah, there's a new and scary edge to what's going on with them. They're awash in dark tattoos and multiple piercings. Some people are frightened by their appearance, but actually it's the serious issues beneath it all that make them scary." She eyed four Apocalypse members heading for the hoops. "We've got two main gangs here, cliques or subsets of larger gangs in a big city."

"And they mingle together here without a riot erupting?" Vince scanned the outside rec area, his slow attention more than cursory politeness. "Pretty damn impressive."

"We all hold our breath every week, but yeah, so far they've declared these gatherings temporary cease-fires. They're probably scoping out the other side for weaknesses, but we're hoping over time walls will start to fall for at least some of them. The cops step up their presence during the events, just in case."

"It looks kinda like junior high when the girls sit at one table and the boys sit at another." He tucked his hands in his jeans pockets, faded denim pulling taut.

She swallowed hard and looked away. "A kinder, gentler image, but basically there."

"What's the scoop on the two gangs?"

Her need for distance from Vince took a backseat to her fervor to help these kids. "Apocalypse and East Street Mercenaries."

He looked back and forth from the basketball court to the parking lot. "I see the similar clothes, almost like a uniform of sorts. But which is which?"

"Apocalypse wears more traditional gang-style clothes, saggy pants and oversized white T-shirts with a crisp crease down the front. 'Tall tees,' they're called around here."

"So those kids with polo shirts buttoned all the way to the top are Mercenaries? That boy, Kevin, wore a T-shirt."

"He also had a brand-new tattoo." She forced the image of his slashed chest out of her mind. "The Apocalypse tat is of the Grim Reaper, hood with the eyes."

"Ah, that's why he carried the machete."

She shuddered. "Exactly. Sadly, the clothes, the darkness, aren't an anomaly. East Street Mercenaries tattoo FEAR across their knuckles on each hand. They also wear an arm torc, a leather thong on their bicep. The wider it is, the more important that person is in the hierarchy. The Mercenaries use guns and brass knuckles with raised letters spelling FEAR, so during a beat down, the bruises leave their tag."

"You really are prepared for this congressional hearing." He stopped her with a hand to the arm. "These kids could be torqued off at you for that."

His callused touch jolted her to a stop and taunted her with a reminder that she hadn't changed so much after all. Somewhere inside her still lived that same screwed-up girl.

She eased her arm free. The neighborhood needed help, but she could well be breaking the thin thread of trust with these kids with her public statement. Hey wait . . . "How did you know I'm speaking at a congressional hearing?"

He hesitated for a blink. "Your father told me."

Her inner lie detector sensed another half-truth. She opened her mouth to push the issue.

Four Apocalypse members abandoned the basketball court and walked toward the back entrance, even though the signs clearly said to enter from the front.

"Nice kicks, Miss Bassett." Two piercings along his eyebrow glinting, Caden nodded toward her yellow gym shoes, signature low rise Chuck Taylors.

"Thanks, Caden." She smiled until he dipped back into the crowd.

Rickie pulled an Eli move and studied Vince through narrowed eyes, especially his bald head. Vince stared him down, both of them like dogs in a pack, alpha holding the longest, taking this past the more normal exchange with Eli.

Rickie shrugged away with something that sounded like, "Fuck you, old man."

Vince turned back to Shay with an *I told you so* look. "Kicks are shoes I assume."

"Oh my, how our own resident bad boy has fallen behind the times."

"Tell that to F-U boy."

"Rickie? Yeah, he's bucking for a higher position in the ranks. But back to kicks." She extended her foot. "Caden's a suck-up."

It helped her tamp down the fear by looking for whatever normal teen behavior she could find in each one.

"So that one is Eddie Haskell busting a sag and packing heat."

"Bingo."

Vince waited while she lifted out a bag of paper plates and cups. "I've heard the baggy pants originated from prison life."

"You heard right. Prisoners can't have a belt in jail, and the clothes are often ill-fitting. Prisoners have to make do with what they get. When they leave jail, they continue to wear their pants low as a testimony to the time served, to garner respect. They went to prison for something they did for the gang."

"Damn." He watched her intently.

"What?"

"You sound just like your father."

"Are you trying to rile me up?" Good God, could she make it any clearer to him that she and her dad were on the outs? "Just because Don and I have both worked with teens does not make us alike in all other ways."

He held her gaze, not as he'd done with Eli and Rickie, but with an elemental buzz all the same. Forget playing the stare-down game. Her ego was just fine.

Vince stepped back into her line of sight. "While you unpack those bags, how about I unload the rest from the car?"

They would spend less time talking that way. Less tumult. "Sure."

"Do you mind if I look around the place after I finish? Check out what you've got going on here?"

All interest in her job aside, his request struck her as odd. "Is this another excuse to play bodyguard to make my daddy happy?"

"I'm just genuinely impressed and curious."

Why couldn't she accept his words at face value rather than assuming he had some sort of hidden agenda?

Suddenly Vince smiled. "Go ahead and say it."

"What?" she snapped this time.

"What Rickie said. Tell me to fuck off. You know you want to."

She bit the inside of her cheek to keep from accommodating him. Denying him access would sound petty. His looking around wouldn't harm anything. "Feel free to wander around. And thank you for your help. People are showing up sooner than we expected."

"You're welcome." He sauntered away, his butt looking too good in jeans that fit.

A baggier fit to those pants would go a long way toward reining in thoughts she did not want when it came to Vince Deluca.

She had other concerns tonight. She looked out over the sea of teens and wondered. Was the boy out there? The one who'd called her earlier this week? No one else on the staff had heard from him. She'd dealt with other calls in the interim. Why did he stick in her head so? Because of her own past? Or Vince's?

Regardless, she had to accept she might well never have closure on a kid who faced machetes and brass knuckle beat downs.

★ ★ ★

Vince ducked out of the Cleveland Community Center, the listening device in place and ready for flight. He'd done his job.

So why did he feel like that bee was stinging him all the way back to the parking lot?

He scanned past the cars to his Ducati loaner. He tensed. Two males were checking out his bike: adult males. Vince relaxed.

A shorter man he didn't recognize stood beside the center's activities director, Eli, the dude with the head full of blond dreadlocks. Vince tucked around the last car between him and them. He needed to make this quick and get to the hangar.

"Anything I can help you gentlemen with?"

The stranger turned first, a young guy in khakis and a yellow polo shirt. Given his uptight haircut and prep school look, the preppy would probably be horrified to realize he wore anything hinting of a gang "uniform." Of course that open top button saved him from totally fitting the bill.

Eli stuck out his hand. "Hey there, Major Deluca. Remember, we met earlier during setup?"

"Eli, right?"

"You got it. And this is Anthony. He's an aide for Congressman Mooney from California." Eli's chest puffed as he hooked his thumbs in his khaki pockets, sporting an outback look. "Anthony's here to check out the lay of the land, gather more information for the congressman to take back to the congressional committee."

The preppy guy thrust his hand forward. Vince clasped back, careful to stay clear of the bandage he noticed on the guy's wrist. "Nice to meet you."

"Cool ride." Stepping away, Anthony stroked the handlebars. "Where did you pick this up? I thought all us public servants made poverty wages."

"A good friend hooked me up with a loaner while I'm on vacation." Vince tied his do-rag over his head, itchy to get to work.

Eli whistled low. "Generous friend. You have a sugar mama?"

"Afraid not." He strapped on his helmet, hoping they would get the hint.

"Ah," Eli answered. "I wish I had your connections. My bike tends to stay in my garage, but I enjoy just owning it, showing it off on occasion. The women do go wild when you crank the engine."

Vince stifled the urge to tap his boot restlessly. "Well, I should be—"

Anthony stroked the leather seat. "What kind of ride do you have?"

Eli shrugged. "Nothing as cool as this. Just a 1098 S Tricolore."

Vince paused. "Not too shabby."

About a twenty-five-K bike, if he remembered right. He eyed the activities director—an activities director for an underfunded community center.

Eli winked. "I do have a sugar mama."

Anthony shoved his hands in his pockets and rocked back on his loafers. "I need to start taking notes from you two."

Eli glanced over his shoulder. "I think I hear Angeline calling for my help. Anthony, get your notepad ready." He nodded to Vince. "Nice meeting you, Major."

The duo walked away.

Vince muttered, "Waxer."

Guys like Eli spent more time washing and waxing the bike than riding it. For guys like that, the bike was all about impressing the babes, not honoring the ride.

And hell no, he wasn't jumping to snap judgments just because the activities director seemed to be exactly the kind of guy Shay admired.

*　*　*

They'd made him come to this stupid "party" even though he might run into *her*.

He wanted to go home, but he couldn't wimp out. Nobody was here for the forced fun. They came to scope out the other side. Get the lowdown in order to make the next hit for their own.

He bounced the ball three times fast before arcing it at the net for . . . a miss.

His fellow banger snagged the rebound and shot. "How lame is this?"

"Food's good." Better than anything at home. Except Shay Bassett had come to restock the tables, and he'd been forced out here in case she recognized his voice from that suicide hotline call. He'd disguised his voice, and it wasn't like she knew him that well. Still, he wasn't risking jack shit when it came to her.

So he continued to shoot hoops with the jag-off he called his brother. He shot again, ball rolling around the rim.

His brother shot. Nothing but net. The chains rattled and settled. "I get food at that corner market anytime I want."

"Not me." He wanted to hurl even thinking about standing beside that building in case someone realized he'd disrespected another gang's tag. *Kevin*'s tag, and now Kevin was dead. "The old bitch that runs the place has it out for me."

"Then pop her. Don't let her get away with dissing you."

He stayed quiet, swatting at a bee buzzing around his head. Memories of his blood-in to the gang made his hands shake and made him long for his inhaler even though he managed his allergies with meds these days.

"You weak with the women?"

He couldn't stop himself from checking out the window where he could see Shay Bassett opening another box of pizza. He looked away fast to scoop up the rebound and make sure she didn't feel him eyeballing her.

At least her big-ass bodyguard had left after his good citizen tour of the place. Was she screwing the guy? The big dude with his shaved head and no-fear eyes looked like a major player. Must be nice to twitch her tail and have all that protection. "Fuck no, I'm not a pussy."

"Are you sure you're not some kinda mama's boy?"

The mention of his ma sent the pepperoni pizza tumbling around in his stomach faster than the annoying bee that kept flying by. "I said no."

"You know what a real man has to do to keep his people safe." He held out his fist.

He bumped fists with his brother, FEAR across their knuckles.

Marked for life. However long that would be.

Anger burned up his throat until he chucked the basketball at that fucking bee. No life. No choices left for him—or Shay Bassett.

Soon, really soon, she would pay the ultimate price for messing in a war where she didn't belong.

* * *

Sitting at the flight controls, Vince flinched as the basketball soared near the camera image. Damn, that was a close call with the thug arcing the ball at their remote-controlled nanosensor "bumblebee." He adjusted the altitude.

The small plane housing the mobile command center was parked at a small local airport, conveniently located near Shay's gathering. Berg, Jimmy, and Smooth sat at screens, monitoring the different angles of video feed and sound. He could have the plane airborne in minutes for alternate sensoring, or he could zoom out on his motorcycle straight to her if things erupted.

Good thing Shay had been cool with him wandering around the center, making it all the easier to plant the nanosensor. Not a surprise, actually, that she'd cut him loose to roam, since the woman only put up with him as long as groceries needed unloading.

How much longer would the FBI agent insist on keeping Shay in the dark? Especially now that all signs indicated she was innocent.

Eventually, she would have to know. What would she think about hearing she'd been observed? Hopefully she would understand the need to keep her in the dark initially. But he suspected otherwise.

He'd heard the zeal in her voice when she'd spoken about the teens and the danger they faced daily.

Working the joystick, he scanned the outdoor basketball

court, recognizing the activities director standing with a trio of teens he'd met earlier. So far, everything in the Eli dude's background check appeared clean. Nothing they'd heard tonight indicated otherwise.

Actually, nothing they'd heard from anyone offered up clues. They would scrutinize the feed again after the event.

He tapped a series of buttons on the controller, easing the bee up a bit higher. Satisfied with the altitude, he programmed the sensor to fly a lazy circle over the court and an outdoor food stand. A few more taps, and he had the pin-size camera on the nano-bug centered up in the area he wanted to watch. *Sweet. Technology rules.*

The suck-up who liked Shay's "kicks" helped himself to three slices of pizza while his friend, the F-U kid, stuffed an abandoned cell phone into one pocket and a snack-size bag of chips in the other. The camera was so good Vince could make out the label. He remembered well never feeling full enough, too prideful to admit it, and gut determined to do anything to gain control of his life.

Vince adjusted the flight so it followed some of the kids in buttoned-up polo shirts and baggy jeans inside. A sweep of the room showed Shay restocking the drink table. He tweaked the focus until her face filled the screen.

Smooth tapped the buttons up and down the edges of the screen. "Your zoom looks a little close to me."

Vince scrubbed his hand over his do-rag, civilian clothes and no shaving a definite perk to this low-profile assignment. "Just trying to hear what she's saying."

"Uh-huh. And you're also swearing off doughnuts." Smooth backed off the zoom with the tap of a button, switching his screen to another view of Shay.

"Easy there, dude," Berg warned. "We don't want to fire up the big guy."

"Does he have a prior claim? I never would have guessed from all the time he's spent watching her."

"Hello, dirtbags." Vince waved a hand. "I'm here."

"Sorry about that," Smooth said without a hint of contrition.

He needed to nip this in the bud. Rumors spread like crazy with his gossip hound pals. They had so much classified information to hold secret that they went to the opposite extreme in sharing every detail about each others' social lives. "No claim, but I do know Shay Bassett. We were in high school together." He couldn't bring himself to call it a brother-sister connection. "I owe her father more than I can repay. He's the reason I'm in the air force today."

"Shit," Jimmy snorted, workout clothes rustling as he twisted in his seat toward Vince. "Who started piping in the violins?"

"Screw off, my friend." Damn, he even sounded like the thug tonight. "How about just take it down a notch."

Jimmy grinned. "Like you did when I met Chloe?"

"I was just yanking your chain." He'd gone easy on the guy, considering what a sap Jimmy was for his conductor girlfriend. "It was obvious you were gone on her from the second you met her a couple months ago. Things are different here."

Smooth typed in commands to scroll through video feed. "Then you won't mind if *I* make a move."

"Of course not." Shay was an adult. She could pick and choose her own dates. He was cool with that. Totally. "She's older than you are."

Smooth whistled while fine-tuning his camera view. "All the better."

A growl started low in Vince's throat before he even realized it.

Jimmy clapped him on the back, eyes still on the screen. "Dude, take it easy. You just got punked."

A phone rang over their headsets, coming from the sensor feed. He followed the sound in flight until it got louder, louder still, bringing the nano-bee to the welcome table manned by the woman with a cane.

Vince pressed the seal of his headset firmer against his ear. "Hey, Berg, can you crank the volume? I'm going to fly closer in so we can figure out if that call's anything of interest."

"Wilco," Berg answered, his fingers tapping in commands that increased the chatter over the headphones.

The microphones on the bee were good enough to pick up the conversation, easily hearing the person on the other line as well. Years spent flying aircraft gave Vince plenty of experience weeding out the chaff in order to listen to what he needed to hear.

The woman at the reception desk nudged aside her clipboard and picked up the receiver. "Cleveland Community, this is Angeline. How can I help you?"

"I want to speak with Shay," a young male voice answered.

Vince straightened, making damn sure the record feature on their control center was working as advertised.

Angeline snagged a pencil, tucking the phone under her chin. "She's busy right now. Could I take a message and have her call you back?"

"I have to talk to her," the teenage voice snapped back, cracking in prepubescent urgency.

"If you will just give me your name and number, I assure you she will call back."

"Maybe I just should have called the suicide hotline."

All background noise faded in Vince's mind as the woman's face shifted, serious, professional.

"Don't hang up, young man. I'm on a cordless phone so we can keep right on talking while I find her. Okay? Stay calm and I *will* find her."

"You'd better, because I don't have much time."

Angeline nodded to an older guy beside her—her husband maybe?—and he helped her to her feet. She clutched a cane and moved with commendable speed for a woman with a bum leg. She shouldered aside teens, and apparently her presence commanded respect, because none of the scary-as-hell-looking kids said a word in complaint. "I can see her across the room. Only a few more seconds."

"You'd better move faster, lady, or you're gonna be sorry."

"Hold on. I'm giving you to her now." Angeline covered the mouthpiece. "Shay, there's a young man on the phone, asking for you. I think he's the one you've been worried about."

Shay dropped the bag of pretzels, snatched the phone, and stepped back by a water fountain out of the fray. Even from two miles away, Vince could see the thoughts race across her expression. The worry. The fear.

"This is Shay."

"Do you remember me?" the young male asked.

"Of course I do. We talked the other night, and I know you don't want to die."

"I'm not going to die today."

"That's good." She sagged back against the silver fountain. "I'm glad to hear you say that."

"If you're not extra careful, Shay, this might be the day *you* die."

Vince straightened in his seat, pressing a hand to his headset to seal in the sound.

"There's a bomb in the building."

SEVEN

The fire alarm shrieked in Shay's ears, echoing through the cavernous gym.

"Everyone stay calm, exit carefully. Stay calm, exit carefully," she repeated, urging teens toward the front entrance. She sure could have used some of Vince's muscle right about now.

Her heart pounded as loudly as the feet drumming away in barely controlled chaos. She spun on her heels for a quick run back through the center. A sidestep kept her clear of Officer Jaworski's line of sight just beyond the door. He would undoubtedly want her out.

Tough. She wasn't leaving until she could be certain all of her charges were safe.

Jaworski's voice blared over the bullhorn with tinny-sounding commands for order. While she wanted to avoid him for now, thank heaven he was on site to keep the peace outside.

"It'll be okay; it'll be okay," she chanted on each gasping breath.

Clearing the center wasn't going as quickly as she'd hoped. At least she could finally hear police sirens wailing at the full moon outside.

Shay sprinted through the entryway back down the empty hall, her gym shoes squeaking along tile. She opened one door after another, an exam room, another, her office.

All empty. And where the hell had she left her backpack? She couldn't waste time searching.

Pressing a hand to the stitch in her side, she dashed into the girls' bathroom, and damn it, third stall down, she found feet clad in a large pair of dusty kicks.

"Out, out, out! Bomb threat."

A gasp sounded from inside the stall.

Two more feet slid to the ground, feminine ones in strappy sandals so small the other shoes took on an even larger—masculine—look.

"Out." She pounded on the stall right by scratches in the paint.

Rickie's a dickhead.

This place sux.

For a good time call . . .

"Open up right now, or I swear I'll take it off the hinges."

The door creaked wide to reveal a red-faced pair of Apocalypse teens.

Caden, wearing his too-cool shoes, buttoned his saggy jeans. "What's the big deal? Somebody just tripped the fire alarm again."

True enough, that happened often, but still. "Someone called in a bomb threat. We have to leave."

"Shit," he barked with a surprise that seemed real enough for her to cross him off her list of suspects.

The scrawny girl went paler than the porcelain john be-hind her. Another suspect down. If memory served, the girl was Toni, a teen she suspected suffered from either ano-rexia or drug abuse.

Toni tugged down her tiny spandex skirt. "Come on, Caden. I've got my mom's car. I'll finish you off there."

How classy. Shay hated most of all that they reminded her too much of herself with Tommy. Losing your virginity in a smelly bathroom stall really didn't make for much of a treasured memory.

Neither said another word as they brushed past, taking their sweet time. Hesitating in the door, Caden clicked his tongue ring against his teeth in a gross display.

Shay resisted the urge to shout out her frustration as she pointed down the hall toward the glowing Exit sign. "Use the back entrance. It's closer."

She would check the rest of the rooms while following them. Only a few more seconds, and she would be free. Not that she was worried. The place really wasn't going to blow up. It couldn't. She was just following routine.

And yeah, if she told herself that long enough, she just might stop worrying about what-ifs during this crazy week.

Finally she pushed through the back door and sucked in mind-clearing breaths that calmed her for a whole two seconds. She coughed on smoke wafting from behind the Dumpster.

Smoke with a distinctive scent rising above even the stench of rotting garbage.

Swatting at an irritating fly buzzing around her head, Shay followed the smell of weed right back to a quartet of Mercenaries toking up behind the Dumpster. She was too furious to be intimidated by the tattooed FEAR across their knuckles.

She kicked her way past a backpack. "That alarm means there's a bomb threat, gentlemen. So move it, unless you want flames smoking out of your ass instead of your doobie."

Her order stunned them silent. Their slow-to-track red eyes didn't comprehend the situation as a chorus of expletives went up from the unmoving crowd. Finally, a kid with swaths of acne got his butt in gear, trudging past her with leaden footsteps. "Whatcha gonna do? Send Jaworski back here? He's probably too busy playing with his rod."

The others laughed at the reference to the cop's tendency to reach for his baton. She wasn't amused.

As the fourth teen—one with a familiar snake tattoo peeking out of his shirt collar—passed, she snatched the hand-rolled from between his pinched fingers.

"Not a chance, Brody." She stared down the seventeen-year-old with professor-type glasses and a scraggly attempt at a goatee. She ground his joint under her heel. "Now move it."

She raced after them around to the front. Eli herded people from the parking area to a lot across the street, where Angeline kept watch over others under the umbrella of streetlights. A fire truck honked in the distance. Officer Jaworski lowered his megaphone as other police cars circled the building.

Shay jerked to halt beside him, panting. "Officer Jaworski? I think I found everyone."

His face pinched with disapproval. "Miss Bassett, you shouldn't have stayed inside."

Okay, whatever. Why argue when she'd already gotten her way? "I grabbed a basic floor plan of the building." She pulled out the flyer from a mini conference they'd held on parenting for teens, complete with a sketch of the building for attendees to use in finding different classrooms. "It's not an exact blueprint, but it has the general layout."

He took the flyer from her. "Good thinking. Thanks. Our bomb squad can use this until we can lay hands on something more official."

She glanced at her pink and yellow striped watch and found that no more than ten minutes had passed since Angeline had made the announcement over the loudspeaker.

Jaworski dismissed her with a wave, crowding her farther away from the building, his hand reaching for his rod—uh, baton. She understood he had a job to do, but the way she saw it, the potential for an equally large explosion simmered around here with the two rival gang members all fired up and mingling. If Jaworski pushed too hard with his hammer approach, things could detonate.

She made a quick scan to count cop cars and found a half-dozen, decked to the nines with guns and more billy clubs. A dog barked from the back of one vehicle. For bomb sniffing or control through intimidation? Her stomach went tight.

Sounds assaulted her already saturated senses: the sirens, the voices, the bustling bodies. All of it swelled with restlessness. She forced even breaths in and out, wishing she could will peace through these kids and make them understand how lethal crowd control could turn. They needed to disband soon before— Damn it.

A fight broke out.

"Fuck you," Rickie shouted, shoving another teen in the chest, scorpion tattoo on his hand flashing red. "Did you really think you could get away with dissing our tag?"

Amber stepped between them, her baby bulge all too vulnerable. "It wasn't him. Webber wouldn't do that."

Caden stalked closer, crowding the pregnant girl. "Do you know something, bitch? Was it you?" The resident suck-up showed his true colors, ones that had nothing to do with gang colors.

Webber chest butted him, a sword tattoo flexing on his bicep. "You started the tag war. We retaliated. Now get the hell away from her."

"Who do you think you are, telling me what to do?"

The exchange and shoves went so fast, in her growing panic Shay lost track of all the kids piling on.

Officer Jaworski barked through a megaphone. "Halt. Step back, or we will be forced to remove you."

The cop's orders all but bounced off the heads of the half-dozen or so teens pushing at each other while the rest of the crowd jeered. Shay could only think of pregnant Amber in the middle.

Elbows jabbed into her side as Shay pushed through, her gaze locked on the vulnerable girl. A heavy foot stomped hers. She bit back a curse.

Eli slid past. "Take it down a notch, Rickie."

Rickie hauled back a fist and let it fly toward Brody. Eli ducked, barely dodging the punch and hooking the kid around the waist. His flailing foot grazed Shay's stomach.

Ouch, shit, damn it.

She knew better than to get in the middle, but seeing Amber cradle her belly . . . Shay shouldered ahead to grasp the girl's wrist and wrap her arms around Amber's huddled body. Thank God no weapons had been drawn yet. This was seconds away from tear gas and drawn guns.

There had to be a better way.

She ducked clear of Rickie and Brody taking on anyone in their path. An elbow nailed her on the cheekbone. Sparks fired behind her eyes, wiping out her sight for a second before she blinked it clear again. She hauled the pregnant girl closer and backed away.

The smell of sweaty bodies and rancid hatred clung to the air. The lot filled with the shouts of their gang mates urging them on, the battle cry of street violence whooping it up until all she could hear were obscenities and shrieks.

Strong hands gripped her waist and ushered her out of the way with Amber. Shay started to scream, then swallowed back the sound in shock.

She sagged with relief. She didn't even need to see his face to know. She recognized those intimidating shoulders in a biker rally T-shirt. The high-end motorcycle parked a few yards behind him only confirmed it.

Vince's face came into sharp focus, a black do-rag over his scalp. "That way, Shay. Go. Now!"

Good God, was this man living in her pocket? How else could he always know when to show up?

He gave a careful but forceful nudge that sent her back and away, her fingers locked with Amber's. Finally, Shay stumbled free of the smothering press.

She clasped the pregnant teen close to her side, surreptitiously checking the girl's pulse at the wrist. A steady throb pushed through the cherry blossoms inked along Amber's arm. "Are you all right?"

The teen swept the back of her hand across mascara-stained cheeks. "Fine, it's no big thing."

Shay wasn't so sure the girl was as unaffected as she claimed, but her heart rate was only slightly elevated, not dangerously so. Shay gave Amber a gentle squeeze, her eyes zipping back to search the crowd to find Vince, her unlikely savior. He blocked a punch then secured his attacker in a headlock.

Now that she had a better vantage point, she could see the cops making headway. Vince's presence helped even the odds, shoving apart the rival gang members. The street began to open up like the Red Sea to divide the warring parties of onlookers. Cops filled in blank spaces as they worked without weapons.

Amber twitched against Shay, the girl's feet inching closer to the brawl. "He's going to get hurt."

Which "he" did Amber mean?

"You need to think about your baby. You're having a little girl, right?"

Tears welled in her eyes. "Yeah, but what about him?"

Shay didn't even know how to answer that other than to tuck the girl closer to her side.

A handful of cops stayed on the fringes, eyes darting, monitoring, hands on their holstered service revolvers. If anyone started pulling guns . . . Part of her longed for her own weapon, and another part of her was grateful the 9 mm was tucked away safely in her backpack somewhere in her office.

Slowly, the tide turned. Eli and Vince restrained Rickie and Caden, while Officer Jaworski and two other police officers snapped cuffs on the other offenders.

Caden gave a final token struggle against Vince's hold, a bruise purpling his jaw, blood trickling from his eyebrow.

"Back down," Vince barked, intimidating through his sheer size alone, "and listen to the cop, or you're going to end up eating asphalt."

"Fuck you, old man."

"Stand in line, kid."

Officer Jaworski took command from the middle, no longer using his megaphone or baton, just the power of a deep bass with authority that added years to his youth. "I want to make it crystal clear. If anything goes down tonight, I took note of who's here, so I'll know exactly who to haul in first for questioning. You'll end up sharing a cell with your 'friends.'"

An uneasy truce settled. Sure, there was mumbled BS and shuffling feet, but fists stayed down. Amber found her sister and gave Shay a wobbly smile. "Thanks, Miss Bassett."

"Call me if anything feels the least bit out of the ordinary with the baby. You have my cell phone number."

"Sure, whatever." The girl bolted away and fell into her sister's arms, sobbing.

A sigh shuddered through Shay as her official role started to ease enough for her mind to slow and question . . .

Vince had actually shown *again*.

And he could have been hurt in a riot gone wrong. Like before. She swayed for a dizzying second before she regained control. She would not, absolutely would *not* bend over and hold her knees.

After he passed Caden over to the cops, Vince powered toward Shay. "Are you okay?"

She rubbed the back of her neck to try to get some blood flowing to her brain again. God, she needed to replace the mental image of Vince injured because of her, of what could have happened, of what could happen still if that bomb threat wasn't a hoax. "I'm fine."

"Are you sure? You're so pale, you look like you're going to pass out."

He thumbed the corner of her mouth, his hand coming back with a smear of blood. She pressed her fingers to her face, fast, suddenly aware of her body again now that the threat had passed. Her cheek throbbed from the elbow jab, but nothing felt broken.

Cool air brushed her stomach, and she glanced down. At some point, a big hole had ripped in the side of her T-shirt, a grubby shirt and jeans now after her trip around broken bathroom stalls, Dumpsters, and dirty cop cars. She smelled like weed, and her hair felt sticky with blood. How could a tiny split in her lip bleed so much?

She pressed the tip of her tongue against the cut.

Vince's eye fell to her mouth. Held. Heated.

She tucked her tongue back in her mouth and looked away. "Just shaken up but okay. You've learned some new moves since we were teenagers."

"Saw it in a James Bond movie." He shrugged dismissively.

He had done that before, made a joke of life when everyone else was on the verge of tears. Yet he couldn't be unaffected by this now. Fights they'd seen and been in seventeen years ago were too horribly parallel to the present. She felt it often enough in her job on a day-to-day basis, but having Vince here . . .

How could she not think of the worst night of all? Bullets had been flying, bodies falling. Vince throwing himself between her and the guns.

Except this time, no one had died. Yet.

Vince gripped her arm, his touch hot and solid. "At least sit down. You're weaving on your feet."

She eased herself to the curb. "Bomb threats and fire alarms are actually fairly common around here. So far, it's always turned out to be a prank. One time a girl flipped the alarm on her way to the bathroom. Her mother had brought her in for a physical, and the teen didn't want her mom to know she was pregnant. She figured tripping the switch would get her out of the appointment."

That had been Amber.

Why hadn't she thought of it until now? Amber couldn't have had anything to do with this threat, too, could she? She'd been lucky to get off with a slap on the wrist before. What would she have to gain from such a risky move now?

Vince crouched down on one knee, his eyes alert, muscles straining at his blood-smeared white T-shirt. "Clearing the room sounds like a temporary fix."

"You know how kids are. Many don't think beyond today." Maybe Amber hadn't needed a reason.

"Any ideas who might be at fault this time?"

She shook her head, not ready to speak on that subject until she had her thoughts together. "I just wish I'd been able to grab my backpack when I checked my office, but I didn't see it right away, and it seemed more important to get the heck out of there."

"We'll go back to the clinic once we've gotten the official all clear from the bomb squad." He squeezed her shoulder, sending a shiver of something besides warm comfort down her spine.

She glanced up at him, into his eyes, eyes very guarded.

What didn't he want her to see? And for that matter, another thought returned to niggle at her brain now that the threat seemed to have passed.

"Vince, I appreciate your help, but how did you know to come back?"

* * *

Paulina had made it through one bomb threat today, but she wondered how she would survive the other bombshell she would have to drop in Don's lap before too much longer.

For now, she decided to be grateful the workday had ended without exploding a congressional witness—and Don's daughter. She'd left the office in capable hands while she ate and slept.

With Don.

She sat across from him at her small dining room table, a Brahms ballade softly coating the thick silence between them. He stabbed his fork through the chicken soufflé, deflating it one poke at a time.

Soufflé?

Okay, so it was a casserole cooked with cream of mushroom soup like her mama used to bake in their tiny Kentucky backwoods trailer park. But the smell comforted her, making her feel loved and relaxed—feelings she'd thought Don would need after a day like today.

She'd figured wrong. He barely touched his food, and he certainly didn't appear in the least relaxed.

Paulina rubbed her cloth napkin along a smudge on the clear glass tabletop. "Have you spoken to Shay?"

"No." Poke. Jab. Bite.

"Why not?" she prodded, a lot gentler than he tore apart his mostly uneaten dinner.

"She's probably busy giving statements." He dropped his fork in favor of the crystal goblet and downed half the sparkling water with a lemon twist. "Deluca called to tell me she's all right and that he's making sure she's settled for the night. If anything, I should be worried about Deluca's boss chewing his ass for turning over the controls to the remote listening device and speeding away to the center. Scanlon's normally cool, but he cursed up a blue streak over that one."

She ignored his attempt to distract her with talk of work. She'd had more than enough of the office with Congressman Mooney's aide calling her repeatedly for security updates. Thank God the overeager aide wasn't in the loop on the air force angle, or her phone would be ringing off the hook. "Seems to me Shay would want to know you're concerned."

Paulina nudged a serving dish of steamed asparagus across the table—Jolly Green Giant straight from the can into a bone Waterford serving dish. She wasn't much of a cook, but Don had never complained before.

He grunted, the glass table providing a clear view of his knee jostling with agitation.

She sagged back in her chair. "You take reticent to a whole new level."

"Then let's don't talk." He dumped half the asparagus on his plate.

"I would ask you to apologize for being rude, but I know you wouldn't mean it."

"How do you know what I mean if I won't talk?" he snapped, using his fork to spear and double over a stalk of asparagus before shoveling it in his mouth.

"I can read your eyes."

A tight smile pulled at his mouth as he swallowed. "A downside to seeing an agent. You have those super-spooky skills at reading body language."

Seeing an agent? Not even dating or being in a relationship. She tried not to let the nuances of his word choice sting. Tried. And failed. "I use my powers for good, not evil. Although it doesn't take an expert to realize you would be upset tonight. Your daughter was in the middle of a bomb scare."

"Shay's all right. It's over. No explosives were found in the building. The fight ended without serious injuries, just some bruises and a half-dozen teens cooling their heels for a few hours in a holding cell. With luck, Deluca's team will figure out who's responsible once they've had a chance to review the footage more closely. Crisis over for today."

He finished his water, eating and drinking as if on autopilot, the way he did everything. Only during sex did she see an entirely different man.

"Stress doesn't work that way. Humans can't compartmentalize like a computer." She'd lost count of how many times growing up she'd run out to the field of goldenrod behind the trailer park and screamed her frustration. These days, she went to the shooting range, letting her weapon shout for her. "And the crisis isn't over until we make it through that congressional hearing."

He set his fork down slowly, with only a small clink of metal against bone china. "Paulina, what are you doing?"

How far could she push him? "We're talking."

"We don't do that. Unless it's about work."

"Maybe we should talk about something besides the current crisis at the office or what position of the *Kama Sutra* to try next."

His eyes went from confused to assessing in a snap that reminded her he had as much interrogation training as she did, plus a few extra years of life seasoning. "Don't go changing the rules, Paulina. We have a good thing, and I would hate for that to end."

A threat?

Would he really walk out the door just because she wanted to commiserate about his daughter being in danger? A daughter she'd never met, only seeing her in photos and surveillance footage.

His face said he was already eying his walking shoes lined up neatly in the entryway.

She hated the spike of panic, even hated Don a little for causing it. Since she'd left that trailer behind at eighteen, she'd trained her butt off to be fearless in every aspect. That training also reminded her of the importance of not pushing too hard, too fast.

Time to backpedal. "Of course you're right about how good things are with what we have." She toyed with the top button of her navy blue suit, giving him a sneak peek at her pink satin bra. "What do you say we take that Sara Lee lemon meringue pie out of the fridge and eat dessert off each other? It'll have to be a quickie so we can get back to work, but I guarantee you'll be satisfied."

Part of being a good agent included knowing when to ease back and regroup for the next push. Because, make no mistake, she wasn't giving up. She'd made it through college eating Top Ramen soup and risen through the ranks in her profession through sheer determination. She refused to be like her mother, totally dependent on a man for everything. And yet, here she stood, realizing she needed this man for what she wanted most, her own little bombshell if she let it slip at the wrong time.

She wanted a baby.

EIGHT

Vince usually tried to avoid cops, but right now he was damn grateful for Officer Jaworski. The young policeman's intervention had saved Vince from answering Shay's question about how he knew to come here.

Leaving his post at the plane hadn't been his most thought-out move ever, but Jimmy was more than capable of taking over as copilot for the listening device. Now he just had to figure out what to tell her after Jaworski finished with his questions. Keeping secrets on the job had never felt this difficult before.

Vince kept a close eye on the baby-faced cop standing with Shay by the cruiser. The bomb threat may have passed, but they still had a perp to find. A perp, not a prankster, because odds made it unlikely that this had been coincidental, coming hot on the heels of a double homicide. These gangbangers were playing in the big leagues, and for some reason they'd picked Shay to be on the other end of that phone right after she'd been hit with the break-in. No doubt about it, she was being targeted.

The registration book for the teen mixer event lay open on the trunk of Officer Jaworski's car. Vince stayed back a step, listening while Shay read over each attendee's name and mentioned anything pertinent she remembered about that person. Angeline had started on the list, but a few minutes in, her bad leg had given out, and she'd ended up parked inside an EMS vehicle.

"Rickie was the one who swung first. He was spoiling for a fight from the minute he arrived, so I'm not surprised he instigated the thing, just disappointed." Shay trailed a finger down to the next entry. "Caden. I found him with the thin blonde over there—Toni—in the girls' bathroom during the evacuation. They were too busy having sex to be concerned about leaving the building."

Jaworski tapped a note into his PDA. "Do you think they believed it was a hoax?"

"Do I think Caden made the call, you mean? It's tough to tell." Frowning, she crossed her arms over her chest and looked out at the dwindling crowd. "The boy on the phone spoke so softly it would be difficult to ID his voice for sure. And this isn't the first time that particular person has called the hotline."

Jaworski's head snapped up as he studied her, then typed the info into his PDA.

"What about the girl, Toni?" Jaworski's eyes dipped to Shay's chest outlined a little too well in the community center T-shirt pulled tight by her crossed arms. "Teenage girls with lower voices can sound like boys."

Vince bit his lip to keep from interjecting—he had heard the call, after all—and to keep from making an ass of himself by telling the cop to take his eyes up twelve inches.

Shay uncrossed her arms, bracing on the car and leaning back, which only served to emphasize her long legs worthy of any jeans model. "It's possible, but the person on the phone definitely spoke with the intention of being IDed as a boy."

Vince forced his own eyes up where they belonged and filed away each nugget of information on the kids for later when he reviewed the surveillance footage.

Jaworski studied a line then added another notation in his PDA. "Tell me about the Mercenary members who jumped into the fight."

"Brody is a professor type, with his round glasses and scraggly attempt at a goatee. Notice the snake tattoo around his neck. I caught him smoking pot behind the Dumpster during the evacuation. He shook off the weed just fine to knock Rickie's hat off his head and start the brawl."

Jaworski scowled. "It would have been helpful to know he's high before now."

"I was busy helping a pregnant girl through a bout of hyperventilation at the time."

"Right, fine, what else?"

"Webber jumped in once the row got going. He's the big kid with a long, dark ponytail and a medieval sword inked on his arm. He was also with the crowd behind the Dumpster lighting up, although I can't recall actually seeing a cigarette in his hand."

"We'll search around the Dumpster again before we leave. There might be something there to match up with evidence we collected the night of the murders. Maybe we can find a blunt and get some DNA."

"Check for paint cans, too. I thought I smelled something else. Huffing? Maybe they left a new tag?"

Jaworski jabbed at his PDA. "They just have to leave

their mark. They're not even subtle about it. Eighty percent of taggers sign their 'artwork.' It reminds me of how dogs piss on trees or how a serial killer leaves a signature."

Vince propped his boot back on the light pole behind him as he studied each face for any hint of what lurked behind those piercings and tats. Were these just kids in over their heads, or a part of taking terror down a new, home-grown avenue? At some point in the near future the Feds would have to bring local police into the investigation, but Wilson insisted for now they needed to safeguard against possible leaks.

Shay's lips tightened. "We'd been making real progress here. I hate seeing so much lost because of what amounts to a small slight."

Jaworski stopped typing. "It seems small to us, but to them, those small nuances are about more than a hat or piece of art. It's about their very identity. All gangs are connected by common traits: intimidation, symbolism, and respect."

Some things didn't change. Vince figured he might as well toss in his two cents for the cop, since he couldn't give him the whole lowdown from their end yet. "Respect through fear."

"Yes, although dissing—disrespecting—can come in such simple forms." Jaworski stepped into a lecturing role well. If he thought his attempt at being an authority on the subject would impress Shay, the guy wasn't nearly obser-vant enough. "Someone tags over another group's tag—graffiti art. Or they paint another gang's tag upside down. No challenge goes unanswered."

Shay's eyes lit. "Caden mentioned their tag being slighted right before the fight broke out."

Jaworski typed a notation into his PDA. "That's helpful. I'll add that to my questions when I interrogate them."

Vince looked the street up and down. "Artwork" abounded on the sides of buildings, bricks scrawled with words, initials, and symbols he suspected would make more sense once Shay keyed him in on the nuances. "If they're all tagging and most of them are signing, why not nip it in the bud?"

"Amateurs"—Jaworski glanced up from his PDA—"or hard-core wannabes tag right away in an attempt to make their presence known. Most groups wait until they're strong and deeply rooted in the neighborhood before they tag. Sure, the tags help us ID some of the members, but that's only the start. We'd rather allow the tagging to develop enough so that by the time we intervene, we're picking up gang members with deeper connections to the larger network."

Vince stuffed down his natural urge to buck up around cops and decided to pick the guy's brain for the good of their investigation. "I get that Apocalypse and the Mercenaries are established. But how do you ID the smaller groups in the making?"

"It's tough, but we're getting better at deciphering their codes. For example, some use location—like the East Side Mercenaries. Others may use area codes or streets and put those numbers on their hats or belt buckles."

"It's like that show *Beverly Hills, 90210* gone way wrong." Although he couldn't say things had been much safer in his old Chicago neighborhood.

Shay laughed low, not a smile in sight. "You're actually not far off. For these teens, it's all about feeding off rebellion and belonging to a group. If we don't offer them safe, positive options, they'll find what they need on their own."

Vince scrubbed a hand over his do-rag, ideas popping into his mind faster than streetlights brightening with the deepening night. "If Caden mentioned a tag dis and he's with Apocalypse, then it makes sense to check out the Mercenaries who signed in. Or it could be an up-and-coming group trying to muscle in."

Jaworski smiled. "Good catch, Major. Thanks for your help." He tucked away his PDA. "That wraps it up for tonight. I'm sorry we couldn't locate your bag. I'll write it up, but I don't expect we're going to recover it or your weapon. Your office is full of fingerprints."

"And here I'd been told to worry about people taking it from me in a fight. I didn't expect to have it removed from a locked drawer."

"I'll let you know if we find out anything, but I would start canceling those credit cards."

Officer Jaworski loped off, joining one of the few remaining cops on the scene. A few feet away, Angeline hobbled away from the EMT vehicle, her husband helping her into a minivan with a catering logo on the side.

The EMTs reminded Vince of something he full well should have thought of before now.

He shoved away from the light pole, his gaze locked on Shay's bruised cheek. How she'd put those kids before her own safety sure didn't jibe with the Shay he'd known years ago. "We should get some ice for your face, or you're going to end up with a whopper of a shiner by morning. Maybe the EMTs have something you can use."

She dabbed her hand along her cheekbone as if testing the tenderness. "I'll take care of it before I go to bed. I promise. Right now I need to catch my breath. A night like this sends me into a time warp. Looking at those three over there"—she pointed to the pregnant girl with two handcuffed boys nearby—"it's tough not to think about how badly we could have screwed up our lives back then."

As much as he preferred to leave the past back where it belonged, her insights could prove crucial in cracking the case. "Why those three kids in particular?"

Shay cocked her head to the side, wind lifting her short honey brown hair. "There's something about Amber that reminds me of myself. Well, other than the fact that she's pregnant, and I never have been. But Amber's in-your-face demeanor with the underlying neediness, a willingness to do anything to get her way? Totally me back then."

"Neediness? I wouldn't have pegged you with that then. I guess I was stuck on the in-your-face part."

"I certainly excelled at that." She plucked at her sweaty T-shirt bearing the center's logo. "Webber and Brody share so many similarities with you and Tommy."

"I sure hope I'm not the scrawny one with glasses and a patchy goatee. Although that snake tattoo kicks ass."

She looked up at him with a hesitant smile, cops starting to clear out behind her. "No worries. Brody reminds me of Tommy when it comes to brains that could have taken him far." Her smile faded. "But there's also a ferocity to him that gives me pause. I don't know if Tommy had that, and I just missed it in my need to glorify rebellion."

Tommy sure as shit had a mean streak when it came to rubbing Vince's nose in the fact he'd slept with Shay. Telling her that now, though, wouldn't accomplish anything, and with Tommy dead, insulting his memory seemed wrong.

"Webber reminds me of you with his size, his bluster and jokes . . ." Her eyes shifted to the teen. "It's been tough getting him to take the world seriously."

Was that how she saw him? Not that her opinion of him

should matter. Her input on these kids mattered. Her insights on the surveillance footage would be invaluable. And that would give him the foundation for his argument to his boss about bringing her into the loop.

No more waiting around. He would get the okay to release some of the information about this investigation to her. Danger had escalated enough around this place that he questioned the wisdom of keeping it open for the coming week. "There are so many potential powder kegs here, I don't know how you're going to sort through it all."

"Not tonight, that's for sure." She stifled a yawn. "I better start canceling my credit cards and figuring out how to get home." She paused. "You never answered my question earlier. And don't pretend you don't remember my asking why you're here."

Vince winged a great big thanks to the man upstairs for the time Jaworski's interruption had bought him to come up with a cover story. "I heard about the bomb threat on the radio."

"But you ride a motorcycle."

"I was in a sports bar."

"That sure was fast."

It was all over the media now. She wouldn't have any real way of checking how soon the news broke. But he wouldn't be able to hold off her questions much longer.

Shay pivoted and walked away.

Just like that? She gave him whiplash.

"Where are you going?"

"To speak with Eli."

He eyed the guy talking down two crying teenage girls. "He looks busy."

"Then I'll wait." She scooped a soda can off the sidewalk and stuffed it in an overflowing trash can.

"Wait for what?"

She pulled up the bag lining the can, tying the ends together with enough concentration to solve a quadratic equation. "Call me paranoid, but I'm not sure it's safe to go back to my town house."

He agreed but hadn't expected her to jump on the safety bandwagon. "Why do you say that?"

"A break-in, dead bodies outside my office, a bomb threat. I'm not sure if I'm just a trouble magnet or if something's seriously wrong." She started walking again, leaving him no choice but to stride alongside. "Either way, I value my life too much to risk it."

That said by a woman who worked in a crime zone? "I'm glad you realize it."

"I'll crash at Eli's for a couple of days."

"What if he's a target, too?" A possibility they needed to consider. Who could they warn without risking the whole operation? "Or if *you* are, you could bring the trouble to his doorstep."

She stopped cold. "Are you offering to help again for dear old Dad?"

He stepped closer, just catching a whiff of her, something citrusy, natural. Sexy. And off-limits, since his mission was to keep her safe. "If I am?"

"Where are you staying?"

This woman could give a man whiplash with her subject changes. "At the downtown Marriott."

"Nice digs. Got enough room for one more?"

What the fuck?

He hadn't expected it to be this easy to keep her nearby, but he wasn't going to argue. "I have a king-size bed and a pullout sofa."

"Perfect." She tucked her slim hands into her back pockets, pulling her shirt taut across two perfect breasts, just the right size to fit his palms.

He swiped sweat from his neck. "What about your yard shark?"

"Buster has a doggy door and self-feeder. He should be fine until I can get the spare key in the morning."

"Not that I want you to change your mind, but why are you giving in so easily?"

"I might be tempted to sleep with Eli. Not a problem with you."

Ouch. "You're great for a guy's ego."

"Yeah, yeah, whatever. You're so obviously a crumbling mass of insecurity, Hotshot. So, are we roomies or not?"

"Like you even have to ask." He passed her a helmet, glad the loaner had come with two. He straddled the motorcycle and fired it to life. "Mount up."

She swung one long leg over the back of his bike, settling in behind him. The heat of her thighs clamped around him, but she kept her hands off, gripping the seat instead. Out of assurance of her balance from riding with others or determination not to touch him any more than necessary?

Either way, just the press of her legs against him was enough for him to know that this was a crappy idea.

★ ★ ★

East Side Mercenaries, FEAR 4-Ever.

Webber shook his head, ponytail brushing his back. Whichever moron had sprayed that by the mall's service entrance had totally screwed them all over. This would be the last time they could hang out at night in empty store units. More of those new task force dudes would be crawling all over the place by tomorrow, taking notes, getting help from Shay Bassett in trying to "analyze" their heads.

As if that would change anything.

He juggled his box of carryout Chinese food as he slid through a slim part in the service entrance door propped open with a broken brick, and tried not to think about how scared Shay had sounded when he'd called in the threat. He'd gotten through the thing undetected, and that's what really mattered.

Thank God their guy had sent someone to spring them out of jail after a couple of hours. Some dudes thought getting jacked up made them tougher in the gang. He worried more about becoming some big mother's bitch by sunup.

At least he had a safe place to stay tonight. Webber padded quietly down the winding halls until he found the right door number and twisted the knob. He held his breath.

Sweet. Open and no alarm.

He put a swagger in his step—a man had to always be represented—and went into the room where Amber already waited, sitting cross-legged on a tarp, her belly heavy and low. He averted his eyes from the reminder that she banged some other guy.

She reached into her fast-food bag. "It would have been nice if you would have whistled a warning."

"Sorry." He screwed up everything else in his life. Why should now be different?

Amber bit into her hamburger, grease and lettuce spitting out the other side of the bun onto the wrapper. The lazy rent-a-cop here usually slept through his shift and rarely checked out these empty store cubicles. The security system was a piece of cake to disarm.

And on the rare occasion they got caught? They hotfooted it away from a groggy security guard armed with just a stick and a radio.

"What happened to Caden and Rickie?" she whispered,

not quite able to keep the worry out of her eyes as she asked about Apocalypse members.

They hadn't always been on opposite sides.

"Pulling an overnight in a holding cell. Pride for Apocalypse and all that."

Cracking open his container of sweet and sour chicken, he leaned back against scaffolding sprawled along one wall and started shoveling in fried rice. At the first bite, his stomach cramped. He'd been too nervous back at the center to eat more than a slice of pizza and couldn't remember when he'd eaten last.

"Hey, Amber? You feeling okay?" He worked hard to keep his voice neutral, his eyes down on his food in case Amber suddenly figured out how he felt about her. Fat frickin' chance, but still.

"I'm good. Miss Bassett made sure I got out of the way."

"Good, you gotta look out for the baby."

She glanced down at her stomach, her layered T-shirts pulling tight across her tummy. He didn't know much about pregnant women, so he wasn't really sure when the kid was supposed to be born. Amber didn't like to talk about it, and neither did he, actually. But wow, she looked about ready to pop.

He searched for something else to say, a joke, anything. He didn't get to be alone with her that often. Maybe if he'd figured out a way earlier, she wouldn't be having somebody else's baby.

"Hey," she said, pointing to his arm. "You added another jewel."

Webber glanced down at the warrior sword tattooed on his arm. He got gemstones inked on the handle sometimes. This time he'd added a golden stone. Amber-colored.

Would she figure it out? If she did, would she think it was hokey?

"I did that last week." He tore the wrapper off his fortune cookie and passed it to her, palm up. "Here."

She looked at it, and her eyes said loud and clear how much she wanted it. "No, it's yours."

"I already ate tons of junk at the center," he lied. "This could be your lucky cookie. Come on. Play along."

She *should* be playing like a kid instead of having one. They should all be kids, but life just sucked for some people. For them.

Amber took the cookie, her fingers soft and cool against his skin that felt too hot and tight for his body these days.

"Thanks." She cracked it open and read, her lips moving silently along. Then she smiled.

"What does it say?"

She waggled it in the air between them. "How bad do you want to know?"

"Hey, it's my cookie."

Laughing, she clasped it to her chest. "What will you do to find out?"

Anything.

"Dude," a voice broke through the room, jolting them both. A person needed to stay on alert.

"Dude," his Mercenary brother repeated, calling through the door before Brody walked inside, too loud and out of control for his own good, "Lewis is here."

Amber shoved the cookie in her mouth and tucked the fortune in her pocket.

Lewis ducked into the room, sweeping aside a tarp hanging from the scaffold. "How's it hanging?"

Amber bit her lip and rolled her eyes where Lewis

couldn't see. The guy was always trying to talk cool around them.

"Good, it's all good, old man."

Lewis walked deeper into the room. "Everyone is old in comparison to you, kiddo." He wore jeans and a ball cap with a team logo, as if clothes would make him one of them. The only way he was like them? He answered to a bigger boss in his chain the same way they did in their gang. They were all just errand boys.

"You guys did well tonight." Lewis was smiling, but something dark and pissed off lurked in his eyes when he watched Brody. "The boss will be pleased with how the bomb threat freaked everyone out."

Brody pounded fists with Webber, FEAR tattoo glaring across the knuckles. "It was balla, dude, hanging out behind the Dumpster and watching everybody run out of there, scared as shit just because of your stupid call."

Lewis propped a foot and elbow on the ladder, a Band-Aid peeking free on his arm. A lot of old bangers hid their tats later. Could Lewis be "cooler" than they thought?

"Webber, you did well phoning in the threat and not showing you knew the truth while you walked around after. We really need to shut up this Bassett woman. Do-gooders like her get people all riled up. Then you've got more cops crawling all over your every move. Slows down business." Lewis paused, the pissed-off part of him sweeping out everything else. "I hear somebody took her purse."

He wanted to correct the guy and tell him it was a chick backpack, you fucking fathead. The guy promised a ton but demanded even more. Too much, sometimes.

The guy also sniffed out lies, and Webber had enough to hold on to. Better to 'fess up, because something in Lewis's eyes hinted he already knew the answer. "That was me."

Amber pivoted toward Webber. "Why would you do that?"

He shrugged, shoving away his sweet and sour chicken. He did it for the same reason he did everything else, just to make it through the day as best he could and figure out how to fix the mess tomorrow.

Lewis stepped closer, as if he needed any help scaring the hell out of them. "Have you used any of the credit cards yet?"

"Nah, I figured she would cancel those anyway. I just used the cash." And kept the gun. "I left her keys," he lied, but Lewis would have no way of checking that, since those keys were in the bottom of Lake Erie, nowhere near the bag. "I know the keys are important."

"But you used the cash." Lewis stared pointedly at the Chinese food.

"That's why I took her backpack. I'm short on food, and Mom is two months behind on rent."

"Give me the woman's bag."

"I threw it in the lake, along with her credit cards." And her keys. He'd wanted to give the pretty backpack to Amber. He'd seen her look at it often enough. "Nobody'll ever find it."

"You better hope so. We need to be careful."

Why was her speech in front of a bunch of tight-ass politicians so important? There were other people who could talk about the local gangs in her place, people who specialized in following them around with notepads trying to figure out what move they would make next.

They didn't have a frickin' clue. Not like Miss Bassett.

And there was his answer.

The woman really did stand a chance at changing things around here with her words and her actions, something

Lewis couldn't afford to let happen. There was too much power at stake, growing every day here.

He snuck a quick look at Amber. He might not be able to save himself, but he would do his best to keep her and the kid safe. "That big guy, though, the air force dude— he needs to go home now. He's too smart. He makes me nervous."

Lewis crouched beside him. "Why do you say that?"

"He doesn't look at us like she does, like she can save us. He looks at us like he knows us."

Keeping people alive around here was tough enough without the mind games. He just hoped Lewis bought his story about wanting the bag for money. Showing a weakness was killer. He knew better. But something about that woman's voice over the phone got to him. For the first time, he felt like somebody really cared.

Stupid lady.

Losing Shay's backpack and everything in it was important. It wasn't the answer, but it would buy time. Because he hadn't lied about a bomb being planted by one of Lewis's butt kissers. Except it wasn't in the center.

It was in Shay Bassett's car.

NINE

★

Shay scrubbed a towel through her wet hair, her face muzzy in the steamed mirror.

One thing was completely clear. Her body hummed with awareness from a simple motorcycle ride along the Lake Erie shore with Vince. What was wrong with her and this disconnect she seemed to have between what her mind knew and what her body wanted?

Well, she had about five minutes to get herself together before Vince returned from whatever errand he'd run, after he'd locked her in the hotel room. He'd even set up a code knock for when he returned, which seemed a little paranoid to her, but the past few days had been beyond bizarre.

Before tonight, she certainly couldn't have foreseen a scenario that would land her in his hotel. All jokes about Eli aside, she had friends. She wasn't a total workaholic. Much. But her friends were all married with families. A call to them meant waking up babies or interrupting couple time for Angeline and her hubby.

So here she was. She tugged one of Vince's T-shirts over her head and shrugged into a hotel robe. In fact, nobody knew where she was.

Maybe she should call her dad, just to let him know she was all right. Shay reached for her cell phone—thank goodness she'd kept it in her pocket rather than her backpack—and typed in his number.

Four rings later, his voice mail picked up.

"Don Bassett," his level tones echoed through the earpiece. "Leave a message after the tone."

"Uh, Dad, it's me, Shay. You may have seen the news tonight about a bomb scare and gang fight at the center. I'm fine. Mom already called to check in. She was pretty freaked out, as you would expect." But it felt good knowing her mom cared, even if Jayne had been a sobbing mess. "So I've had a chance to speak with her." Unlike Don, a man who hated rambling messages. "And uh, I guess that's it. Bye . . ."

A knock sounded at the door. Her chest tightened. Two more quick taps, pause, one more.

It was Vince.

She shook her head to loosen her short, damp curls— damn her vain lapse—and rushed over. She slid the chain, the safety bar, and the dead bolt before tugging the door open.

Vince filled the entrance. "You should have asked who it was to be sure."

"I just love being reprimanded like a six-year-old." Damn. That sounded snippy. "Thanks for the T-shirt to go under the robe."

He slid past, two bags dangling from his hands. "The

laundry service will have your jeans ready before morning. But I also picked up some things for you from Wal-Mart."

"Thank goodness for twenty-four/seven hours. Your shirts are a little, uh, roomy on me to wear out in public." Tomorrow she would get her super to unlock her apartment so she could get to her clothes and the spare set of keys to her car. Tomorrow, in the daylight, with lots of foot traffic around for safety. "I hate feeling paranoid."

"It's not paranoia if somebody's really gunning for you. We live in a world of big-ass scary threats." He walked past and tossed his helmet into a chair.

He swept a hand over his head to clear away the do-rag and tossed it on top. Her fingers itched to test the feel of his shaved head.

She pivoted away on naked feet. "Duh, why else do you think I invited myself to stay in your hotel room? I'm pretty tough, but this week has pushed even me to my limit. I care about my safety, and this is about the last place anyone would look for me." The hotel room suddenly felt very empty. Very intimate. She rushed to add, "Besides, it's not like you're going to make a move on me."

"Are you so sure about that?" His voice came from right over her shoulder.

She started. How did such a big man move that softly?

He reached for her. His fingers stopped just shy of her face. Another inch, and he would be touching her. Would he go so far as to cup the back of her head and urge her toward him? She swayed, her bare toes curling into the carpet. A flash of Amber's sad neediness stabbed through her mind, steadying her.

Shay ducked his touch. "You've always had a twisted sense of humor."

"Hold still." His knuckles grazed her cheek, his hands

smelling of oil, musk, and man. "You really do need to ice that bruise."

She flinched away. From pain? Or the lure of his touch? Curiosity was a dangerous thing. "I'll live."

His face closed up. "We hope you'll live." He turned away and walked toward the mini fridge. "You stay in that job, even though they try to kill each other, try to kill you, steal from you."

He knelt to pull out the small ice bucket, his jeans outlining his firm butt.

She shoved her hands deep into the robe's pockets. "You stay in the air force even though they send you to countries where they keep shooting at you, trying to kill you." She'd fought hard for these kids. She wouldn't surrender now, not even in a discussion. "Nights like this only make me more determined. The clinic and the work here must be making progress for someone to want to destroy it that much."

Vince poured ice into a plastic cup and walked back to her. "What if these kids don't want to be saved? What if the work destroys *you*?"

He pressed the cool glass against her arm.

"I won't let it." She glanced down to find a long scratch stretching from either side of his makeshift ice pack. "That's nothing. Must have come from Amber's fingernails when I pulled her out of the fight."

"Or someone had a knife drawn, after all."

Bile burned the back of her throat. "I must have been too distracted to feel it happen."

She refused to accept the alternative, that she'd somehow become numb to pain again. That she would have to push harder, deeper until she felt something. Her knees folded under her, and thank goodness the bed was so close, or she would have landed on the floor rather than on the edge of the mattress.

Vince steadied her at the waist. "Deep breaths. Adrenaline letdown, I would guess."

She dropped her head between her knees, her wrist throbbing with that phantom sting from a long-ago slash. Something she definitely didn't want to explain to Vince. At least her dad had enough respect for a person's privacy to keep that bit of horror in the family. "I resent feeling like a wimp."

He rested the cup of ice against the back of her neck, and God, that felt good.

Vince rolled the cup lightly against her neck. "My buddy Berg is a hardened combat vet, cool as can be during battle, and yet more than once I've seen him hurl the second he steps out of a plane. You're right about these street gangs being at war."

Her head drooped forward as she sank into the comfort of his care . . . Wait, what was she doing?

Shay straightened, putting a couple of extra inches between them. "Most of the time I try to think of the kids as regular teens so I don't go running for the hills."

"A little more caution wouldn't hurt." He gestured to the long scratch, not touching this time, simply brushing the air over her with the cup in his fist. "At least you weren't seriously cut."

"True enough." She knew just how deep to slice before inflicting serious damage. She had faded scars on the inside of her thighs to prove it.

His eyes held her intently, firmly, until her chest went tight again as if squeezed by a strong embrace. What was going on here that she couldn't even freaking breathe around this man? Was she just caught in a time warp of unresolved feelings from their teen years? Or simply feeling sorry for herself because her father didn't care enough to call and her mother had been so hysterical Shay had ended up comforting her?

Or did she want Vince now in a very adult way?

Regardless, she may have made a big mistake in coming with him. "Should I call the front desk and ask for another room?"

He blinked. Just a simple blink, but enough to release all the oxygen that had somehow been held hostage from her. He looked away, rattling the ice in the glass for a second before setting it on the bedside table and standing. "I'll find a plastic bag for your ice pack."

She struggled not to gasp for air. Simple breaths. *In. Out.*

He dumped his purchases out of the Wal-Mart bag: sandals, sunglasses, a hat, and a frilly shirt. "You're easier to watch over here. No arguing about another room or the sleeping arrangements." He picked up the ice bucket, poured the rest into the bag, and tied a double knot at the top. "I'm on the sofa bed since it's closer to the door."

She decided to ignore the dictatorial tone rather than risk more sparks. "You won't hear me arguing over taking a comfy bed."

"Good." He passed her the ice bag and a hand towel.

"Thank you." She lifted the bag in salute, but she really meant so much more. Like thanks for not pushing her to admit how much she wanted to be there.

He clicked off the lights, plunging her in total darkness, alone in a hotel room with Vince Deluca. She burrowed under the downy comforter. The sofa bed creaked under his weight, covers rustling for what seemed like forever.

Totally surreal.

And totally agitating.

Which left her totally awake.

Where was that ice pack? Oh, in her hand. She pressed it to her overheated face.

"Why did you shave your head?" she blurted.

The sofa bed squeaked from what sounded like Vince turning away from her. "Go to sleep, Shay."

"I seriously want to know." Knowing suddenly seemed so important she couldn't possibly sleep until he solved the mystery for her.

He sighed, mattress groaning again as he rolled onto his back. "I started going bald at twenty-two. I trimmed it short for a while, but that meant I had to go for haircuts all the time. It was easier just to shave it."

"I didn't recognize you at first." He'd scared her then. He scared her now in a completely different way.

"It's been seventeen years."

"For some reason it doesn't feel that long."

"Working with the teens brings back lots of memories." Some of those memories were actually good.

"So you mentioned earlier. Those kids do make everything feel more immediate."

Silence settled again, her eyes growing accustomed to the dark until his bulk took shape across the room. "Thank you again for your help."

"I would have done it for anyone in the same position."

Her BS-ometer started niggling again. "I appreciate you're interested in what I do, and I'm thankful for the help you've given, even if you make me crabby while you're doing it. But I still don't get it."

"Get what?"

"Why you're here, hanging out with me during your vacation. And please be honest." She rolled to her side, plumping the pillow. "I spend so much time with these kids I've developed an internal lie detector. I call it my BS-ometer."

He hesitated.

A horrible possibility blindsided her. "Are you dying?"

"What?" He sat up, his big body a blur in the dark.

She held herself completely still, not sure how she would deal with the worst kind of answer. "Do you have some kind of terminal disease, and you're on a pilgrimage to make peace with your past? I thought maybe the bald head could be a result of chemotherapy."

"Shay, you always did have a wild imagination."

To go with her wild side? "Am I right or wrong?"

"I absolutely promise I do not have a terminal disease, and my head is shaved completely by choice."

She exhaled. Hard. "Then I'm not sure what you hope to accomplish with these catch-up sessions."

A thought scampered through her brain, every bit as outrageous as her assumption that Vince had lost his hair from chemotherapy. What if he'd come to Cleveland because of her? What if he had as many unresolved feelings from the past as she did?

Her stomach tumbled. Too much.

He reclined back on his two stacked pillows, his arm under his head. "Everything will make sense soon. I promise."

Another no answer, and one that sure didn't lead her to believe he had feelings for her. Especially since she'd given him a gold star opening if he'd wanted to confess some kind of lingering affection.

She eased up—abandoning the ice pack before her face went numb—and hugged her knees. "What aren't you telling me?"

Tension hummed from him almost as loudly as the air conditioner on full blast. "You were right about tonight being a bumpy trip down memory lane."

Her BS-ometer didn't miss his abrupt subject change. He was definitely hiding something from her. If her stomach fluttered much more, she would levitate off the bed. "I look at each one of them as an opportunity to rewrite history."

"Have you had any luck with that yet?"

"I see some glimmers of hope here and there, but the jury's still out. I have to admit Amber's pregnancy struck me hard, but I still have hopes of getting her settled into a dental hygienist training program with on-site babysitting. It'll take time to see how much of what we've done at the center has stuck. One thing's for certain. We need more help."

"More people like Officer Friendly?"

"I assume you mean Jaworski."

"None other."

"He's, uh . . ."

"Arrogant?"

"Brusque." She smiled, her first of the night. A short-lived levity. "Since I've been sitting on the other side of this situation, I've seen how easy it is to grow a hard shell. It's a tough balance between caring and caring too much. The people that care too much end up self-destructing or slapping up walls so thick, nothing can get through."

"Like Officer Friendly."

"Exactly." Her arms tightened around her knees. If she could keep herself from flying apart, maybe . . . "Five Mercenaries caught him outside his apartment. Their brass knuckle beat down left him covered in FEAR bruises."

"Damn," he whistled low and long. "That explains a lot about the guy. Back in the day we may have resented cops, but we never took it to that level."

"We pushed it close, though, that night Tommy died."

After a Civil Air Patrol meeting, Vince and Tommy had been fighting, the cops caught them, and Tommy pulled a gun. Bullets started flying. Bodies falling. Dreams dying.

A friend dying.

"I really am grateful you saved my life that night." But if she hadn't played them against each other, would that fight have even started? "Even if you did it for my father, I should have thanked you back then, rather than scream at you to go away."

Vince swung his feet off the bed, sitting on the edge, unmistakably studying her in the dim shadows. "Is that why you came to the hotel room tonight? To *thank* me the old-fashioned way?"

His words slapped her. She might be curious about the new Vince, but that didn't mean she intended to jump into bed with him. She'd changed, too.

She grabbed the ice bag and pitched it toward his shadowy shape. The sack settled beside him with a rattly thud. "I'm far past the age of offering sex in lieu of gratitude."

"Damn shame." He scooped up the ice pack and pressed it to either side of his neck slowly before tossing it in the trash. "G'night, Shay."

What the hell was she to make of that?

She suspected she would spend most of the night awake trying to figure it out.

* * *

With a flick of his foot, Vince downshifted, slowing the motorcycle on his way past the Rock and Roll Hall of Fame. Shay perched on the seat behind him, still not touching. Tourists rubbernecked at a snail's pace past the row of overlarge sparkling guitars out front.

Would Shay remember rides they'd taken years before, their hormone-revved teenage bodies hepped up by close contact? The memories may have faded for her but he knew damn well the attraction hadn't diminished.

Only an idiot would have missed the awareness snapping between them the night before. He could blame it on adrenaline and circumstance, but he wasn't into lying to himself. This woman had always stirred an unwise— flat-out dangerous—craving inside him.

Except in less than an hour, things would become all business, and there would be no going back.

He wanted her in the loop. He'd lobbied for this when he'd left her alone in the hotel room the night before. She knew these kids in a way nobody else did. Her insights could be invaluable in getting to the root of who else might be involved.

Yet he found himself wanting to roar off with her, tucking her away until the congressional hearing passed. Now how would that desertion play out? Landing him in a questioning room like his dirtbag father? But that wasn't who he was anymore, a rule breaker. He worked every day to leave that jailhouse legacy behind.

So after they went to her place for clothes and keys, he took the long route to the command center where the briefing waited. But even the long route ended eventually.

He slowed the bike into the small airport parking lot where the military Pilatus painted in civilian colors waited inside an open hangar, hiding in plain sight.

Shay walked beside him, but her kicks were no doubt dragging. "You're expecting a lot on faith from me. You tell me we need to make a quick stop before you take me back to work, but you won't tell me where or why."

"Will it help if I tell you this involves your teens?"

She looked up at him sharply, the morning sun glinting off her golden brown hair scraped back in a short ponytail. "Okay, you've hooked me, but my trust only goes so far. I'm not going on some cross-country junket with you."

With those few words, he wanted to take her up in a plane. He could see it, her adventurous spirit, winging this earth girl up to touch the heavens. But not now. Probably never. "We're only going to sit in the plane and have a conversation with some important people."

She shaded her eyes with her hand, looking ahead to the innocuous-looking plane. "Who are the other guys inside?"

"A few of my friends."

Her arm fell to her side. "Did you hook up with some others for your road trip?"

"Could you hold your questions for fifteen minutes? Then I will answer anything you ask."

About the mission, anyway.

His past was as off-limits now as it had been then. As a teen, she wanted to use him to get back at her father. If she got to know him better now, she would see what a mess he was inside, always wondering if today would be the day he stepped over the edge like his own father. He liked to think he'd channeled his inherited aggression into his job. He got to push boundaries, break rules even, all for a positive result that wouldn't land him in a military prison.

Walking across the tarmac toward the parked plane, she had a regal way about her, even in jeans, long legs slowing with each step.

He needed to throw her a line. "I have some people who want to meet with you about your upcoming congressional testimony."

Her brown eyes widened. "How are you tied in with that? Have you been tapped to testify, too, as a success story about making it out of that kind of life? You're certainly a poster child for someone who's pulled himself up by his bootstraps."

"Biker bootstraps, huh? Guess the image works."

"Don't laugh this off. You have a chance to witness to these teens." She grabbed his forearm, her touches so rare it more than caught his attention. "I may have problems with my father, but I respect what he's done for kids. He didn't save them all. No one can. But lives changed because of what he did."

"Believe me, I know that. But that's not what we're all here for." He offered her his hand to steady her on her way into the plane.

She ignored his hand and hauled herself inside.

Vince gestured to his three workmates inside the aircraft, all wearing civilian clothes. "Their hideous fashion taste aside, these are top-notch guys from my squadron, and in spite of the casual shorts, we're not here on vacation." He palmed Shay's back as he guided her to the copilot's seat. "Guys, this is Shay Bassett. Shay, the guy in the Hawaiian shirt is Jimmy." He pointed to his lanky friend folded too tightly into a seat in front of a monitor. "He's a pilot, too."

She stayed quiet, her pert nose scrunched in confusion.

He pointed to his somber pal behind a computer screen. "Berg is a top-notch navigator and fire control officer. He's a man of many talents, although right now he's knee-deep in seeing what your teens are up to on Facebook." He gestured to the last guy, lounging back in a pink shirt. Somehow the player managed to make the color work for him. "And Smooth is our flight engineer. He monitors engine health. In a pinch he's one helluva loadmaster."

Smooth winked, leaning forward to extend a hand. "Pleased to meet you, Miss Bassett."

Jimmy clapped Smooth on the back. "How's your girlfriend? I enjoyed meeting her last time we were back in Vegas."

Smooth just laughed and leaned back. Vince gestured for Shay to sit while he took his place at the keyboard, bringing the screen to life with an empty room. Don Bassett strode across the monitor image, their gateway to the teleconference where all would be revealed soon enough.

Shay stiffened in that way Vince had come to realize was customary when her father showed up, even if only a virtual arrival. She shot Vince a tight-lipped look before gluing her attention to the screen.

Could she resent her dad because of the problems between her parents that seemed to have started long before their divorce? He didn't consider himself über in touch with his feelings, but he'd once dated a woman who had what she'd called "abandonment issues" because her father walked out. Those issues of hers had made for plenty of problems between them whenever he had had to go dark and couldn't call her for a few days.

These days, it wasn't unusual to go dark for weeks.

Not that he was looking for a relationship with Shay. He just couldn't figure her out, which frustrated the hell out of him. He liked answers, order, fixing puzzles and engines.

For her safety, he needed to ignore the attraction and focus on the job.

Don took his seat as the Fed they'd been working with entered the room as well. She stepped up to the microphone. "Good morning, gentlemen. Hello, Miss Bassett, it's nice to finally meet you face-to-face, even if long distance. My name is Special Agent Paulina Wilson. I'm with the FBI, and we believe you could be the target of a terrorist attack."

TEN

Two hours later, Shay walked toward her car, working like crazy to keep her temper from exploding and to keep from falling to her knees in abject terror.

Barely, just barely, her steps stayed even with Vince's on her way across the community center's parking lot to get her car. She'd held her silence so far, but she wasn't sure how much longer she could seal the lid on her feelings if she didn't get away from Vince very soon.

For days, he and her father had been keeping her in the dark about an unthinkable danger lurking. She'd been deluding herself by imagining Vince might be here to put the past to rest, to make peace.

To reconnect with her.

Her feet pounded the steaming asphalt even harder.

Idiot.

All those warm fuzzy moments of sharing back in the hotel had meant nothing to him. He'd simply been distracting her to keep her off track until it suited him to bring her in the loop.

And oh God, if she started thinking about possible terror attacks at that hearing, she would hyperventilate.

Vince's arm shot in front of her to stop her, his eyes shaded behind badass wraparound sunglasses. "All right, spill it. What's pissing you off? And don't bother denying it. I'm developing a BS-ometer of my own."

She pivoted on her ridiculous gladiator sandals she'd put on with him in mind. Only a dozen more steps, and she would have been home free, cranking her car for her big escape. "I have no intention of denying a thing. I was only paying you the common courtesy of not blasting you in front of your work friends."

"None of them are here now. Blast away."

She hadn't expected him to agree. Shay looked around to make sure nobody was listening, privacy ramping up to a whole new level. Other than a few stray cars and the old lady across the street painting over the side of her white brick building, everyone else must be sleeping in on Saturday morning.

But still. "Let's sit in my car."

Striding away, she thumbed the Unlock button, Vince's biker boots thudding behind her. She settled behind the wheel, waiting until Vince slid into the passenger seat, folding his bulk into her compact. She considered turning on the engine and cranking the AC, but the morning hadn't heated up the inside yet. Vince waved for her to continue.

"So you and your friends are some kind of special flyers," she blurted. What the hell? She wanted to know more about the threat, about her kids, not about him.

He paused, obviously measuring his words.

"Damn it, Vince." She lowered her voice if not her anger. "I get that there's a big investigation going on, and I'm supposed to help the Feds by spilling my guts about these teens after I've spent years doing everything I can to get them to trust me. But I'm still a little confused on what *you*'re doing here."

He thumbed the cracked dashboard. "My friends and I are pitching in with surveillance. We belong to a test squadron that brings new aircraft and equipment into the military's arsenal. Sometimes we're called upon to use those toys in conjunction with other governmental venues."

"Like my CIA daddy."

"It's best we guard our words carefully outside of secured rooms. You've already been given special consideration because of your father."

"Thank you," she said tightly.

"Wish you meant that."

"Wish you would answer my questions."

He folded his arms across his chest, the vinyl seat crackling beneath him. "Fine. Ask what you want, and I'll answer what I can."

How much truth would she get? "I thought you were a pilot."

"A test pilot. I have a degree in mechanical engineering. I like to fly, but I like to play with how it all goes together. My mom said I started taking apart my moving Happy Meals toys at three years old to see the machines inside. Taking apart dirt bikes then motorcycles naturally followed. And here I am."

Charming, but not the point. "Quit trying to distract me with cute little childhood stories. And quit hiding behind those sunglasses." She tugged them off his face. "I'm mad and I'm scared and I have just cause."

He took his glasses back with a surprisingly gentle hand

and hooked them on the neck of his T-shirt. "You saw that a search of Kevin's apartment turned up information linking him to a possible terrorist plot directed at the hearing. It's likely he tried to rob the clinic that night to raise cash to leave town after the Feds searched his place. I wish the threat could have died with him, but everything indicates otherwise."

"What things?"

"I can't tell you all the details, but suffice it to say we have picked up on enough cell phone chatter from known terrorist entities to be . . . concerned . . . but we haven't been able to pinpoint the direct source yet. I hope you realize your father and I are doing our level best to keep you safe."

"My father. Right." It always came back to what Vince felt he owed her father. "I understand more than you think." Like how easily she could be led off track by his intense eyes and quick smile. Not this time, Hotshot. "My father knew *before* Kevin broke in. You knew before I gathered that powder keg together under the clinic roof. I know you used a conversation with me to plant a listening device in my place, on my turf."

He leaned closer, close enough he had to look down to meet her gaze. "Think, Shay. If we went ballistic hauling folks in for questioning, we might have lucked into nabbing someone lower down in the chain. But we wouldn't have found the people responsible, and the hit could very likely still carry through with hundreds, even thousands dying. Including the visiting members of Congress. And including *you.*"

She blinked back tears of frustration and anger and even helplessness, because he could be right. "Did it ever cross your mind that I could have helped?"

"That's the only reason you're in the loop now. But never forget you're a civilian. You don't have a need to know everything. If you want the right to know that comes with a uniform, feel free to join up any time."

Her tears dried in the face of his cool tones that echoed too closely to overheard fights between her mother and father. "You can't even bring yourself to say you're sorry."

"What do I have to be sorry for? We were careful not to violate anyone's rights. The bomb threat should make you realize more than ever the urgency of what we're doing. I was called in to do a job, and I have done it to the best of my ability in the very short time frame I was given. I *am* sorry that people are dead, more than I could ever express, and I'm going to work my ass off to make sure no one else is killed." He angled closer still, crowding her in the already tight confines of the compact, his voice rumbling low, deep. Intimate. "We're just trying to round up the right people so they can be put away."

She backed from him, from the urge to flatten her palm to his chest. "Okay, so you want my input. Fine. It's more complicated than simply arresting or deporting these people. Take MS-13 for example, an L.A.-based gang comprised mostly of immigrants from El Salvador. It started out as a group looking to protect themselves and morphed into a street gang. Cops deported some of them back home, but the country was in the middle of a civil war. Those gang-bangers became experts in guerilla warfare, skills they brought right back here to the States. Now we're dealing with drugs, human trafficking, weapons smuggling."

He clasped her arms. "That should tell you right there the scope of what we're confronting. People are already terrified of these kids. If these gangs cause a major event during this televised hearing, how jazzed do you think taxpayers are going to feel about giving tax dollars for more of your pizza parties and small group sharing?"

"Is that really all you think I'm doing? Throwing pizza parties and hosting campfire chats over s'mores?"

His silence said too much.

God, she'd had enough. Of this. Of him. She needed to go home.

Shay grasped the key in the ignition. "I guess we're at an impasse."

He put his hand over hers. "We still have to work together."

"I know what's important." She put his hand back on his knee. Even if her retreat could only be temporary, she needed to regroup. "I'll do my job. Thank you for getting me back safely to my car, but I really need some time alone to think."

★ ★ ★

Just go?

Did she really think she could dismiss him that way? Standing by his bike, Vince watched Shay rest her forehead against the steering wheel in her rust bucket of a car. This woman was wreaking havoc on his mind.

He hadn't even found out where she intended to go now that she had her car and a lone credit card retrieved from her apartment.

He would not let his hormones affect his judgment.

Vince charged back over to her car and knocked on her window. "Shay, get out."

She turned her head to the side, still resting on the wheel. A sigh shuddered through her so visibly he didn't even need to hear it. Her mouth moved with a clear *no*.

"Come on, Shay. We're not done here." Not by a long shot. He opened the door. "Step out."

She stayed put and silent.

He sighed just as hard as she had and added, "Please."

She sagged back in the seat. "Where I come from, no means no."

He grasped her hand and tugged her out. "Please listen without interrupting for once." She opened her mouth with a gasp, and he tapped it closed. "Maybe you have a point about your input being valuable earlier on, but this isn't some paint by numbers deal where everything just fell into place. There are real world, big stakes here, and I fucking care what happens to you."

Her mouth fell open again, but this time in total shock.

Screw it all. Adrenaline flooded reason.

He sealed his mouth to hers. She went stock-still. For all of two seconds.

She fisted her hands in his shirt, twisting, tugging him closer. Oh yeah. He swept his tongue along the seam of her lips, and she parted, opening, inviting, meeting the thrust with a bold taste of her own.

He pressed closer, anchoring her against the side of the car, all the pent-up heat from the very long and sleepless night pouring out of him into this kiss. A kiss that beat the hell out of anything he'd fantasized about as a teenager.

Her arms slid around his neck, her hips rocking against his in an unmistakable answer to the frenzy roaring through him harder and faster than any souped-up bike. He palmed her head, fingers spearing through her silky hair until the short ponytail came free. The hair band fell to the ground. Whispery curls teased around and over his fingers, as sexy and elusive as Shay.

The soft give of her breasts against his chest only reminded him how vulnerable she was. He fit his leg between hers, the reins on his restraint getting thinner by the second.

Much longer, and they would need to take this somewhere else, somewhere less public.

He eased his mouth from hers, and her forehead fell to rest on his chest. Thank God she wasn't ready to talk yet.

And she wasn't bolting.

He forced ragged breaths in and out, his hand still cradling her head, testing the glide of her hair against his fingers. Willing his heart rate to slow, he scanned the deathly quiet lot. He would have expected some kids to be shooting hoops on the weekend, even in the morning. The bomb threat last night must have scared everyone into staying clear today, because he saw nothing more than the occasional car.

A four-door compact slowed on its way past the center, darn near crawling, like tourists rubbernecking to check out the Rock and Roll Hall of Fame. Except there sure wasn't much to see here, other than that old lady sweeping a roller of white paint up and down her brick grocery corner market. He checked out the sparse foot traffic: an old man walking his dog, a young guy jogging.

His eyes went back to the car. A truck roared around a corner, speeding to pass the four-door. Vince tried to make out the driver in the slowing vehicle but couldn't see through the tinted windows. Very tinted.

"Shay," he whispered against the top of her head, a bad feeling dumping acid in his gut.

"Vince," she answered, her voice soft and husky, "no talking. Not yet, please."

"Shay—"

The window on the sedan rolled down. A glint showed with raising arms pulling—

"Shit."

A gun.

"Shay, down, damn it! Down!"

Vince tackled her to the ground just as gunfire popped through the air. They landed. Hard. Asphalt tore up his elbows, but better that than the lethal rip of a bullet into flesh.

Shay wriggled beneath him. "The guard. We need to warn him."

Gunfire sprayed, pocking the ground, ping, ping, pinging off her car.

"I think the guard already knows," Vince barked in her ear, tucking her closer, pressing as near to the car as possible. He considered climbing in but didn't want to risk rising. "Don't move. Do. Not. Move."

"Believe me"—Shay wriggled beneath him—"I'm not running anywhere."

The air roared around him with the sounds of war. A scream echoed from across the street, the squeal of tires, and still the shots continued. From more weapons? Other shooters?

He turned his head and looked under her car, trying to assess the threat from his limited vantage point. She wriggled again. "Be still."

"I'm trying to look," she shouted. "Maybe I can see who it is."

Him looking was one thing. Shay exposing her face was another matter altogether. "An ID won't mean a thing if you're dead."

"I'm more likely to smother," she muttered, her breath hot against his cheek.

Her heart pounded against him, hard, fast with a fear she wouldn't let past her bravado. His arms convulsed around her. Breasts to chest, her hips cradled against him, and yeah, his body was hepped up with adrenaline and still hard from their kiss. He would worry about the erection later, once the bullets stopped.

He clutched her closer, her citrusy smell filling what little air there was between them. Screw waiting for these thugs to quit shooting. What if the shooter left the car? He had to get Shay out of here. He slid his arm up to open the door . . .

Just as brakes squealed, and the car sped away.

That fast it was over. Silence surrounded them. The neighborhood echoed with that wounded quiet after a storm. He scanned the parking lot, the basketball court, across the street . . .

Abandoned. Everyone had run for cover.

And Shay was still alive. He kissed her again, firmly.

Slowly, the air around them cooled as a siren sounded in the distance. He eased up onto his elbows, lifting himself from her, even as their mouths held until the very . . . last . . . second. Shay stared up at him with confused but passion-fogged eyes. He started to apologize, but apparently his voice wasn't working right yet.

He turned his head to the side, coughing to clear his throat and hopefully his mind. A glint on the asphalt on the other side of her car tripped his attention. He stared harder, his brain on a fucking gerbil wheel trying to process everything barraging him. About six feet away lay something he recognized well from his first night in town. Their shooter had used and tossed.

The gun from Shay's little backpack.

ELEVEN

Fifty yards away, Officer Jaworski sealed the little gun in the evidence bag.

Shay hugged her stomach while crowds gathered and gawked across the street. There had been a time when she didn't care if she lived or died. That time had long passed.

She looked at her bullet-pocked car and shivered. Police had roped off the scene, marking shell casings on the ground, more bullet holes in the center's street sign and a billboard. She was seriously starting to hate this parking lot.

At least no one had died this time, which was somewhat comforting, but the increasing violence brought a thick cloud of impending doom she couldn't shake. She snuck a glance at Vince standing solid and steady beside her. The past hour had been filled with giving statements, and while she hated what had happened, she welcomed the distraction from speaking about what happened *before* the shooting.

A kiss that still had her body on edge, her senses already

on total overload from the shots, the danger, the fear. She plowed her fingers through her hair, remembering the urgency of his touch as he'd freed her short ponytail.

Vince moved closer, the heat of him warming her back, his head dipping toward her ear. "While we're stuck here cooling our heels waiting for Jaworski's questions, you and I should talk."

Not in this lifetime, Hotshot. "Talk about what?"

"Don't play coy here. We can't ignore that kiss. Hell, probably half the neighborhood saw."

"Then half the neighborhood witnessed a mistake. Quite frankly, I'm more focused on the drive-by."

"A mistake?" he hissed as if he hadn't even heard the rest of what she'd said. "You can't tell me you didn't feel something last night in the hotel room. Even before that. This has been building for a long time."

"And now we know."

"Damn straight. There's a chemistry here that needs to be dealt with."

"I am dealing with it. By staying away from fire." This man had already burned her once without laying a finger on her. She didn't want to think of how badly he could singe her to the core given free rein over her body. Or worse yet, her feelings.

One thing was certain. She couldn't trust her own willpower anymore. She needed to put distance between them.

Without a word, she strode toward . . . she wasn't sure what, except the destination would be somewhere away from Vince.

She made it all of three steps.

He gripped her upper arm, his touch nearly as hot as the fire it stoked. "You can't just put your fingers in your ears and chant, 'La, la, la, I'm not listening.'"

"Says who?" She shrugged to tug free, but he held firm.

Just her arm, for crying out loud, and already she ached deep and low to dive right back in for round two of wrapping herself around Vince's hard-muscled body.

"Pardon me?" the community center guard interrupted, giving Shay the edge to jolt away. A retired police officer, he wore his new uniform with crisp precision. "They're impounding your car and need the keys."

No car, no apartment, no purse. She couldn't even have her dog for comfort, since she'd given Buster over to her neighbor to watch. All of which seemed petty to complain about when she could have died. "The key is still in the ignition. I was about to leave when the shooting started."

"Thank you, Miss Bassett." His eyes blazed with the excitement of being back in the thick of things. "I'll bring it around for the tow truck." The old flatfoot launched into a light jog back toward the crime scene.

Shay was alone with Vince again, but not for long. "I think it's best that I stay with someone else."

"Because of that kiss that doesn't exist."

"I can stay with Angeline. In fact, I should go ahead and call her now."

"I thought you said she already has a full house."

"Can you promise me that if we're alone in a hotel room, we won't kiss again?" Or more.

His silence answered loud and clear.

"I'm calling Angeline." She pulled out her cell phone, the tow truck beep, beep, beeping as it backed to hook up her car.

Her thumb hovered over her cell phone keypad as she watched the guard slide into her little car to move it into a better position for the tow truck. Her ten-year-old compact wasn't much, but it was hers. Pocked with bullets, it had protected her well this morning. How odd to feel such a swell of nostalgia for a car she'd planned to replace when the end of the year sales rolled around.

She forced herself to look away, turning her back and focusing on her phone again. Vince scowled at her, obviously not one bit pleased about being overridden.

Tough.

She hit the preprogrammed number and snuck one last look at her soon-to-be-towed compact, the guard cranking the engine. The phone rang—

And her car exploded.

★ ★ ★

Don guided his car through the landscaped entrance leading into his condo complex and wished raging thoughts were as easily steered.

He had a couple of hours for a shower and power nap before he needed to return to the office. He wouldn't have left at all, but his people wouldn't have their take on the video feed ready until then. He suspected it could be a long time before he saw the inside of his place again.

His heart jackhammered a litany of denial in his ears, but he couldn't ignore reality.

Some bastard had tried to blow up his daughter.

Had he and Paulina been so focused on concerns about an attack at the hearing, they'd missed a sign? His screwup could have cost Shay her life.

He wound along the narrow road, inching past a rent-a-cop doing rounds in his cart. Yet another reminder of how close Shay had come to dying. If not for that too-thoughtful-for-his-own-good old guard moving her car for the tow truck . . . There had to be more they could do.

At least they had a lock on a cell phone from those responsible. Now they had to hope the kid didn't toss it. Their intel showed it was a prepaid sort, but unlike the mob, these thugs didn't have disposable income. He wanted to grab the little bastard and rattle his cage.

Paulina, however, had vetoed him. She thought that would alert others in the chain, causing them to close ranks. She insisted they could learn more by cloning the cell phone, enabling them to trace all the other numbers it called. The dark ops team's advanced technology expanded the scope, speed, and reliability of sniffing out a network through electronic cloning. Now that Paulina had fast-tracked the secret FISA warrant needed to cover their butts legally, they were ready to roll. Vince and his fellow aviators would be spending a crap-ton of time at their workstations.

Impotence roared through his veins as fiercely as his high-powered engine sped up. He powered down lanes leading him deeper into the gated neighborhood of three-story mock brownstone condos.

He whipped up the driveway in his corner unit, headlights sweeping across the minimalist yard and the front stoop.

A front stoop with a woman waiting for him.

His shoulders slumped.

Jayne sat on the top step, her long legs tucked to the side, porch light glinting off gray blond hair held back from her face in a clasp. She'd worn her shoulder-length hair that way since the day he'd met her in college. She'd always been perfectly groomed, perfectly composed, perfectly pissed at all the ways he hadn't been the perfect husband.

He glanced down the row of condos, and sure enough, there was a car parked in the guest spot. If there was anything in this world that would give him a heart attack, that woman topped the list.

He turned off the engine and stepped out with a heavy

sigh he reserved especially for his ex-wife. "I have to shower, change, eat, and head straight back to work. You're going to have to take a number."

"If I listened to every time you said that, we would never have a conversation."

Sounded like a good plan to him.

"Don, we have to talk."

"Fine." He brushed past, catching a whiff of her Chanel perfume.

His senses tumbled into a time warp of naked memories that left him twitching below the belt. He tamped down irritation. He'd been married to the woman for nineteen years. They'd slept together, had great sex before their relationship dried up. It was only natural his body would occasionally go on autopilot when she walked in the room.

He absolutely refused to feel guilty. He and Paulina had never asked for nor expected exclusivity.

Still, he had been sleeping with her for four months, respected her in the workplace for a year now. She deserved better from him.

Don pushed inside his condo, Jayne hot on his heels with tut-tutting.

"Wow, Don, love your cookie-cutter decorator. I must get his number. I've always longed for a place with nothing more personal than a razor and food."

"I like brown and black. So sue me." He wasn't here enough for it to matter anyway.

He pitched his keys on the black lacquer dinette table. Jayne still had baby pictures of their two kids on her key chain, for God's sake. Of course she also used that as a reminder to their adult children of how they'd failed to do the expected thing of marrying and having children. Which usually lead right into how bad he'd fucked up in raising them.

She hitched her purse higher on her shoulder. "Don't you want to know why I'm here?"

Damn, the woman was so good with the guilt, she should hire out. Right now any issues he had with his kids took a huge-ass backseat to making sure he didn't lose a child altogether.

His gut burned. "Not really. But if you're going to tell me anyway, make it quick."

"As polite and sensitive as ever, I see."

Maybe the whole thing was just indigestion from the casserole Paulina fed him.

He tossed his roll of antacids beside his keys. "I thought when we got divorced we would spend less time together?"

Standing behind the sofa barricade, Jayne straightened a pillow on his leather sectional. "You were in the air force then. There isn't any way to spend less time together when you were gone all the time."

"Yeah, yeah, old script. I took care of Sean's tuition. We're done here." He gestured toward the front door.

She dropped her leather purse on the couch. "Don't you dare ignore me."

"No worries, Jayne, you've always made sure no one ignores you."

"Are you trying to pick a fight?"

"We never needed to try." As much as he wanted to send her on her way, he couldn't waste the time standing around. "If you want to talk, you're going to have to follow me around, and you'd better speed things up, because I'm going to be naked and in the shower within the next five minutes."

Jayne grabbed him by the arm, stopping him as much by her grip as by the fact that they never touched each other at all anymore. He stared down at her smooth hair and furrowed brow.

Her Chanel perfume wafted up again, another thing that hadn't changed. He remembered the scent well after buying the requisite bottle every Valentine's Day.

Her trembling, however, tugged at him far more than her scent.

Don gripped her shoulder. "Jayne?"

"It's all over the news. I had to hear it on the *car radio* that someone tried to kill our daughter. And then when I spoke to her, she tells me this threat has been going on for days? *You* let her wander around without knowing what kind of danger she was in."

And Jayne didn't even realize the worst of it.

"She knows now."

"When did you tell her?"

He forced himself not to look away like some disobedient toddler about to pitch the remote control in the commode. Lord, but Shay had been cute when she waterlogged their electronics. "We couldn't risk her tipping anyone off."

"We? *We?*"

"The FBI, the government." He was skating on thin ice acknowledging that much. He couldn't go so far as to out the air force or how he, a CIA agent, had tangled himself up in an operation on U.S. soil.

She shrugged free of his hand on her shoulder. "Damn you and damn governmental obligations. I put up with your BS when you *were* ignoring me. But when the job comes before your own flesh and blood, our children you are biologically obligated to protect . . ."

She shoved against his chest. Once. Twice. Hard.

He captured her wrists. "I'm doing what I think is best for her."

"You're doing what you always do." Her fingers curled into fists against him, digging deep until her manicured nails disappeared altogether. "You view the world through analytical eyes, because it's easier than actually feeling anything."

"What the hell do you mean by that?"

She pulled her arms free slowly, eying him with incredulity. "Are you really so clueless that you don't get it? Even your children know. I believe the air force suspected, too, but you were of better use to them numb."

Numb? She thought he was some robot? Just having her here and talking about Shay in danger had him roaring inside with hellish memories of that night their daughter had tried to kill herself.

The doctors had all made it clear Shay hadn't been "acting out." She'd been serious. Days after that boy Tommy had died, she'd taken amphetamines bought off some street corner, filled the tub with icy water, and made a longitudinal cut along her wrist to sever more arteries and veins.

Anger, impotence, and yeah, *pain* threatened to explode him. "Screw you, Jayne. And screw this. I don't need you probing around inside my head. So what if I don't go all Joe Sensitive like that nice, safe accountant you've been dating? For all *his* sensitivity, the loser took six fucking years to put that engagement ring on your finger, and he still doesn't have the balls to set a date."

Don turned to snatch up his antacids.

"Ever heard of PTSD?"

That, he couldn't let pass. He turned back to face her. "Yeah, I've heard it from *you* non-fucking-stop, even after we divorced. You're the one who needs to listen. I wasn't a POW. I never got shot down. I may have been . . . overtaxed at times, but that's a long way from PTSD."

"You keep telling yourself that." She stood her ground in her pretty flowered skirt with her cotton top hugging her willowy body, pearls at the neckline. "Just like others told themselves because they were afraid of missing out on a promotion. I had to stop caring about you a long time ago, but I do care about our children and what happens to them."

Like he didn't? That horrible night still fresh in his mind, he felt anything but emotionless. "Ah, I see where this is going. You're blaming me again for Sean's aimless life, for Shay slashing her—"

"Stop." Just that fast her composure faded. Tears swelled in her blue eyes. "Do not go there just to hurt me so much I can't think. I'm talking about today. Right now. Making sure that you're doing everything you can to keep our baby girl safe." Her voice faltered. "I can't risk her again," she gasped. "I can't—"

Ah hell.

He reached for her. She shoved at his chest again, but this time he didn't restrain her hands or move away. He just tucked her against him, her tears flowing so fast now they soaked through his shirt to sear his skin. There came the guilt pouring over him in buckets full. He hadn't just failed the kids. He'd failed her.

"Jayne, honey, shhh. It's okay, Jaynie. She's okay now. Strong and whole." Probably more so than him if he took his ex-wife's assessment of his mental stability to heart. His arms twitched tighter around her. "We've got everything under control. She's being protected. Nobody's going to get through Vince Deluca."

She swiped her wrist under her nose and sniffled. "Vince, huh? You always did have a lot of faith in him, even when other people didn't. I admired that about you."

There was a time he and Jayne had liked a lot of things about each other.

"Vince is a good man." Don reached into his back pocket for his handkerchief and pressed it into her hand, the

same way he'd done the day he'd proposed and she cried
her eyes out then, too.

And it hadn't taken him six years to pony up the ring or
the date.

"Thanks." She knuckled away the tears, her fingers
stained with mascara. She inched back, a wobbly smile in
place at odds with the tear streaks in her makeup tugging at
something inside him. "I can't believe you still carry these."

"A guy never knows when he'll have a pretty girl crying
on his chest."

"Girl?" She snorted on another sniffle. "Good Lord,
Don, I haven't been a girl in . . . I don't even want to say
how long."

Something shifted inside, something that compelled him
to say, "You're still pretty, and you know it."

He only looked into her eyes for less than a second, and
then he was kissing her.

When had he even lowered his mouth to hers? He'd just
acted by instinct born from years of marriage. Her mouth
felt the same, soft and fitting at just the perfect angle to give
him access, and he couldn't stop his response to her, to the
familiarity triggering some sort of sensory memory.

Feel those subtle curves.

Taste her peppermint toothpaste.

Smell more of her Chanel scent until it was as if she
filled every inch inside him.

His body went on high alert, and damn it, damn it, damn
it, he needed to get his head on straight and his ass in gear.
He deserved every bit of that guilt she'd been heaping on
him.

Casserole churned uneasily in his gut even long past
when it should have been out of his system.

He broke away. No easing or niceties. He had to put an

end to this. He set Jayne away from him, both of them gasping. She looked as horrified as he felt.

"Don, that was wrong."

"I know, and I am sorry. It won't happen again. I'm doing everything I can to keep Shay safe, and I'll make sure you're kept in the loop as much as is legally possible." He gripped his bedroom doorknob. "I have to shower. You can see yourself out."

The front door clicked closed before he even made it to the bathroom.

* * *

No more rides around town on his bike.

No more leaving Shay out there in the open.

Vince would make sure she stayed in protective custody until she delivered her congressional testimony and they had had the people responsible for these threats in custody.

She rode in the rental car beside him, staring out the window at Lake Erie, picking nervously at her clothes, covered in grime from hitting the dirty parking lot. "I don't think I'm ever going to get over the horror of how that dear old guard died in my place."

Words weren't going to fix this one. Vince kept driving.

The FBI had arranged a safe house setting for her at a hotel, even transferring her dog to a kennel and gathering necessities for her rather than risk showing her face *anywhere*.

Vince turned on a side road, each glowing streetlamp taking them farther from the East Side. He couldn't even think about how close she'd been to those bullets, how close she'd come to turning that car key. Sure, he'd been in the vehicle with her, but he'd faced death often enough in his life to shake off the near brush.

Her near misses with the bomb and the drive-by, however, shook him to his boots at a time when he was already reeling from the impact of her mouth on his. He eyed the rearview mirror, checking again for a tail.

Still clear.

Within the next five minutes, he would have her locked up and secured in an exclusive hotel with police protection throughout the building. He would feel better if he could stay with her 24/7, but he still had a job to do, a job that would hopefully put an end to all of this.

Even now, Don had his people following up leads.

Vince winced from thoughts of Shay's dad. Thinking about her father only brought back old scripts of staying away from Shay out of respect to him. Old habits were tough to break.

But after that explosive kiss against the car, he suspected this was one avenue he would have to travel if he ever expected to put thoughts of Shay to rest. She, however, didn't appear so inclined.

He paused at a stoplight right outside the hotel, even though the street was deserted so late at night.

Sighing, Shay shifted her eyes from the window to his face. "It's going to be a long night if you're not talking to me."

"Fine then. What do you want to talk about?"

She tapped her chin, eying the hint of a goatee he'd shaved into his five o'clock shadow. "I thought military guys couldn't have any facial hair other than a mustache. My dad was always complaining about having to shave so often."

Ah, she wanted to make small talk to dodge the obvious. Still not willing to acknowledge what had happened between them. Something rare, by the way.

Her avoidance spoke more of how much the kiss had rattled her.

He stroked his short beard. "We call this category one relaxed grooming standards. There are situations where something like this is acceptable. Suddenly my bald head doesn't look so hard-core military, does it?"

"You're right." She fidgeted with the sleeve of the shirt he'd bought her just the night before, nodding toward his arm. "Just that small change and the biker tattoo peeking from under your sleeve would throw me off the track if I passed you in an airport."

His biceps flexed. Sometimes he forgot the Chinese lettering was even there. "When I look like this, I'm not such a glaring target for people hating on the military."

"How much more can you let it grow in?"

"Depends on the assignment." The light changed, and he drove ahead, shifting gears, his knuckles brushing her knee. "Special Ops dudes looking to blend into the Afghani countryside can go category three, with bushy beards and long hair."

She scooched closer to the door. "I can't envision you with long hair."

"There's not much to grow out." He ducked the car into the underground parking garage.

"Ah right, you don't do this"—she stroked her hand along the air over his head, not touching his shaved scalp, but she might as well have—"to look badass."

His fists clenched around the steering wheel as he whipped the car into a reserved spot by the elevator. "Do that again, and we're going to finish what we started right here."

She twisted her fingers in her lap, but her eyes held, pupils widening with undeniable desire. "We should find something else to talk about."

Shay could play at small talk, but her body betrayed her with signs of arousal, like her widened pupils and the flush to her skin. The beading of her nipples just visible through the whispery flowing shirt he'd bought for her at Wal-Mart. The way her tongue kept tipping along her lips as if tasting, remembering.

He turned off the car and faced her, arm draped over the wheel. "You're still pretending to ignore the fact that we were a tongue stroke away from saying to hell with it all and getting busy in a public place. Admit it. You're as completely turned on as I am. It's been an edge-of-the-universe day, and adrenaline is still stinging through your veins. Even beyond that, what we felt was abso-fucking-lutely more than any sane person can resist."

Leaving her slack-jawed, he slammed out of the car and around to her side. He gripped her arm to help her out and to keep her safely by his side.

Her chest rose and fell too fast to be mistaken for anything but arousal. "Vince—"

"Not now." Keeping her out of danger was his number one priority.

Vince hauled butt through the parking garage and into the lobby. His local contact had already signed them in under false identities and given him a room key, so he headed straight for the elevator.

He would figure out what to do about the raging attraction between them once he got there. Sadly, it would most likely lead to a raging fight instead. God help them both, he needed an outlet for the building steam.

He entered the elevator—empty and safe—and punched the button for the twelfth floor. The doors started to slide closed only to bump back open again. A panting young couple in bathing suits charged inside. Since they weren't carrying even so much as towels or a beach bag to conceal a weapon, he decided they were safe enough. That woman couldn't hide even a nail file in a string bikini at least two letters too small for her cup size, much less anything with more lethal firepower.

Vince tucked Shay to his side, silencing her tiny huff with a quick scowl. The couple wedged themselves in a corner and promptly tangled themselves around each other.

His eyebrows shot upward. Shay stiffened against him.

Vince shifted. "Uh, dude, what floor?"

The overeager swimmer came up for air only long enough to gasp, "Fourteen."

Fan-fucking-tastic. They would get to hang out here in close confines with a peep show.

Overeager dude grabbed near-naked woman's ass. If she wriggled much more, her silicone implants would fall right out of her top. Between kisses and strokes they mumbled rambling little sighs.

"Want you."

"Can't wait."

"You're so hot."

"Soon, baby, soon."

It would have been funny if it weren't for the fact his sexual frustration had pegged out halfway to the hotel. He hauled in air that suddenly felt about a hundred and ten degrees. The man's hand slid from her waist to cup her hip.

Vince glanced at Shay, and tiny pearls of sweat dotted her brow. Her tongue started playing peekaboo again.

Ding.

The doors opened. Shay sprinted forward. He grabbed her hand and tugged her back against his chest while he checked both ways down the hall. Clear, other than one man he recognized as the guard assigned to watch over her. The man didn't so much as glance up from his paper, looking the part of a disgruntled husband hanging out in the hall for peace.

Vince slotted the key card in and out. The green light flashed. He swung the door wide and clicked on the lights. The room was exactly what he'd ordered, the space expansive and open so he could see in a glance that no one lurked. A dim light glowed over by the king-size bed. He swept a hand for her to enter.

Vince strode past. "Shay, I believe you're going to have to rethink that policy on not discussing what happened—"

She grabbed a fistful of his shirt and pulled him to her. "Make the first move."

"What?"

"You turned me away last time. If you want me as much as I think you do, you need to come get me this time."

Kind of a moot point, since she had his shirt in a death grip. He should say no. He should explain about the aftermath of adrenaline. "Shay, this is a—"

"Bad idea? I know. I don't care."

He'd turned her away before. The toughest thing he'd ever done. "You're the one who said we should pretend that mind-blowing kiss never happened. If we finish this, do you think *that*'s something we can ignore?"

"Quit thinking. Quit talking. After a day like this, even I can't deny what I'm feeling." She let go of his shirt. "So I'll say it again. If you want me, come get me."

All right then. He cupped her head and powered them back toward the closed door. He'd done his gentlemanly best to make sure he wasn't taking advantage. He wanted her and intended to have her. Now. And again later on that big bed. Beyond that, he had no idea.

But one thing he did know for certain. She wouldn't be able to ignore the detailed attention he planned to devote to pleasuring every inch of her body.

TWELVE

★───────────────────────────────

Shay felt the hard press of the hotel door against her back, the even harder length of Vince against her front. He anchored her in much the same way he'd pressed her against her car earlier.

Her car.

The bomb.

The dead guard.

Oh God, that could have been her. Or worse yet, Vince.

She dealt with death on a regular basis on the suicide hotline, even with these kids so hell-bent on killing each other. Maybe that's why she felt this connected to Vince, because they both dealt with life and death as a routine part of their jobs.

And she really didn't want to think about that now. She inhaled the musky scent of Vince and some kind of rosy air freshener, desperate to erase the tinge of smoke still stinging her nose and memory.

She ached to sink into sensation, tingles prickling over her like a sunburn, slightly painful, her skin tight and over-heated. In need of relief. A relief that couldn't come close to being satisfied by the gusts from the air conditioner vent.

Vince nuzzled her ear, his light beard rasping her tender cheek. "I thought we were pretending the kiss never happened."

"We are." She slid her hands over his chest, the king-size bed just visible over his shoulder.

She liked the door just fine. Shay slipped her hand lower to caress him.

He swayed for a second before planting a palm on the door by her head to steady himself. "Consider my mouth closed."

"Oh, I wouldn't go that far." She traced his lips. "Your mouth can do some amazing things. I'm already imaging all the possibilities with your category one beard."

His eyes widened with shock, then totally wicked intent.

She grappled with his belt buckle, the metal biker emblem warm from his body. Her fingers started to shake as she worked the top button free, then the zipper.

His eyes met hers, his face shadowy with only the dim glow of the bedside lamp, but the gleam in his eyes shone brightly. Watching him watching her, she tucked her hand inside his boxers and molded her palm to him, thick and hot and throbbing in her hand. She slid her fingers down his shaft, lingering at the base to massage farther, deeper, until he went even unbelievably harder beneath her touch.

She cupped the back of his neck to taste and swallow his groan. She tapped her way down his chest until she could torment him two-handed, massaging the base while caressing up and down. Her thumb glided over the bulbous head, smoothing nature's lubricant until he growled.

He gripped her wrists just above her wide watchband.
"Stop."

"No."

His smile caressed her kissed-sensitive lips. "I didn't
mean permanently."

Oh. Good. Tackling him might have been problematic,
given his size. And my, the man had some size on him in all
the right places. "Condoms?"

"Wallet. Back pocket." His hand slipped from her, and
she gripped his wrist to stop him.

"I'll take care of it." She dipped her fingers into his
pocket with slow deliberation, his buttocks taut to the touch
even through denim. She wanted to explore him leisurely,
in the light. But time would invite reality, and light would
bring questions. She would be satisfied with this, and, oh
my, how she had the feeling he had the ability to satisfy her
so very much.

She filched his wallet and passed it over. He plucked a
small square wrapper free, which she promptly stole from
him.

Vince yanked her shirt up and off, sweeping aside her
bra before her senses could unscramble enough to catch up
with his hands. Cool air teased over her bare chest, tightening her already puckered nipples to near-painful buds.

She wanted his touch, his mouth, but wondered if he
would find her smaller breasts enough. And God, she hated
that shallow thought, but how could a woman avoid it in a
world obsessed with glorifying boob jobs?

He cupped her breasts in bold, callused palms. "Perfect."

Her BS-ometer detected only total honesty. Vince's com-
pliment soothed lingering insecurities leftover from long-
ago rejections as sensually as his hands sketching along her
hypersensitized skin.

He ducked to take one nipple in his mouth, working her gently with his teeth while he stroked the other just enough to keep her from screaming for him to pay equal time . . . and he did . . . until his talented mouth had her head thunking back against the door.

She tugged at his shirt, bunched it in her fingers until it floated free. She flattened her hands to his chest and soaked in the molten hard feel of him, sagging, starting to slide down the door but unable to stop.

"Shay," he rasped his bristly new beard against her ear. "We need to ditch those pants of yours."

They both reached at the same time, sweeping her jeans and panties down. She kicked them aside.

"Much better," he growled.

He hooked his fingers behind her knees, lifting her, bringing her flush against him until her legs locked around his waist. The aching damp core of her pressed fully against his erection, his open zipper rasping a delicious friction against the vee of her thighs.

He flattened his palms up the length of her thighs, settling behind to cup her buttocks in a securing grip. "Your legs are the things fantasies are made of."

"Keep talking like that, and I'll think you're trying to get into my pants."

"Considering your pants are already on the floor, I must be doing something right." He nudged against her, his hardened penis working tantalizingly against the heated nub of nerves. "I need to hear exactly what you want and make it happen."

"Yes, it's working. In fact if you keep that up, I'm going to finish . . . here . . . and now." She shivered. She gasped. She totally *wanted*. "Can we please shut up?"

"Never. I intend to let you know with each and every

stroke just how fucking amazing you feel inside, around me . . . your hands on me and mine on you. There aren't enough ways to feel every bit of you at once."

He slipped a thick finger back and forth along her slit, slickening, tormenting, until she wriggled herself into position for him to sink inside her with one, then two.

Finally, finally he positioned his erection against her and plunged deep. He filled her, stretched her, sent ripples of pleasure through her. She desperately wanted to harness it before she flew apart too soon. She'd waited too long for this with him to have it end so fast.

Then he moved. And moved again until she couldn't think about restraint or the past or anything but milking the most out of this moment as he thrust inside her. Deeper, harder, faster, everything she demanded and more, all the while giving him the words he wanted.

Arching to get closer, deeper, she skimmed her hands over his shaved head, the smooth texture so different from anything she found on a man before. But then he wasn't like any other man.

More than anything, she wanted this moment. Sure, she would likely deny it tomorrow. Without question, she wasn't ready to bare all to him, of her body, her scars, her soul. All of which were scary-as-hell things she didn't want to think about. She didn't want to think at all.

She writhed against him, clawed at his shoulders, couldn't get close enough because nothing would be enough until she found release. She buried her face into the curve of his neck, his raspy whiskers lightly grating against her forehead in sweet pain. Hot breaths puffed over her, faster, riding words of how much she pleased him, turned him on and inside out.

Ecstasy that far outstripped any street drug swelled inside, building, bigger, until she felt ready to shed her skin and burst into the wash of pulsing sensation. Ripple after ripple rolled through her, throbbing along all her over-revved nerves from a day fraught with an adrenaline dousing.

Slowly, her body cooled and went boneless in the aftermath of explosive sex at the end of an intensely explosive day. She felt hollowed out inside, exhausted.

And a little scared.

She sagged against him, her legs sliding to the floor, her limp arms around his neck doing less to hold her upright than his hands molding her to the door. Over his shoulder in the dim light she saw her shirt and his scattered over the carpet by her bra. They hadn't even made it to the bed or turned on more than the one dim light.

A blessing as far as she was concerned. Because here in this dark room, her body and privacy still shielded in all the ways that mattered, she could hold on to her secrets for a little while longer.

★ ★ ★

Creaking back in his desk chair, Lewis had major deals in the works, and he wouldn't let any piece-of-trash kid risk that.

He saw a weakness in that boy, the one in love with the pregnant slut Amber. He'd been ordered to make sure Shay Bassett didn't survive, whether it be through car bomb or drive-by. But again, the kid had missed.

Of course little did Webber know the deeper implications of his role. Hit or miss, he'd still managed to steer attention away from Lewis's real goal, the true money-maker.

Lewis fired up his computer while fishing another of his

disposable cell phones from the bottom drawer. He might be new in his career field, but he could handle these teens, understood how to maneuver them with the right carrot. He was just starting to gain some power, and he refused to lose it. The people he worked with could give him everything he wanted. More money and clout than his picayune junior position now.

One day he would be at the head.

Yes, he had a major deal in the works. Getting rid of Shay Bassett was merely a fortunate sidebar. She had proven herself to be an annoying hindrance.

The last thing he needed was for her policies to gain support and momentum and effect. He depended on the international freedom of movement these gangs enjoyed. If Congress started pouring money into crackdowns the way they had into security against terrorism, his business dealings would shut down altogether.

Meanwhile, he needed to put Webber to the test, make sure he had the stuff to see this through. He had too much invested in the kid to simply scrap him altogether. Convincing a kid to do what Webber ultimately had to do . . . that took time.

Webber just needed a little toughening up, along with a reminder of how badly things could go for the people around him.

* * *

Paulina hip bumped the door of her Mercedes convertible closed, basket of food in both hands. Okay, so it was lame bringing her "boyfriend" food in the middle of the night, but as the mission coordinator in D.C., she knew they had about an hour's downtime before things revved up. Food at the site would be pathetic pickings and mostly forgotten in the rush to get things done.

She worried about him.

Don looked like hell these days, handsome in a refined way but haggard. At least she could make sure he ate.

Even her best investigative skills likely wouldn't stand a chance at finding out what was bothering him, other than the obvious with Shay. But Don had been wearing this gaunt look long before bombs started exploding in his daughter's car. As much as he tried to hide it, the longer she spent with him, the more she realized he felt things. Deeply.

That knowledge teased her with possibilities. Maybe he was more committed than she realized. If he could pour half that drive and determination he showed at work into being a parent, he would be the perfect father for her child.

Paulina elbowed the doorbell, longer and harder than she intended. Her balance wobbled between her teetering heels and the awkward basket packed with her ham and mushroom soufflé and a fruit cocktail Jell-O mold.

Don's footsteps pounded down the hall, louder. She started to announce herself.

He yanked the door open. "Damn it, Jayne." His hair wet, he jerked his bathrobe tie tight. "I already told you I'm sorry for—" He looked up. His eyes went wide. "Shit."

Jayne?

Jayne!

"Jayne?" Paulina pushed inside, her steps and voice far more controlled than her churning stomach. "Your ex-wife was here."

He held up his hands. "Hey, calm down. She was waiting on my doorstep when I got home. She saw about the explosion on the news and wanted to know why I hadn't told her what was going on with Shay."

Perfectly reasonable. But she hadn't gotten this far in the FBI by accepting half the story as the whole truth.

She knew guilty when she saw guilty. "And you're sorry for not telling her, which is why you barked, 'Damn it, Jayne,' when you thought she'd come back."

"That's pretty much how conversations between us roll." His eyes skipped away and back. Liar.

Paulina circled him, her job-honed instincts blaring.

Even with the scent of his fresh-washed body and spicy soap, she smelled . . . another woman. "So you got your shower."

"Uh-huh,"

He dodged her eyes.

"Did you sleep with your ex-wife?"

He met her eyes, wary. Weary.

She slammed her basket on his black lacquer dinner table. "Answer. Me. Now. Did you sleep with Jayne?"

"Hell, no. Even if I'd wanted to—which I didn't—you may recall you wore me out last night. I'm not exactly in my twenties anymore, and I don't resort to those little purple pills."

Dating a CIA agent totally stank. His evasive maneuvers were pretty darn convincing. "*Something* happened."

"Don't you think we should head back to work? I need to get dressed."

"I couldn't locate you on your phone. You were probably too busy sucking face with your ex to hear."

"I was asleep," he snapped. "If anything, you should be chewing my ass for not hearing the phone when I'm on call."

She stepped closer, crowding him, even if he didn't retreat. "Right. Whatever. So I came by to feed you and let you know you can snag a couple more hours' sleep. There's been a glitch with the technology, and it's going to be a while before they're up and running again to track the data. Now I deserve to know what happened here with you and Jayne."

He hesitated.

"Don't hand me any bull about how we're not in a relationship." She held her temper in check, because if she lost control of her emotions, she might just cry, and she would not humiliate herself that way. "We've been sleeping together for four months. That entitles me to a straight answer."

He scrubbed a hand over his face, then along his steel gray hair. "We had a fight about Shay. Things got heated and"—he hesitated, swallowed, threw back his shoulders—"we kissed."

THIRTEEN

She blinked once. "You kissed your ex-wife. You *kissed* her?"

Don could see the hurt in the furrow between her brows—coming from a woman who never showed softer emotions.

That cut him off at knees far more than buckets of Jayne's tears. "I accept responsibility."

A tic started at the corner of her eye. "How can you be so calm about this? I know we don't have some great romance going here, but when I sleep with a man, I expect exclusivity. And I'm absolutely certain this isn't okay with Jayne's accountant fiancé."

He felt compelled to offer her some reassurance. "I did not sleep with Jayne."

"A mighty big technicality. My mama always said close only counts in horseshoes and hand grenades. In case you were wondering, this qualifies as a grenade."

Best to divert this conversation ASAP until she cooled down. "Your mother? That's the first time you've even referenced a family."

"I didn't crawl out from under a rock." The tic twitched faster.

"So, if you didn't crawl out from under a rock," he pressed ahead, "where are you from?"

"I grew up in Kentucky." She eyed him warily, fingers toying with the handles on the picnic basket. "Mama and Daddy worked in the local car factory. They divorced when I was five."

"Did your father cheat on your mother?" He risked a step closer. "Is that why you're so fired up over one kiss?"

"Hell, I don't know if my father cheated or not." She slammed the wooden basket handles down and faced him full on. "I was five freaking years old. I'm ready to explode because we're sleeping together, and you plastered your mouth all over another woman."

"I'm sorry." He still didn't understand what had happened with Jayne, but he knew full well it was going nowhere. "It meant nothing. I was comforting her because she'd heard about the bombing and drive-by. She was terrified for Shay and . . . Again, it meant nothing."

"Absolutely do *not* pull out that cliché shit with me." She tucked her hands on her hips, started to talk, shook her head, and turned away, then spun back. "Do you love her?"

"No! Fuck no," he answered without hesitation.

"Do you hate her? Did marriage make you some kind of commitment phobe?"

His neck started to itch. "I'm not that complicated."

"You couldn't be more wrong about that. Don, there *is* a limit to how many cans of cream of mushroom soup I'm willing to waste on a man."

He held his tongue, gauging what to say next that wouldn't send her spiraling into a full-tilt rage.

Her face went red anyway. "Don't you dare ask if I'm PMSing, or I'm going to unleash some serious tae kwon do on your ass."

"You think you can take me?" he couldn't resist taunting.

Her eyes narrowed with sexy lethality. "In more ways than you can even imagine."

He shoved his hands in his robe pockets, suddenly feeling damned vulnerable, given he was naked underneath. "I should have kept my mouth shut. Excuse me for having a shitty week due to gangbangers with terrorist connections gunning for my daughter. The kiss was a fluke, and no way in hell will it ever happen again."

"Don't insult me with more of those cliché answers." She stepped closer.

"Pardon me?"

"No, I'm not going to pardon you this time." She began circling him.

"You have to know I was only speaking in a figurative sense." Where were his pants?

"Oh, I know full well that you won't commit to so much as an *authentic* apology." She stopped in front of him, legs spread and planted, killer heels dangerously close to his bare feet. "That makes it a little tough to believe you're not still carrying around feelings for the woman you were married to for nineteen years."

"The woman I *divorced* fifteen years ago."

"Excuse me for thinking you might have feelings for her. I assumed that must be the reason you've never been seriously involved with anyone else for as long as anybody can remember."

Fine. He got it. He was inadequate when it came to anything a female would call meaningful. "You're the one changing the rules, not me."

She snorted her disgust. "You're a freaking train wreck, Don."

Frustration detonated inside him. He'd taken it when Jayne pulled that PTSD crap on him; hearing it again, from this woman . . . "Fuck off, Paulina."

Her face went into deep-freeze mode.

Ah, shit, shit, shit.

Had he said that out loud? But he couldn't take it back, and she'd made it clear his apologies didn't mean jack. So he stood his ground and waited for the retribution he knew was com—

She slapped him.

Yeah, there it was; however, even expecting it hadn't prepared him for the pain hammering his jaw. The woman was *strong*.

He anchored her wrist. "I'll give you that one. But do *not* try it again."

She flipped him on his back.

Holy hell. He saw stars dancing around his ceiling fan. This was not his day.

But he wasn't going down easy. He still held her arm, lucky him. "Don't say I didn't warn you."

He hauled her down.

She slammed on top of him, tucking and rolling, tumbling again. His back crashed into the dining room table. Her basket slid across and hurtled to the carpet.

China shattered. Food splattered. She launched to her feet panting, only a second ahead of him.

He'd never seen this side of her before. So out of control. So damn hot.

Her hair twist slipping loose, she crouched, ready. Watching. "No dessert for you."

Don stalked closer, careful to keep his body loose, his moves nonthreatening. Easy enough to appear vulnerable when his robe tie had long ago given up, leaving his Johnson waving in the wind. "You're hurting yourself by denying us that treat, princess."

Slowly, he touched her stomach, her muscles gripping beneath his touch. When she didn't move, he stroked upward, slowly, until she straightened, her feet still immobile. Pinning her with his eyes, he slipped his hand down, lower still, until he stopped between her legs in a none-too-subtle reminder of where he'd laved away lemon meringue from their last meal together.

Paulina pressed his hand more firmly to her, molding her skirt between her legs. His body throbbed in response, hardened, his erection clear to see. Yeah, baby, this is what they were about. This was how things were supposed to be between them. She guided his hand back and forth against her, farther, sliding it just free of her body.

She flipped his hand around.

And bent back his pinky.

Pain screamed through his body even as he locked his jaw up tight. She pushed harder, just about drove him to his knees.

She leaned closer, her mouth a kiss away from his. "Who's on top now, baby?"

He blocked the agony and swept his foot behind hers, knocking them off balance. He twisted just in time to catch the brunt of their fall. She got to be on top, but he wasn't letting those lethal hands of hers loose. He locked a leg over hers for good measure.

Panting, she loomed over him, her face flushed, her hair

a frazzled, fiery mess. Her hips offered the perfect cradle for his raging erection.

He smiled up at her. "What now, princess?"

"Shut up." Her mouth slammed against his, nothing gentle or giving about it.

Paulina nudged aside his bathrobe with her teeth. She nipped and kissed her way down, stung and soothed with her teeth and tongue. He hiked up her skirt to her waist, slipped his fingers under the string of her underwear, twisting, tighter, until snap, the scrap of satin fell free. She teased her damp core against him, lubricating him with her essence, almost sending him over the edge like a trigger-happy teen.

He arched back and slammed home deep inside her. A groan slipped between his gritted teeth. He paused. *Restraint. Restraint. Restraint.*

She struggled to free her hands, wriggling against him with needy insistence. The woman worked out, and it showed. "I need you hard and fast and out of control right now."

Thank God they were on the same page.

"Glad to comply." He released her wrists and gripped her hips, hauling her down as he thrust upward, letting her take this as far as she wanted. The carpet chafed his ass, no doubt leaving rug burns, not that he cared as long as she kept . . .

Sliding . . .

Up . . .

Down . . .

Faster and faster.

The slap of skin against skin echoed in the room along with their gasps and elemental grunts. She scored his chest, and he growled his appreciation. He arched up to take one pert nipple in his mouth, drawing, teasing, working it until her rhythm grew more frantic.

Her face went tight with pleasure. He watched her release slam through her, tearing a scream from her throat along with a litany of louder "Yes, yes, yes," as her eyes fluttered shut.

The tight pulsing squeeze of her pleasure massaged him, wrenching the last of his control away. She locked her knees tighter against his hips, milking his orgasm again and again until it nearly hurt, but he wasn't ready for it to end.

He was so screwed in more ways than one.

She sagged over him, a sweaty, sated blanket of soft female. His head still tumbled from the intensity of how they'd come together, unlike anything he'd ever experienced before. All antacids aside, he wasn't ready to give up her soufflés yet, and that blindsided him on a night when he needed all of his wits to get through what the coming hours held at CIA headquarters.

This woman had a way of throwing him off kilter until he forgot practical concerns.

He went still, searching his mind, because something was off. He'd missed the boat somehow . . . He sat bolt upright, rolling Paulina off him and onto the carpet.

Both of them bare. Totally bare.

Because damn it all to hell, he hadn't worn a condom, and she wasn't on the pill.

★ ★ ★

Finally, they had a break in the case.

Airport lights cut through the dark night heavy with heat and tension. Vince pounded pavement, biker boots thudding on his way toward the Pilatus painted in civilian colors with a civilian registration number. Going to battle in jeans rather than his flight suit chafed sometimes, but the under-cover persona came with the boundaries he got to push in the air.

He stroked his jaw. Skipping shaves rocked, too. Which made him think of Shay's questions about category one grooming standards and what her nervous conversation had led to.

He couldn't let himself think about the way he'd left things with her, hauling ass out only seconds after brain-stunning sex against the door. He'd barely had time to zip his pants after the emergency call from Berg, much less coax Shay out of the shell he could see her retreating into at mach speed.

The air force had never cared much about convenient timing.

Jimmy jogged up alongside him, eyes sleepy lidded, but a gleam of excitement shone through the fog. "Hey, Vapor, you ready to roll?"

"Seems I'm more awake than you are, my brother."

Years of working together settled them into step silently along the ramp to the yellow and blue Pilatus tied down between two White Cessna Citations. Monitoring equipment had been moved into a corner of the hangar for a makeshift command center the day before. Vince and Jimmy would transmit data down from the plane to Smooth and Berg.

Smooth had been monitoring the cloned phone channel from the teen mixer. The phone had gone active again. Now Smooth and Berg were logging every number stored in the phone's history, working their asses off to follow the path of the calls and put together a network that would lead them to whoever was orchestrating this nightmare in the making.

If one of those phone lines was in action while they had the plane in the air, they would be able to get an up-close peek at the speaker. Photos often spoke a lot louder than words when people were careful not to use their real names.

But he couldn't ditch protocol, or he risked the whole mission. Preflighting the plane was his responsibility, one he intended to accomplish as fast as possible.

Vince looked over to Jimmy, the breeze blowing in off the lake doing little to cool the stress steaming through him. "I'll get the walk-around, and you take the interior."

"Sounds good to me."

Vince grabbed a checklist from his publication bag and began the mandatory preflight ritual. He started at the entry door and moved in a clockwise direction around the air-craft, checking for any sign that something was amiss. Even a bird's nest clogging an intake duct could cause a crash. He didn't want to end up in a safety report where the cause of the accident was a yellow-breasted anything. He spotted no leaks and nothing with boobs, yellow or otherwise, around the airplane.

He entered the cabin just as Jimmy sat in the copilot seat.

Jimmy shot him a thumbs-up. "The snooper system in back is in the green. Let's get this baby off the ground."

Vince wedged himself into the left seat and strapped his waist belt. "Read it, and I'll run it."

Parking brake, yoke unlocked, the steps continued to get the plane prepped before engine start.

Tension ratcheted, clouding his vision. As much as he wanted to be airborne pronto, he knew these steps were about more than safety. He needed this ritual, here in the craft, even if for sixty seconds, to get his head in the game and relegate everything else—especially Shay—to the back of his mind.

With each call from Jimmy, Vince fell into the rhythm, sliding into the zone.

Jimmy moved on to, "Engine start checklist."

He checked the radio frequency and keyed the mic. "Burke Ground Pilatus niner-six-eight-foxtrot-uniform, Charlie Row, Spot Four starting engines."

The radio crackled, "Copy foxtrot-uniform, call when ready to taxi."

"Prop."

Vince peered over the nose. "Prop clear." Some things didn't change, even after a hundred years of flying. He moved his head over to the open window and yelled, "Clear."

He pushed the starter switch, and the big turboprop on the nose spun to life. They cleaned up a few minutes more of call and response and readied to taxi.

Jimmy read back the instructions to the controller and scanned the right side of the airplane. "Clear right."

"Cleared left," Vince answered then advanced the throttles and started the aircraft moving.

He tapped the brakes for a check then eased off with a minuscule lurch forward. Routine. Ritual. Block out all else.

Jimmy dialed up their second radio to the automated terminal information service frequency for the latest weather. He jotted some info down on his kneeboard and checked the takeoff data. "Takeoff data looks good. About a three-thousand-foot roll."

Vince braked to a stop just short of the runway. "Burke Tower, Pilatus niner-six-eight-foxtrot-uniform number one with information bravo, ready for takeoff."

"Foxtrot-uniform on takeoff hold runway heading until three thousand feet," the tower responded, continuing with the takeoff instructions, which Jimmy repeated back.

Ready to ride.

His body hummed louder than the plane in anticipation. He applied power and turned onto the runway. He nudged the rudder pedals and nosed the aircraft onto the centerline. He moved the throttle forward, and the aircraft rapidly accelerated. Jimmy watched the instruments, while Vince handled the airplane.

Vince pulled the yoke back, and they slipped into the air. "Gear."

Jimmy pulled up the gear handle. "Gear in transit. Gear up, lights out."

The night sky stretched ahead with a sickle moon and blanket of stars. Hell yeah, hogs and planes. Nothing like flying along the road or the clouds. Nothing except sex with Shay?

Head back in the game, moron.

He circled through the departure and received clearance to the area they were going to snoop. Flying at 9,500 feet, lights off and in the dark, no one would even notice them from the ground. Jimmy cleared out of the copilot seat and moved to the rear to turn on the snooper equipment. The machine would scan the preset cell phone numbers gathered by Smooth and Berg.

"Damn," Jimmy grumbled into the headset, "none in use. They just couldn't make this easy for us, could they?"

"I guess it was too much to hope for that we would immediately hook onto the signal of someone spilling their guts."

More waiting. For how long? Usually he would welcome the extra flight hours, but tonight he wanted answers.

Cloning the kid's cell phone allowed them to retrieve codes from the phone and ID who the person was speaking to. After grabbing the cloning data, it was a piece of cake to listen in, just like tuning a radio or planting a bug. They shared the valuable technology with the Feds for tracking paths of mob transactions and with the CIA to follow a terrorist path until they had a picture of the group being monitored.

All well and good if someone was actually talking.

Jimmy tweaked the tuner on the listening device. Still nothing but silence. "Remember back when you and I were testing the snooper and hooked into the boss's phone instead of the one we had set up to test?"

Vince grinned at the memory. "Scanlon sure was torqued, but it was well worth it to find out his wife called him Big Stallion."

"Still cracks me up thinking about his face when he walked into the room, and everyone started snorting like a horse. Classic."

Their squadron commander had doled out payback by putting the two of them on every flight with a middle-of-the-night show time for three months. Then Scanlon's wife had died, and the boss stopped joking.

Jimmy shifted in his seat. "What's the scoop with you and your babe, Big Stallion, Jr.?"

Vince keyed in new navigation points to the computer system. "Broken record, my brother."

"You're not going to get away with that 'just friends' story anymore." Leaning toward the front, he jabbed a thumb at Vince's neck.

Vince glanced down. A hickey at thirty-four? He'd been like a teenager so into the moment, into her, he'd lost control.

A smile tugged at his face. And he wouldn't change a second of it.

His smile faded. Would Shay agree? He would just have to persuade her that they could not go back to the way things were.

"I'm also not into locker room talk."

"She's that important?"

Shay always had been, in her own way. Even when she torqued him off, made him want to run for the hills—or make love to her against a door—he never forgot her. Shay left a large and lasting impression.

So how would he reconcile who she was? Who her father was? Who his dad was? He didn't know how to put the pieces all together and wished this flight would crank up so he had less time for ruminating and more time for acting.

Jimmy reached across and knocked him on his bald head. "You're overthinking."

No shit. "Ah, stupid me." He thunked his forehead. "I should have just consulted my Magic 8 Ball. But I keep getting, 'Reply hazy, try again.'"

"Hmmm, I get the sense it's saying 'Better not tell you now.' Sometimes we guys just aren't ready to accept what we already know deep down is going to happen."

"Did you get a degree in Magic 8 Ball psychology during those two weeks of leave you took to hang out with Chloe?"

"That's me. Captain Sensitivity."

His headset filled with a ringing sound. A phone call.

His gut clenched. Finally. "Here we go. He's making a call. Heads up in the hangar, Berg and Smooth."

"Roger," both men responded over the headset.

Four phone chimes in, the sound stopped.

"Hello?" a deep male voice answered.

"Hey, dude, it's me," the teen responded.

Vince worked to place either of the voices but came up blank. Maybe Shay would know if they replayed it for her. He blocked thoughts of her and focused on the moment, gathering as much data as possible.

"Are you on a throwaway phone?" the adult male said low.

"Of course."

The kid had lied, because they knew full well this phone had been used before. Interesting.

Had he done it to save money, the arrogance of youth assuming the odds were for him? Not that it mattered. The kid's carelessness was their gain.

"So," the deeper voice came on again. "Make this quick. I've got work piled up on my desk."

Someone who worked at five in the morning? And for that matter, what was any teen doing up this early? All the ones he knew slept until noon in the summer. He tuned out thoughts and tuned in his ears.

"I know who she's banging, and it's not good."

"Were you careful?"

"Duh, of course."

Vince sat up straighter. They couldn't be talking about Shay sleeping with him. No way had her location been outed—much less what they'd been doing. That would mean a security breach of horrific proportions. He forced his attention back to flying the plane. It would be too easy to get sucked into the content of the conversation.

Jimmy fiddled with the control screen and keyed up the secure link to Berg and Smooth back in the hanger. "Sounds like their call is going to be quick. Do you guys have what you need so we can get a flyover look of this kid?"

A short hiss sounded in his headset telling him the encryption was synced up. "We got it," Smooth answered. "Finishing the trace. Sending you coordinates now."

"Received," Jimmy answered, affirming the coordinates had popped up on the screen. Jimmy punched some buttons to point the surveillance cameras. "The kid's call is coming from about three miles behind us, Vince. Come around to heading zero-eight-five. While you do that, we'll try to get a lock on who he's speaking to."

"Wilco, in the turn." Halfway through the turn, the camera locked in on a park in the middle of the city.

The rest of the phone discussion sounded benign enough, something about changing their meeting place—leaving the mall?—then the man signaled an end to the conversation. "Hang tough, kid. We're in the homestretch. You just have to make it to tomorrow afternoon. Prove yourself, and you know the payback will be worth it."

The line disconnected.

Tomorrow. The date for the congressional hearing. Vince's fists tightened around the yoke. They needed to find that little prick who was terrorizing people—terrorizing Shay—just for some payoff or payback.

Jimmy zoomed the image, Vince's smaller screen up front giving him a bird's-eye view of their first look at the caller, pulling the cell phone away from his ear. Or at least it looked like a male.

Whoever it was wore a hooded sweatshirt, leaving little of his face clear. Damn that breeze blowing in off Erie. They could have used a boiler night.

Or maybe the person didn't want to be identified?

Vince pushed some buttons to stream the video back to the hangar where Berg and Smooth could use editing software to capture still photos of the caller. Hopefully they'd caught enough to run a facial recognition program and check against a database maintained by the Feds.

The airwaves crackled before Berg droned, "We're getting good data down here. Working photos now."

A successful mission. Photos of their person of interest and a new cell phone to monitor. They could start building a picture of the network of plotters.

Vince leaned back in the seat to revel in the success. He looked up and out the windshield.

"Holy shit!"

FOURTEEN

Vince stared through the windscreen right up the ass of what appeared to be a huge buzzard.

He violently broke left just as the swooping bird seemed destined to become a permanent part of the Pilatus. Which might have been funny, except a bird to the windscreen at this speed was the same as taking a cannonball hit.

Still diving left, he ducked his head and braced for the impact, the noise . . . and heard nothing but the hum of radio wave static. He peeked out with one eye and saw only starry night sky cut by the first finger rays of sunrise.

"What the fuck?" echoed not over his headset but from right behind his ear.

He glanced back to see Jimmy crumpled up against the back of his seat.

"Sorry about that, old buddy." Vince leveled the wings. "The buzzard must have been on an FAA clearance. He was fricking huge."

"Yeah, yeah, buzzard, shmuzzard. Let me know if you need a real pilot." Jimmy settled back into his seat at the snooper screen. "Ya know, Buzzard might not be such a bad call sign for you."

"Vapor, Hotshot, Buzzard, it's all the same to me, as long as I land at the end of the day." What would have happened to this investigation, to Shay, if he'd crashed? He'd never worried beyond the weight of the mission before.

"I thought for sure I had one that would piss you off. You take all the fun out of razzing."

"I live to please." Vince leveled out the plane and checked panel readings. "All set to shut down back there?"

"Hold on a second," Jimmy answered, humor gone. "I think I've got something. Swing back around for a sweep over the park."

"Wilco." Vince banked right, eyes out for that buzzard, although it was more likely the bird died from a heart attack. "What do you have there?"

"Almost got it . . . I'm fine-tuning. Damn," he hissed. "Take a look at your screen. We're gonna need to call for backup."

What now? Vince looked down, snapped back in his seat. The kid in the dark hoodie sprinted through the park, running full-out from three attackers with machetes.

* * *

Shay had always known to be careful in her work, but never before had she felt like she had a huge bull's-eye on her back.

Stepping out of protective custody for this parent meeting at the community center was scary, even with security from the FBI. Plus she had the added watchful eye of Officer Jaworski's finest because of the bomb threat.

Canceling her presentation scared her more, though, because she knew what could happen to these kids if she gave up. Vince would be speaking at a start-up meeting for a new Civil Air Patrol squadron, a part of her plan for bringing order to this corner of Cleveland. She'd never thought to adopt any of her old man's tactics in her own life, but maybe remembering some of the public good her dad had done would help her forgive him for checking out on fatherhood.

She searched the crowd for Vince. He was already a half hour late. She'd stalled as long as she could. Much longer, and she would need to cobble some kind of talk together with Eli. She found him still in a back corner chatting with a decked-out young mom.

Too bad Angeline couldn't have joined them, but according to her husband, the stress from the bombing had taken a serious toll on her blood pressure, so they were both camped out in front of the TV indulging in nonstop sports network.

She checked her wristwatch. If Vince didn't show soon, she feared the crowd would get restless and leave. Many of them were on a lunch break from work. Others worked the night shift and were giving up sleep.

He'd called an hour ago to say he needed to talk with her about something important. Something he couldn't discuss over the phone. But he still hadn't arrived from whatever work had called him away last night.

After they'd had sex against a door.

She'd never been so glad for an interruption as she was when her cell phone rang. *Chicken*. Yep, that was her, but didn't she have enough on her plate right now? She was entitled to pull a Scarlett O'Hara and worry about it tomorrow. These kids needed her undivided attention. And if she kept making excuses long enough, she might actually convince herself she wasn't running from the intensity of being with Vince for the first time.

A hand cupped her shoulder. She jumped, then looked back.

Vince crowded close to her from behind, hot and bulky and intimately familiar. "Look out for spiders, and watch what you say."

Spiders? Her eyes went wide. His friends were piloting their surveillance insects in here. Now. Her skin itched worse than if the real things had been crawling up her leg.

He tugged his day planner from under his arm and pulled out a grainy black-and-white photo. "Do you recognize this person?"

She squinted. A sweatshirt with the hood up obscured most of the face. Was the listening spider recording her now? Could the eyes on the other end see how her body hummed with awareness from standing beside Vince? "I can't see enough of the face to be sure."

Vince pulled another photo sheet from beneath it with a series of smaller snapshots scrolled out like movie frames. The cumulative picture coalesced in her mind.

"That's Brody." She glanced up sharply.

"The professor-type kid from the Mercenaries, right? Is Brody's family here?"

Oh, God, what had he done? "Why do you want to know?"

"Later." He nodded toward the wall where a tiny spider crawled along the edges of a bulletin board. "Can you answer my question please?"

"His grandmother is over there"—she pointed to the last row of chairs—"wearing a purple shirt, sitting by the water cooler. That's Webber's mom beside her."

"They're friends?" He edged closer to the spider. Feeding information?

"Neighbors." She hated being kept in the dark, but she had to trust him. Strange how she trusted him so totally when it came to her teens but couldn't relax her fears when it came to her heart. "They take different shifts on the city road work crew so one of them is always around for the kids. Is it him?"

Brody? Her caller? The bomber. It didn't gel for her, but she should know better than to rule anything out when it came to these kids.

"Shhh. Not now. I need you to watch the adults and note anything that seems strange for our friends." He planted his hand on the wall beside the silvery arachnid. "I should present my part of the talk now."

She scanned the room, her eyes snagging on twitchy Officer Jaworski, who never let go of his nightstick.

"Who's that with Jaworski?" She pointed to the young man in a sharp suit standing with the cop in the back of the room. Another undercover guard? Maybe. But maybe not. It seemed to her anything out of the ordinary should be noted for the folks on the other end of the eight-legged listening device. "I've never seen him here before."

Vince cocked his head to the side. "Oh, that's the congressional aide from California getting the lay of land. He came to the meet and greet. I ran into him in the parking lot checking out my Ducati with Eli."

"I must have missed him. I wish Eli would have mentioned that." She made note of the California aide for future reference in her quest to put her agenda forward. A personal appearance from the political staff boded well, and she intended to make the most of it by speaking to him before he left. "Let's get things rolling."

She stepped to the front of the room. She would have to trust that the metal detector they'd installed at the door after the bomb threat had kept any guns and knives out of the building. "If you'll all return to your seats, we'll continue on with the second half of our program."

The crowd shuffled around, jockeying for seats, a good showing of maybe a couple dozen parents, most of whom seemed genuinely concerned. Except for the one flirting with Eli. The young mom had more bling than interest in the meeting, perhaps somebody too caught up in the successful lifestyle she thought gangbanging could bring.

Focus. Breathe. Shay gripped the podium. "We appreciate your interest and participation in the process. As you already know, things have reached a critical point for the youth in our neighborhood. They've moved beyond beat downs and drive-by shootings to planting bombs. Obviously, everyone on staff here feels deeply for the safety of your children."

She trained her eyes on the crowd to keep from looking over too often at the spider. Or Vince. Or that freaking young mom who was now digging in her designer purse and punching numbers into her cell phone. "We want you to understand we know this isn't easy. These kids are tough. Some of them are dangerous. Some of them are hurting. I hear them, and I understand, because I was there. I suffered from a litany of teenage issues, even flirting with crime."

The mom with her too-perfect nose and what looked like an overdone boob job brought the cell phone to her ear.

Rage swelled deep, pushing up her throat and demanding release. Before she realized the words were forming, they tumbled out of her mouth. "I emotionally hit the wall and tried to take my own life."

She stole a moment to catch her breath and keep her

eyes steadfastly off Vince until she could tamp down her anger. Still, Shay could feel Vince's presence growing, emotion swelling from him. Maybe it hadn't been fair to spring it on him this way. Okay, it definitely wasn't fair.

And she needed to get her brain in gear again rather than stand around like an idiot. Time to improvise. "I survived only because my parents found me in time. I got a second chance, thank God. We need to find a way to give our youth a second chance."

She risked a glance at Vince, currently studying her through squinted eyes.

"Here with us this afternoon is someone from my old neighborhood who found his second chance through a new group, a new gang if you will, the type of positive option we would like to implement here. But I'll let him tell you about that. Ladies and gentlemen, please join me in welcoming Major Vince Deluca, a pilot in the U.S. Air Force and a combat veteran."

She gave him a wide berth to take the podium, not sure of him or herself. Didn't they have enough to worry about just staying alive? She grasped her wrist, twisting the wide green polka-dot watchband around and around over her faded scar.

Searching the room for those clues to collect, she realized it wasn't just anger at the mother pimped out on the drug-dealing lifestyle who pissed her off. It felt like the whole neighborhood was boiling over in a pressure cooker, ready to blow. Everything was coming to a head, from suicide calls to the FBI's presence in town.

Would Brody call her again? Was he out to get her or seriously thinking of taking his own life because of what the gang was forcing him to do?

A part of her balked at the phone tapping that she knew

would happen from now on, but they weren't breaking any laws, and people's lives were at stake.

Vince stepped in front of the podium, no barriers between him and his audience. "The Civil Air Patrol is an all-volunteer organization with an air force affiliation. The uniforms are almost the same, as is the ranking system. The opportunities kick butt. It's not just about learning how to march. Teens will have the chance to participate in everything from learning to fly to search-and-rescue missions."

He paused, leaning back against the podium and crossing his biker boots at the heels. "You can tell by my appearance I'm not your run-of-the-mill clean-cut guy."

Laughter rippled through the crowd, taking the tension down a notch.

"I was a member of a motorcycle gang as a teenager—not the good kind, either. I did things that should have landed me in jail. If not for Shay Bassett's father and his openness to taking on hellions like myself, I *would* be in jail. Instead, by seventeen I was on board a flight that located a missing father and child who'd gone off the road in a snowstorm. Today, I pilot multimillion-dollar aircraft. There isn't an easy quick fix here. But I'm sure glad no one gave up on me."

He reached for the glass of water beside him and took a long swallow before continuing, "I could ramble on for hours about how freaking cool my job is, but I imagine my time is better spent answering questions you may have about Civil Air Patrol and my own journey off the streets."

Shay scanned the crowd, while mumbling a litany of observations for the surveillance device. She watched the parents, listening to their questions and watching their reactions. Some interested. Some skeptical. A few frowning with outright disapproval. For that matter, the young mother with the bling and boob job had just left the building, making her wonder why these parents couldn't be more supportive.

Could one of these adults be involved?

She'd just assumed an older teen, a high-ranking member in one of the gangs, was calling the shots to increase power and establish dominance over other gangs. The possibility that one of these parents could be orchestrating their own child's life into crime shouldn't surprise her, but it did. She could only think of one reason why an authority figure would get involved in this juvenile level of violence.

Money.

Her eyes gravitated to Brody's grandmother sitting with his sister. Lord knows they didn't look like they were rolling in any surprise windfalls, but many got sucked into the criminal activity before realizing that gangs rarely brought much to anyone other than those at the very top of the chain.

Why would they risk notice with something as high-profile as disrupting a congressional hearing?

She tried to pull her thoughts together, making mental notes for later when she could speak more freely. Thank goodness Jaworski was here to keep the peace if need be.

To make sure Vince didn't throw himself in front of a bullet for her a second time.

* * *

Webber jogged down the cement steps leading to the cellar below a condemned brownstone, his ponytail slapping his back. He whistled the preselected top ten song of the day. He didn't want his buddy in the cellar jumping him.

The late afternoon sun beat on his head like a powerful fist. Only twenty-four more hours, and this would be over.

At the bottom of the stairs, he pumped the handle, the heavy metal door squeaking on its hinges. His mouth dry, he licked his lips and kept whistling. The cooler air underground stank like mold and rotten food.

The slice of light from outside combined with the beams of a fat flashlight glowing in the corner. No shadows. Just one person.

Brody rolled to his feet. "Dude, I owe you." He jogged across the cement floor and gave him a light one-two slug on the shoulder. "You really saved my ass out there. It was like something out of a movie the way you drove up just in time before those whacked out Apocalypse dudes laid into me."

"No big thing." He knelt to jam a brick against the door, propping it open. "I happened to be in the right place at the right time."

"Funny coincidence."

Not funny and not a coincidence. He'd been tracking Brody.

Webber stood, grabbed Brody's hoodie, and slammed him against the concrete wall. "Who did you call?"

"What?" Brody squeaked.

"Come on, brother." He twisted the sweatshirt tighter. "Speak up, or there's nothing I can do for you."

"Just Lewis," he whispered.

"I know that much. He told me about the call." Lewis had actually set up the whole thing to see if Brody would take a used cell phone. Webber was supposed to pretend to use a phone, toss it in the trash in clear sight of Brody, then wait and watch. Lewis was always looking for weak links, and Brody had already used up his second chances.

And now he'd forced Webber to betray his friend. A test for Webber, too.

He was walking on the edge here, trying to keep Amber

and his mom safe. Shay Bassett, too. "You're not supposed to call him. Only I am." He was even keeping Brody alive. "Lewis wants to know who else you called and what you did with the phone."

"No-nobody," he stuttered, the lie written on his face.

Webber released his hold long enough to dip his hand in the front pocket of Brody's sweaty hoodie. "This phone, I'm guessing. We're supposed to toss 'em after we talk. You know that."

"I will." Brody reached to get the phone back, but Webber was quicker.

"It's all old." He turned it over and over in his hand. "Scratched up like. Used." He knew, because he'd marked it ahead of time. "Where did you get it?"

"I found it." He looked away.

"You just found it? Be straight with me, man. If I can tell, then Lewis is going to know for sure." He squeezed his friend's shoulder hard. "I'm trying to help you."

"Just don't tell him then." Brody bucked up.

"The only way you're going to survive this is to tell the truth." A fact that scared him snotless, since he'd told his own lies to Lewis. Except Brody wasn't smart enough to pull it off. Selfish lies showed most.

His foot sank into a soft pile of trash as he stepped closer. "Come on, brother, own up. You can trust me."

Yeah, he was learning to lie well.

Brody dipped his head and whispered, "I saw you throw it away. It seemed like a waste."

"What did you do with the money Lewis gave you?"

"Bought some food and stuff."

Bull. He looked into his friend's eyes, and yeah, Brody had done exactly what Lewis suspected.

"You bought blow." Webber pinned him to the wall

again, arm across his neck. He wasn't risking Brody going ape shit on him. "Only question is, did you snort it or shoot up?" Coke or heroin, bad news either way. "Lewis is going to kill you if you don't get yourself under control. I wouldn't be surprised if somehow he already knew and sent those Apocalypse badasses to finish the job for him."

"He wouldn't do that." Brody shook his head, his pupils wide, even for a dark cellar. "He's with us."

Webber wasn't as certain.

He leaned in nose to nose. "Are you that much of a pinhead you don't see he's playing all sides, whatever brings him the biggest payoff?"

Brody started shaking. Hard. Worse than the time ten years ago when they'd gotten stuck in a snowdrift trying to sled down the drainage ditch. A long time ago.

They weren't kids anymore.

Webber eased the choke hold and reached into his own deep pocket, his fist curling around brass warmed from his body. His throat hurt like when he used to get strep all the time, but he had to be a man and see this through. It was Brody's only chance at staying alive.

That's all he could do now, try to keep the people around him alive. He wasn't sure exactly when he'd grown a set of balls and decided to do something other than just roll over and die. He only wished he didn't feel so alone in seeing this out.

Webber waved his free hand out the door and snapped. Three long shadows stretched down the stairs. Drawing up in the entrance. Two brothers and a peewee looking to blood-in with the Mercenaries. All wearing the same brass knuckles he pulled out of his pocket.

Webber thumped Brody on his chest, lightly for now. "You know we have to put you in check."

Tears pooled up in Brody's eyes. "I won't do it again, man. I'm your brother. You can trust me."

Not anymore.

"Lewis has to see we take care of business, or he won't be respecting us. You need to remember you ain't nothing but a soldier." He tapped Brody on the chest again with the brass knuckles: thump, thump, thump. If he didn't lead this, someone else would do it. Much worse. "When you disrespected him, you dissed us all."

Webber threw the first punch.

Before his fist met flesh, he shut down. He blocked the whimpers, the flailing, the pleading. He blocked it all. He was two people right now. Like two halves of a brain. Or two sides of nature. He had logic, the part that told him what he had to do, no matter how much it made him want to puke. And he had rage. Years of it bottled up with nowhere to go.

He let the fury pour out of him now, used it in a way that could bring some good. Brody would hurt like hell, but he wouldn't end up with a bullet behind his ear. That counted for something. His fist slammed in time with the other arms pumping up and down, driving Brody to the floor.

Then it was over.

Brody lay limp on the ground, eyes closed. Webber knelt down to be sure, and yeah, his friend was still breathing. And groaning. They knew how to deliver a beat down that didn't damage internal organs.

He swallowed back puke.

Webber reached in his pocket and pitched a wad of rolled bills to the other three. "Go party." He nodded to the peewee who'd wanted his blood-in so bad. "You done good. You're a brother now."

Poor little fucker.

Whooping and high fiving, the three sprinted up the concrete steps. They faded away, high on the smell of blood and whatever they'd pumped into their veins.

Webber walked toward the flashlight and snatched it up, along with a bottle of water. He walked back and poured it all over his childhood friend's face.

Brody moaned, rolled, and clutched his stomach.

Webber leaned low. "Lewis has a message for you. Quit screwing around and do what you're told, or he's going to make sure your sister's nothing but a toss-up for every Apocalypse piece of shit to plow through."

Brody cried. He just curled up and sobbed like a baby.

The puke fisted harder up his throat.

Fuck. Webber wanted to cry like a big baby, too. Like the pussy he was trying so hard not to be anymore. But he had to think about the money that would keep his mom and Amber from being tossed. God, these people knew how to find just where to hurt a guy. Lewis had sure found his weak spots fast enough.

He kept kneeling beside his friend and waited until Brody's heaves slowed.

"I'm gonna take you to the emergency room now. Okay, dude? It's over. You just gotta keep your mouth shut and do what you're told. You need to remember you're a foot soldier. Follow orders, and you'll stay alive."

Brody wasn't half as smart as he thought, and that was dangerous.

Webber stood again. He'd taken a chance in planting a cell phone that actually *had* been used for Brody to "find."

Lewis hadn't counted on that. The older guy had told him to use a new one and fake out Brody. Risky thing, disobeying Lewis. Too easily Brody could have been the one delivering the beat down.

But Webber knew he was smarter. His planned disobedience had a purpose. For sure the cops had to be tracing calls after that bomb threat. Setting up Brody to use the cell phone that had been used for the bomb threat, hoping for a trace . . . it was their only chance at taking Lewis out.

And maybe even figuring out what else Lewis had going on that he wasn't sharing.

Hope. He hated that feeling most of all.

Webber stuffed his hand in his pocket and shook off the brass knuckles. He extended a bloodstained hand.

Brody clasped on tight and tugged himself up, barely, leaning most of his weight. "Doesn't seem fair I get the beat down when nothing happened to you for taking that bitch's purse."

"Life isn't fair, and if you think it is, then you're even dumber than I thought, my brother."

Lewis had given him his orders and made the consequences clear. A suicide bomb explosion would have everyone looking for terrorists and paying less attention to jacking up gangbangers. Shutting up Shay would make for one less—very persuasive—do-gooder who'd somehow snagged big government attention.

And if Webber didn't comply? Lewis would shoot Webber's mama full of the coke she'd fought so hard to kick, then cut out Amber's baby, leaving them both to bleed out.

All Webber needed to stop everything?

Do exactly what he'd threatened on the phone with Shay Bassett that first day he'd been told to call and get under her skin. He had to kill himself. Strap a bomb to his chest and blow himself up, along with an auditorium full of people.

All during a nationally televised congressional hearing.

FIFTEEN

Don wished the pieces of this investigation would come together faster. Instead, it seemed every time they figured something out, the puzzle expanded as wide as the web of cell phone numbers they'd collected by building networks from that banger's call.

And they had less than twenty-four hours to complete the picture.

Their broadening scope of law enforcement now included the Cleveland Police Department, and the D.C. contingent had shifted to Ohio in preparation for the hearing. He'd been given full use of a station interrogation room for a secured meeting while Paulina settled the Congress members at the hotel.

Although it didn't take much effort, given the California congressman's aide seemed to have taken care of everything from a private guard to mints on the pillow.

Don glanced at his watch again, waiting for Vince,

Vince's commander, Shay, and Officer Jaworski. He needed work, in fact welcomed the chance to avoid Paulina and the discussion of a possible pregnancy. She had to have noticed the lack of a condom, but after their explosive sex, she'd hauled out of his place pronto. That was okay by him since he was still reeling at even the thought of a baby.

Another child.

Another chance to fail.

Something was cracking wide open inside him, and he was slapping emotional Band-Aids all over himself to keep from hemorrhaging out faster than coffee gurgled in that old coffeemaker in the corner. The hell of it all? He couldn't figure out what else to do.

The door clicked open. He jolted to a stop. Whoa.

Officer L. Jaworski was truly and thoroughly torqued off. You'd think the guy would be happy they'd brought him into the loop. Of course, calling the baton-clutching cop had been a no-brainer when Vince had reported from the air about the attack launched on the boy. They'd followed Brody as long as they could until he slipped into a back alley. God only knew what had happened to the kid. Hopefully Shay could offer insights to help them.

Shay, Lieutenant Colonel Scanlon, and Vince followed the young officer who flexed his muscles like an action hero wannabe. The door snicked shut behind them.

"Thank you for meeting with us." Don nodded a welcome to the familiar faces, shook hands all around. He'd billed himself as a part of Paulina's team, since technically the CIA had no jurisdiction here. The role of "concerned father" wouldn't get him the same level of attention. All the more reason to focus on the job at hand rather than checking how Shay was holding up. "We're looking forward to working together to ensure everything goes smoothly tomorrow."

"So I hear, Agent Bassett. Let's get right to it." Jaworski gestured for everyone to take a seat then set a digital photo frame on the table. He clicked to the first image. "Major Deluca tells me his technology indicates that the boy in this photo made a call today on the same cell phone that was used to place the bomb threat at the community center. It's important that we be sure. Are you certain that's Brody? I can't make out anything from this."

Vince waved for him to click to the next. "There are more here than she got to see on the printout." He turned to Shay. "Brody's the professor-looking one with the scraggly beard, right? 'Cause it appears there's some facial hair on the chin."

Shay leaned closer on her elbows, tucking her short brown hair behind her ears. She'd done that as a child when nervous. An image of her as that sweet little tomboy side-swiped Don with questions of what a kid of his with Pau-lina would look like.

His daughter rubbed the lock of hair between her thumb and forefinger. "Sure, but that's not what tipped me off. Honestly, it's just something about the way he's standing." She pointed to a tiny smudge on the kid's neck. "And the head of a snake tattoo wrapping around."

Jaworski and Vince nearly missed bumping heads look-ing back at the photo. Vince tapped the magnify feature to zoom in. "Sure enough, there it is."

Jaworski spun the frame around to fully face him. "We'd have figured it out."

Ungrateful ass. Don looked at his daughter to give her an atta-girl, then stopped. "You seem surprised by what you're seeing, Shay."

She was really working to make that hair stay behind her ear. "I just wouldn't have thought he would be the one.

Other than his drug use, he doesn't fit the personality type of someone who's suicidal."

Suicide. Just the word slammed him back in his seat. He wasn't sure he wanted this peek into his daughter's psyche, but had to ask, "What do you mean?"

She tipped the frame toward her, tapping the zoom in on the partially revealed face. "Brody doesn't seem depressed or isolated. The times I've spoken with him face-to-face, I didn't pick up on any verbal cues. Of course, I could be wrong."

What cues? Because God, he wished he'd known what to look for and couldn't hide from the fact he might need to learn so he didn't screw up again. "Could the hotline calls be a setup? Maybe the kid really doesn't want to die."

Maybe Shay hadn't really meant for it to go so far back then, in spite of what the doctor had said.

Vince rested a hand on the back of her chair. "Your dad may be onto something. A setup to get to you somehow. Put you on edge. Maybe they plan to call right before the hearing. They've got you carting your cell phone around with you, taking calls from the kid no matter what's going on. What would you do if a call came in right before the hearing?" He tapped her shoulder absently. "No need to answer."

"Sure, it's possible, but there was still such helplessness, desperation even, in this boy's voice." Shay pivoted toward Vince as she made her point.

Very close. Vince's wrist was still draped over the back of her chair, almost touching her.

Don eyed the two, and sure enough, their body language spoke loud enough it didn't take a trained agent to see something had shifted between them. Although he'd thought there was something between them years ago and had been dead wrong about that, too.

Shay traced the outline of the image with one finger. "Brody's more reckless, in your face. When I caught him behind the Dumpster toking up during the bomb threat, he totally didn't care."

Jaworski tapped his club absently. "That could be the drugs talking."

Don felt a tickle in the back of his brain. Something about the Dumpster . . . He shot upright in his seat. "The night I stumbled on the two bodies—Kevin and the student—I smelled marijuana by the Dumpster. There were stubs all around."

Shay scooted her chair back, as if putting distance between herself and the image of Brody.

"Oh God." She clapped her hand over her mouth.

Vince's hand on the back of her seat slid to massage her neck lightly. "That evening of the bomb threat, Shay said something about Apocalypse being after the Mercenaries because of a tag getting dissed. Then there was Mercenary talk of that just being retaliation."

The cop pulled his PDA back in front of him. "So let's say Kevin disses a tag, signs his work. Mercenaries up the stakes by painting over Apocalypse art *and* killing the original tagger. The college student was just collateral damage."

Don lined up the clues and events in his mind. "That feels right. All this activity makes me even more certain they still plan to go through with disrupting the hearing, even with one of their key players—Kevin—dead."

Jaworski turned off the digital frame. "The time has come for me to pick up Brody for questioning. Maybe we can even get a DNA match off those blunts left at the Dumpster."

"Just you?" Don could already imagine the steam rising

off Paulina if she was shoved aside in the investigation. And if she was dismissed personally? He knew her temper well. They would have to talk soon. "We brought you this information. The murderer will pay in good time. For now our focus has to be security at the hearing."

Jaworski snorted. "Don't piss on my shoes, and I won't piss on yours."

Vince stepped in. "Officer, it doesn't appear as clear-cut as picking up this Mercenary kid. Sure, the cell phone network my guys are putting together starts with Brody, but already we're building a larger pool of numbers that includes far more Apocalypse members. The calls are each cryptic individually. Yet Brody's the one who made the bomb threats. Both groups are clearly at work here. The question is, are they actually working toward the same end? Or are there two plans in motion?"

Jaworski's eyes lit. "Then let's start rounding them up—"

A cell phone interrupted the standoff, a generic ring that sent Jaworski unclipping his cell from his belt. "Excuse me for a moment."

He flipped open the phone and tucked into a corner, mumbling low before he turned back around, scowling. Not good news.

"You win, Agent Bassett. That kid Brody is going to be a piece of cake to watch. He was just found in an ER waiting room, passed out and beaten to a pulp. He's in surgery now."

* * *

Still rattled, Shay curled up in the overstuffed chair in her hotel room, stroking her fingers back and forth along her laptop keyboard. She'd been reviewing her speech, but she wanted to be at the hospital. If life hadn't gone so wildly insane with all this security, she *would* be there now checking on Brody, sneaking a peek at his medical chart.

Sitting in a hotel room with her butt nailed to this stupid chair made her want to scream.

Except that would freak out her current protector, Vince's crewmate Smooth, otherwise known as Mason Randolph. The young sergeant was watching over her while Vince slept.

At least Smooth never lacked for anything to say. She just let him talk while her mind tumbled with confusion. She still tried to reconcile Brody's face with the voice on those calls. It didn't make sense. Of course, none of what these kids were doing made any real sense. Did they have any clue about the terrorist involvement, or were they so oblivious to what was going on they unquestioningly followed orders, no matter what the higher-ups requested?

Right now she was just grateful Brody hadn't died.

Knowing the two Congress members leading the forum were only a few doors down made her all the more eager to scoop up her laptop and plead her case now.

Smooth snapped his fingers. "You still with me? Do you need a nap? I can stop talking."

Go to sleep with him in the room? She trusted him, but ewww. She needed this fishbowl feeling to end. "I'm wide-awake." In spite of the soothing mug of decaf tea in front of her. "So, Smooth . . . uh, do you prefer to be called Smooth or Mason? I never thought to ask."

He flashed a grin. "Smooth or Mason, either is fine by me."

"Okay, Mason." Calling him by a real name made things feel more normal. "I've heard Vince called Vapor by the crew. I thought he and his friend Jimmy were Hotshot and Hotwire."

"That's more of a recent joke." He stretched his legs out in front of him, penny loafers and jeans, bare ankles, seeming casual except for the tense flex of his shoulders and the way he always kept himself between her and the door. "For now anyway, his call sign is still officially Vapor, and Vapor it will stay, unless there's a keg party renaming ceremony."

"But why is he called Vapor?"

"A number of stories are out there. For a big guy, he walks spooky softly, like vaporizing from one place to solidify in another. Or when he's had enough of the world he gets on his bike and roars out so fast there's nothing but vapor left behind."

"Enough of the world?" She cupped her mug with both hands, the AC chilling her back. "Vince has always been so easygoing."

"He's laid back, sure, and God knows there are days when his humor hauls us through. There are also days it's impossible to joke. Some people think that when we watch through a camera, we're distanced from what's happening. Physically, that may be true." He tapped his temple by a thick head of gorgeous hair that did absolutely nothing for her. "But when it comes to the head games? This isn't like parking yourself in front of a television."

She could only imagine what they'd seen in combat. Or worse yet, what they'd seen over a monitor and been powerless to intervene.

What her father had seen?

Her mother had said for years that he must have some form of PTSD. Shay had even mentioned it to the shrink who helped her put her life back together in college. Not that her dad had ever joined in a session for her to have a peek into what he might or might not feel.

She tuned back to Mason, grateful yet again that he liked to talk. Grateful for these insights into her father, who never spoke, and Vince, who joked so much it was tough to tell what he actually felt. Shay sipped her tea, inhaling the soothing minty smell, complete with three sugars.

"We all know this is real, the people are real. The stakes and dangers are real." One of his penny loafers started to twitch. "People who've never even set foot in a church before will find God fast. Most folks get this impression of Vince because of the bike and tats, like he's scary."

She stared into her mug, guilt tweaking. She'd almost run screaming from him that first night he'd come back. "I know that bikers go to church, too."

"Good. But the difference with Vince is that when he prays before combat, he's not praying for himself."

She looked up at him. "He's tight with you guys. I can see that."

"Yeah, yeah, we're all one big happy family, but that's not what I meant." His twitchy penny loafer went stone still. "He prays for the other guy. The one he's looking at in the camera."

His words curled through her veins much like the warm tea heating her system. As if she wasn't already confused enough about her feelings for Vince.

"Well, Mason, for a guy who supposedly hits on every woman in sight, you sure are doing your level best to sell me on your friend."

"Shhh . . . That'll be our little secret. As much as I enjoy a kegger, I want to keep my call sign."

She turned the imaginary key on her lips and tossed it away. "I won't rat you out."

"Smart lady. When you get an inside track, it's always wise to cultivate your contact."

"Sounds like you prefer those assignments that call for category three grooming codes."

"Hell yeah." He stroked his own contoured beard growing in. "Hey wait. How did you know about that? Hey, you're really good at that espionage crap. You must get it from your old man."

"Thank you."

His perfect smile faded. "It's not a good thing, not if you want to have a relationship with Vince. We do things we can't talk about. We go places you'll never know. The wives and girlfriends who can't be at peace about that end up leaving."

The already frigid temperature dropped in the room by at least ten degrees. "Who could ever be totally at peace with that kind of life?"

"My point."

A knock on the door cut through the silence. A knock in code.

Vince was awake.

* * *

Vince waited outside the hotel room, his gift for Shay tucked under his arm.

Smooth opened the door. "Hey there, sleepyhead. What do you have there?"

Vince shouldered past, his grip loosening as the dog—Shay's gift—leapt free to race across the room.

"Omigod!" Shay jumped from her chair to kneel down and scoop up Buster. "I've missed you, buddy."

She nuzzled the dog's neck, talking more nonsense phrases and looking totally beautiful doing it. Her brown eyes glimmered with more life than he'd seen in her all day.

And he wasn't the only one who'd noticed. "Eyes off, Smooth."

The flight engineer held up his hands. "Why does everyone always assume I'm after their woman?"

"Because you are." Vince clapped him on the shoulder with a bit of extra force on his way to the vanity. He filled up an ice bucket with water for the dog and set it in a corner of the bathroom.

"You are so toast," Smooth said low.

"Stick it, my friend."

"You brought her dog, dude. That's better than flowers." He winked. "I should know."

Vince gripped the doorknob. "If you hang around much longer, you'll end up walking this mutt instead of the bell-boy I paid off."

Smooth waved on his way out. "Heading to work as we speak."

"Hey, Smooth?" Vince stopped in the doorway. "Thanks."

His crewmate shot him another wave over the shoulder on his way down the carpeted corridor. Vince closed and triple locked the door. He'd actually taken the dog with him to the hangar to pull his shift watching the screens, logging numbers and forwarding them to Wilson's people for the Feds to link together.

Part of him wanted to work through the night. The other part knew his crew had it under control, and he'd gone beyond bleary-brained an hour ago.

Shay pressed her cheek against Buster's head. "How did you get him and manage any sleep?"

"I caught a catnap." A lie, of course. He'd been working before he picked up her dog. He was supposed to be sleeping now.

Vince looked at her open laptop. "Do you have your speech ready?"

"I've been ready to give this talk for months." She stood. "I'm just glad to finally have the chance."

Buster leapt from her arms and into the chair.

She laughed low. "Apparently he hasn't missed me as much as I've missed him."

Her laughter hung in the air, tempting him as much as her long legs. "I would imagine he feels safe now that he's with you again."

"Ah, you're turning into a regular dog whisperer."

He laughed. She laughed again. The sounds echoed lightly, then faded, leaving just the two of them alone in a room with a bed and not much else.

A cart rattled outside the door, louder, sending him on alert until it passed. Buster hadn't even flinched. "You really ought to think about getting Buster a pal, preferably one with some guard capabilities."

"I would probably wreck that dog, too. I spoil pets." She settled on the arm of the chair, her leg swinging.

"Have you considered obedience school? Or at least watch those dog training reality shows."

"He's perfectly obedient. He's just too sweet for his own good." She stroked Buster's neck as if soothing herself as much as the dog. "What about you? What kind of pet do you have?"

He leaned back against a wall, arms crossed over his chest. "I don't."

"Why not?" Her hand slowed, her fingers long and graceful like the rest of her. "You obviously love animals."

He was in serious trouble if he was getting turned on by her fingers. Except he remembered well how high those fingers could take him. "Heavy travel for my job doesn't permit."

"That sounds like a cop-out from committing to me."

Commitment talk. "I'm away seventy-five percent of the time. How fair is that to a pet?"

"Seventy-five percent?" Her eyes went wide.

Way to go, dumb ass. Was he subconsciously trying to sabotage any chance of getting her into bed? "Between field tests and operational missions, it doesn't leave much time at home." He dropped into the other chair. The bed was apparently off-limits for now.

He knew how he wanted this night to end. How he *needed* it to end, given that tomorrow looked so unsure. But with her life on the line, her needs had to be top priority.

She held his gaze. "That can't leave much time for a social calendar."

"That's part of why those of us in the squadron are close. We spend so much time together."

"Is anyone married? Does anybody even manage a relationship?"

There she went with talk of relationships again. What had happened to the woman pulling away as fast as she could pull on her pants? "It's possible. Our squadron commander is a recent widower, but before that, he and his wife had one of those perfect marriages. Berg is married, rocky, though. They have small kids, which makes the separations tougher on his wife."

"And dating?" Her chest rose faster, her breasts outlined in that pretty pink shirt.

"Jimmy Gage—Hotwire—met someone a couple of months ago. They're working out the commuting deal until she can move to Vegas."

"Two whole months. Wow. Serious long term stuff there."

He shrugged. "They seem intense about each other, but time will tell."

"What about you?"

Well, she couldn't be blunter than that. Of course they probably should have had this discussion before they ditched their clothes. "I don't have a girlfriend tucked away in Vegas, if that's what you mean."

"You'd better not, if you're sleeping with me. But actually, I was asking about your past."

"Oh, hell. Okay." He worked to keep up with her words when all he wanted to do was look at her legs. Naked. "Wait. We're sleeping together?"

SIXTEEN

★ ——————————————————————————————————

Vince's stunned look stayed put long after his words faded.

Shay bit her lip. Had she really said that part out loud? Of course she had. Since the conversation with Smooth, she'd gone soft inside over the peek into Vince, a peek that left her hungry to know more about him.

"I said I wanted to hear more about your past. Back when we were teenagers, we were so busy trying to be cool, we didn't spend much time talking about things that mattered. You, in particular, were tight-lipped about anything but jokes."

"Maybe I had good reason."

She'd spent most of her teen years fantasizing about his hot body and most of the present avoiding any feelings for him because of past rejections. Hiding out in the dark not only covered her scars, but it also kept her from clearly seeing the person in front of her. "I would like to hear that reason."

His eyes took on a predatory gleam. "Would it increase my chances of getting you in bed?"

"Saying things like that sure won't."

He relaxed back with a laugh. "Fair enough. History of Vince coming up. I was the first in my family to graduate from college, a shocking accomplishment in and of itself. Nobody would have thought I stood a chance at getting a master's."

"Congratulations! That's an awesome accomplishment. Your mom must be so proud. It's a shame your father died before he could know that."

His eyes dropped for the first time. "Actually, my dad didn't die like my mom told everyone." He looked up again, a flicker of the old defensive Vince shadowing across his face. "My father went to prison by the time I was seven. I even remember visiting him."

A thousand questions scrolled through her head. She settled on, "Is he still alive?"

"He did die, just not when or how mom insisted we tell everyone. He died in a jail yard fight at Leavenworth when I was ten."

"Leavenworth?" Shock echoed through her. "A military prison?"

Defensiveness morphed to a chilling, detached expression, a look that scared her, more because of the resemblance to her own dad than the fact that a cold Vince looked mighty intimidating.

"My old man was court-martialed for smuggling drugs into the country in his military cargo plane. Mom had already divorced him by the time the verdict came in. She hated the military, blamed the military."

"How does she feel about you being in the air force?"

"Mom doesn't return my calls."

"That's really sad." She could understand the woman's frustration, but to so categorically lump all military people together for a hate fest? That didn't make sense. A tiny, insistent, and annoying voice whispered she was doing much the same because of her own father. "What did she want you to do with your life?"

"Not be my dad." He shoved away from the wall toward the window.

Could the people on the floor below hear his boots thundering?

He adjusted the air conditioner. Paced. Tweaked the part in the curtains. Paced. "My mom was a receptionist at an oil change garage, and I hung out with her after school. She told me she took that job to give me male role models who would start me on a solid career, living in one place, away from temptations."

His mother's rationale made sense. What a tough position for her to be in with so little support and a teenage son running rogue.

He checked the locks again. "For a while, it worked. I learned to take apart any engine and put it back together. I could have used that as a way out. Instead, I started jacking cars."

"You stole cars?" She couldn't hide her gasp. She'd known he skirted the edge before her dad recruited him for CAP. He'd even pushed boundaries for a while after meeting her father.

"You know what's strange?" He dropped to sit on the edge of the bed. "I didn't keep them. I drove around, sometimes popped the hood to give it a tune-up, then put it back."

"That's unusual." Although not surprising to her, since she knew he didn't have the heart of a criminal.

"Then I got caught. At that point, jail would have been fine with me." He glanced up with a wry smile. "But like most teens, I wanted to rebel against the parent trying hardest to help. When the judge offered community service by joining Civil Air Patrol, I figured the military angle would push my mom's buttons way more. God knows I didn't magically settle down the minute your dad passed me my first uniform."

All these revelations about his past were only making her realize her initial instincts about him back then had been right. He was a good man. Now she just had the proof from Mason and Vince's own mouth to support it.

And, oh God, she was hovering so close to the edge of falling right back into that huge vat of confusion that came with having feelings for Vince. "Something must have changed to make joining Civil Air Patrol be about more than pushing your mom's buttons. I remember you being totally into the program, even when Tommy tried to tempt you to do otherwise. What happened to make you clean up your act?"

He leaned forward, elbows on his knees. "I got to know you."

* * *

Paulina usually enjoyed her job. Not so much tonight.

Once Don had shown up at the luxury Cleveland hotel and continually ignored her, job satisfaction had taken a serious downswing. She swept her briefcase off the round corner table in the hospitality suite designated for their use and eyed Don a few feet away dialing his cell phone.

They'd cordoned off a floor of rooms for the Congress members, their aides, and security. Shay, Deluca, and his crew blended seamlessly into the mix of check-ins.

Of course business should take priority, but some kind of acknowledgment of their explosive sex at his condo wasn't too much to expect. Sure she'd rushed out of his place quickly. She'd been too emotionally raw to talk to him after sex, definitely too upset to discuss forgetting about birth control. He hadn't seemed in the mood for talking either.

Once she'd pulled out her day planner in the car, she'd realized the timing was wrong in her cycle. And if she turned up pregnant anyway? She couldn't let herself get excited over the possibility, especially with things so unsettled between her and Don.

Damn it, she was the one who had every right to be prickly and distant. Not the big jerk chatting on his cell phone. Forget waiting for him to approach her.

She took charge on the job. She took charge in all other aspects of her life. She would take charge of this. If that meant the end of things with Don, then so be it.

Her throat closed up.

Her feet plowed forward all the same. Stalking past a silver coffee carafe and spray of hothouse flowers, she spiked divots in the plush carpet as she set her eyes on Don. She tapped her moody lover on the shoulder. "Don? A minute of your time."

He flipped his cell phone shut. "Sure, but we should make it quick. I need to meet up with Lieutenant Colonel Scanlon."

That ripped it. "We need to talk."

Slowly, he tucked his phone inside his sports coat. "Actually, I was planning on talking to you right after I finished up with Scanlon."

Yeah right. "If you're worried about your daughter, that's fine. If you're mooning over your ex and wanting to end things with us, that's not okay, but either way, speak up like a man."

His eyes narrowed at her final words. The air crackled between them with that same dangerous spark they'd succumbed to last night.

"You don't pull any punches, princess."

"I think we already established that with our *workout* at your condo." Her body still simmered from the intensity of the coming together, a heat that could swallow her whole if she didn't tend it carefully.

His face stayed closed, too classically handsome for his own good, attractive in that way that just grew better with age. She thought for a moment he would walk away right here and now.

Then he crossed his arms over his chest. "I forgot to use a condom."

"Right. I noticed. I was there, remember?"

"Damn it, Paulina, what if you're pregnant?"

His words sank in with a thud. Because of his heavy-with-doom tone? Or because she suddenly realized she didn't want his baby, not this way.

She looked deeper into his expressionless face and found a glimmer of something in his eyes, something that looked incredibly like outright horror.

"It's fine." Words tumbled out of her mouth ahead of her brain. "I started my period this morning."

Of course she lied, but she couldn't live with this awkwardness for even a few days until she started for real. Or didn't.

Right now she needed to focus on not slugging him for the mammoth relief flat-out shuddering through him. She might not want to get pregnant this way, but the thought of carrying his child did *not* fill her with *horror*.

Dumping his ass would be a lot more satisfying than any punch.

She threw back her shoulders and thrust her chest out just enough to give him a peek at the lilac lace he would not be seeing up close later. "I think we both know it's time to call it quits."

"What?" His incredulity was almost ego soothing.

"Last night was . . ." She struggled for words and could only come up with, "Too much. Destructive, even. We need to end it while we can still be civil to each other."

He stepped closer, sliding a hand along her neck, stroking his thumb behind her ear. "Come on, Lina, we had a fight. We'll do better next time. When this is all over, let's crawl into bed for a week."

She stared at him through narrowed eyes. "Did I ever mention I really *would* like to have a baby?"

He jolted back like a man struck by a live electrical wire.

"Exactly." She fought tears. Angry tears. *Not* the other kind. "Now go away, to your ex-wife or your own lonely corner. I don't care. But please do not insult me by going on about how I'm wrecking a good thing." So much for not having words inside her. Now there were too many to contain. "You think this is a good thing? Never talking about what's important? Never going anywhere together except work and our apartments? I think what we have is crap." Paulina spat out the last word and turned on her heel away from him.

He gripped her shoulder. "Can't we agree to finish this conversation later?"

"I don't have time for this now or later, Don. I have members of Congress and their aides to keep track of, as well as your daughter. Then I have a life to live."

She jerked free, determined to make it to the door before

he could see the tears gathering behind her eyes. She would hold on to her pride. She wasn't that poor, needy little mountain girl in the Kentucky trailer park.

* * *

Don watched Paulina stalk away. There was no other word for it. Certainly not *swish* or *sway* or anything at all meant to entice him. He stood stunned. He hadn't planned on forever, and he was relieved about the baby issue.

But he hadn't foreseen her reaction or his disappointment.

A rattle in the hall startled him—for all of two seconds until he saw a maid pushing her cart down the hall. Thank God this was a secured area, or anybody could have taken him down. Some agent he made today, no good to Paulina, Shay, or himself. He was always careful. Always in control.

Last night, nothing had been about control.

Don pressed his palm against the pinch in his chest. Had all the females in his life gathered to stage some collective intervention to convince him he was a fucked-up dude? He looked down at his hand and wondered for the first time if maybe those chest pains had less to do with age and more to do with stress.

Somebody needed to alert the media.

He didn't need persuading anymore.

* * *

Shay didn't need any more persuasion.

Hearing Vince say meeting her had changed his life for the better delivered an aphrodisiac stronger than anything she could imagine. His words soothed the old hurt inside her.

But thinking about that hurt, that night, made her wonder. "How can you say that when I slept with your best friend?"

"That event happened later, if you recall."

She stared down at her dog, sleeping peacefully in the chair beside her. What a thoughtful gift from Vince. He'd seemed perfect to her back then. He still seemed amazing, but more real. "If I was so important to you, why did you turn me away?"

"Respect for your old man. Respect for you."

Oh God, she needed air. She'd been so mired in insecurities then she'd missed out on a chance for so much. With her restraint already falling fast, this tipped her the rest of the way over the edge. "If I could go back to that time . . ."

"Well, I have to admit I wasn't all that sure you really wanted me as much as you wanted to piss off your dad. That stung my pride more than a bit. Little did I know it would hurt a helluva lot worse when Tommy threw your panties at my chest."

She squeezed her eyes shut, her fingers burying deeper in her dog's fur. She'd wanted something like that to happen, having no clue how much she would regret it now from an adult perspective. "I'm so sorry."

Silence hung heavy with her memories of driving over to see Tommy. Of intending to tell him she'd made a mistake sleeping with him. Instead, she'd found Tommy and Vince circling each other, knives drawn. The fight had sucked in more teens, until finally the police arrived.

A gun was drawn.

Bullets flew, and Tommy dropped.

A horrible possibility bloomed in her mind. Her eyes snapped open. "Were you two fighting about me?"

Vince stared back at her, his dark eyes totally somber for

once. "He threw your underwear. I threw a punch. Things went downhill from there."

As if she hadn't already felt guilty enough about that night. The truth was even worse than she'd imagined. The stab of guilt went deep.

That night rolled back over her. How much she'd hated herself for giving away her virginity out of anger. The ache in her heart and between her thighs over how raw the rough, brief encounter had been in the arms of someone who didn't really care about her.

Now to hear that Tommy had lorded it over Vince . . .

She sat up straighter. Tommy had arranged for her to meet him that night. Could he have planned the whole explosive event? As much as she wanted to hate him for that, she couldn't scrounge anything more than a deep sadness. They'd all been so young, reckless, even outright stupid.

No one deserved to die because of the ignorance of youth.

Shay saw the same weight of guilt etched on Vince's bold face. "How do we get past feeling responsible for what happened to him?"

His fists opened and closed on his knees. "I wish I had the answer."

She couldn't even hold his gaze and looked down at her dog again, her sweet little spoiled pet that Vince had gotten for her. Somehow he'd known how much she needed the comfort Buster would bring in the middle of this chaos.

An image of Vince from that night came back to haunt her. Vince wrapping himself around her to shield her after the cops came. That vision collided with memories of the drive-by shooting at the center when he'd covered her yet again. And here he was again, putting himself in harm's way for her, protecting her, comforting her even.

Shay stood and walked to his chair. She wrapped her arms around his shoulders. He stiffened in her embrace, but she forged on, urging him to rest his head against her chest, hugging him close, offering comfort.

His hands slid up to palm her waist, then circled around. She wasn't sure how long they held on to each other. Nobody cried or spoke, but the air thickened with something she couldn't quite define.

But it was something she absolutely couldn't miss.

He tugged, catching her off guard and off balance. She tumbled into his lap as he sealed his mouth to hers. Urgency pulsed from him into her. She blinked through her surprise to find her body already burning for more.

Her chest rose and fell with ragged breaths. Raw emotions from the past and from the present scoured through her, and she couldn't resist the outlet his kiss, his body offered. She suspected much the same feelings stirred through him.

Twisting, she knelt to straddle him without breaking their kiss. The bold sweep of his tongue over hers sent a fresh jolt through her.

Her legs clamped against his as she wriggled to get closer, yet she was already as close as she could get without crawling inside him. He cupped her head, palmed her bottom, wrapping her in heat.

She stroked her fingers over his smoothly shaved scalp. So sleek. So sexy. She nipped the corner of his mouth. "Don't you want to ask me fifty questions like, am I sure this is what I really want?"

He teased her earlobe between his teeth. "Or why the change of heart?"

"Or what are we going to do once tomorrow is over?" She arched her neck to give him better access.

"Or how about, when are you going to stop talking, because tomorrow is the very reason we need this?"

"I can't argue with that."

She stripped off his shirt, and wow, she'd shortchanged herself in not taking the time to look him over last night. The hard cut of muscles twitched under her gaze, the tattoos shifting with the roll of tendons as if coming to life. The phoenix tattoo draped over his shoulder, wings down his back, was familiar. "I remember this from when you used to strip off your shirt to work on your motorcycle. Did you know how we girls drooled over you?"

"God, I loved that rat bike." His fingers rasped up her sides, his thumbs grazing her breasts.

"Rat bike?" She shivered at the wash of tingles.

"Rat nasty," he explained between nipping his way down her neck, into the vee of her shirt, "held together with baling wire and a prayer."

Shay kissed her way over his shoulder for a better look, and yes, she'd remembered correctly. The wings flowed down his back with the word Freedom interwoven in the feathers. An amazing piece of art, it must have taken a full day to create.

Shay skimmed her hands over his broad shoulders, thinking of that first night of his return when he'd walked in and nearly scared her to death with his intimidating size. Now her mind filled only with memorizing every inch of him. She crawled across his chest, Carpe Diem etched on his abs, another mark from his teen years, an earlier tat, this one not as expertly scrolled.

He peeled away her shirt and unhooked her bra in a smooth sweep and toss, teasing over her skin. She gripped his arms and found the roughened texture of another tattoo on his other biceps. Could she have forgotten? No. She remembered everything about him. She broke the kiss to look.

"Yeah, it's a new one," he growled, his hands rising to cup her breasts, plucking lightly on both until she beaded harder with pleasure.

Her lashes fluttered shut for an instant before she forced them open again, determined to look her fill this time. She found a dagger with Chinese lettering on the handle.

The blade gave her pause.

She forced herself to lean forward and press her lips to the tattoo, to own it as a part of him and not a part of her past. "Any other new inkings I should know about?"

"You'll have to find out for yourself." His callused hands rasped along her skin as he stroked from her breasts around to her back, fingers dipping below her waistband. He gently snapped her thong.

She would have to get naked soon, totally bared in the light. Her scars would be out there for him to see. She should tell him. She wanted to and didn't at the same time.

Maybe he simply needed to rediscover the new and different her the same way she was relearning him.

SEVENTEEN

✦ ─────────────────────────────────

Who the hell needed sleep?

Vince had never felt more completely awake.

He wondered how the woman kissing him senseless could feel so intensely familiar and new at the same time. Not that he intended to waste even a second thinking right now.

He had a willing Shay in his arms and a bed a few steps away.

She clutched his shoulders, urgently wriggling against him. He scooped her up and carried her to the wide bed. Finally. He propped his knee on the edge and eased her onto the mattress, holding their kiss as he positioned himself over her.

He'd spent so many years avoiding thoughts of her, he'd missed out on the possibility that she'd changed, too. He'd focused on thinking about the negatives they brought out in each other, until he'd lost sight of her positives that had enticed him in the first place. The way she always listened, really listened to what he and other people had to say.

Her uninhibited laugh when she rode on the back of his bike.

Vince elbowed up to keep the bulk of his weight off her. The feel of her smooth hands on his body, exploring his tattoos, sent his pulse into overdrive. Not many women understood, just seeing them as a sign of danger, either a turn-on or turnoff. Shay seemed to understand how the markings were simply a part of him, past and present, with maybe more in his future.

She reached for the fastening on her jeans.

He placed his hands over hers. "I've got it."

Smiling, she let her arms fall to rest above her head. With her shirt and bra already on the floor, she made for pinup material. Her pert breasts high and creamy white with pretty pink tips. Her tousled curls fluffed around her face in a halo belied just a little by her hint of a wicked smile.

She kicked off one shoe then the other, and they tumbled along the carpet.

He palmed both tempting mounds at once, and she arched into his touch with a gasp. Slowly, gently, he massaged her, enjoying the way her head dug back into the pillow. She kept her arms over her head as if pinned by invisible cords, her fingers flexing open and closed.

Trailing his hands until he stopped at the top of her jeans, he slid the button free, exposing another inch of tantalizing flesh. And, ah, what a time to notice her belly button ring, a simple gold rod offering a hint of the old rebellious Shay. No way could he resist leaning to press his mouth against her there, clicking the metal against his teeth with his tongue.

She rocked her hips. "You're really good at that, you know."

"I'm giving it my best effort." He glanced up at her as he took her zipper between his teeth and pulled . . .

Down.

Down.

Down until her pants parted and his chin rested right against her sweetest curve of all. Her fingers stretched straight and open and taut. A flush swept her body. He would have liked to see her brown eyes open and locked on him, pupils widening with pleasure. Still, she appeared so intensely in the moment.

A total turn-on.

He tugged her jeans along her hips, nuzzling briefly against her soft curls. The scent of her threatened to send him over the edge, and he shifted his attention to peeling her pants off her legs. A tantalizingly long task as he worked his way down her killer gams.

She kicked her jeans and panties free, bowing up off the bed and kneeling to reach for his belt buckle.

Again he smiled. "Let me."

She hesitated, then leaned back onto her elbows to watch. She eye stroked him with appreciation as firmly as if her hands roved his body. Words seemed scarce, but he was so busy taking in the nuances of seeing her, smelling her, feeling her, his brain lacked the capacity for much else.

Then his pants were gone, and he worked his way back up her body, nibbling her hip, down to her thigh. She'd mentioned enjoying hiking and camping, and the exercise showed in her long, defined muscles. He knew well the power of her legs locked around him.

He skimmed his mouth down to the back of her knee, nudging between her legs with his shoulders. After a second of hesitation, she parted for him. Caressing her calf, he crooked her leg to give him access to her pretty ankles, pink-tipped toes, and yes, spreading her wider for his journey back up. Nip after nip he retraced his path. He worked his way along creamy skin, past her knee to the inside of her thigh.

His mouth met slightly raised lines.

He opened his eyes and saw pale scars, thin striations faded by time until they were barely visible. But he didn't question for a minute what they represented, what she'd done to herself.

She tensed against him. He buried his face harder against her in counterpressure to the pain that had led her to do this to herself. He stroked her carefully until she relaxed again.

God, it ripped him up inside thinking of how much she'd suffered, too. After the night Tommy died, they'd never spoken again. Shay had dropped out of Civil Air Patrol. They'd gone to different high schools for senior year. He'd never called.

And here they were seventeen years later, even hotter for each other.

He kissed her intimately, as close as he could be to her, letting her know how much he wanted her, past and present. Her sigh spurred him.

Her head flung back and her hips arched. He drew in her scent, wanted more and took it, stroking and laving. Her moans massaged him higher, harder, coaxing him on because he wouldn't stop until she found her completion, even though holding back was just about killing him.

She gripped his shoulders, her fingernails digging in deeper, insistent. Her groans swelled, her hips writhing against the anchoring pressure of his hold. He teased his tongue and teeth against her until her whole body went taut, bowing upward with her uninhibited release. Moans built to cries, louder and louder until she flung her wrist across her mouth to muffle the sweet sounds.

He stayed with her, working every last ounce of pleasure for her, even though his body throbbed with a driving need to be inside her. With a final sigh, she sagged back, and he crawled up her body. Her deft hands slid a condom over him before he could even think to mention it, much less reach for the packet. He covered her, entered her.

And he didn't want to leave.

* * *

Shay didn't want to leave the hotel bed and face the uncertain world outside.

She kept her eyes off the clock and on a magnificently naked Vince. The alarm had been set. Egyptian cotton sheets tangled around their bare bodies, and Buster slept at their feet.

Perfection? Maybe.

Scary? Definitely.

Her head resting on Vince's phoenix, she toyed with his dog tags. *Tink, tink, tink.* "I wish we could stay here for a week."

"That can be arranged." He trailed a rose from the vase up and down her spine.

Her stomach flat-out pitched. "First, I have to get my life back together." She would much rather focus on Vince's hard-muscled body and the pleasure they could bring each other. "I never realized how difficult it could be to replace everything in a wallet. I'm definitely going to have a plan B backup in the future."

He teased the rose over her nose, the sweet perfume mingling with the musky scent of sex. A heady combination. "Are you planning on getting mugged on a regular basis?"

"You know where I work. It's a possibility."

He skimmed the rose between her breasts, back and forth. "I would offer you money, but I suspect you wouldn't take it."

"You're correct." Especially not now that they'd slept together and with the possibility of that week in bed together looming.

"Why not ask your parents for a loan?"

"I'd rather sleep in a tent." She cringed at even the thought. Her brother was the one who asked for money in his constant quest for another degree. Not her. She had her own realm for disappointing them.

He set the rose aside on her pillow. "You really do resent your father that much?"

She rolled to her back, studying the crown molding bordering the ceiling. "We have our problems."

"I'm surprised you didn't end up in the air force, too. We may have only spent six months together in Civil Air Patrol, but you really were a first-rate flyer."

She turned her head on the pillow and faked a smile. "I was only there for the boys."

He grazed his knuckles along her jaw as if to soften his words. "Stupid me, I thought you were there to get your father's attention."

Her smile pinched as tight as her chest. "If that had been true, I would be flying right now, don't you think?"

"You're following in your old man's footsteps, whether you realize it or not."

"I'm a nurse, and he's some spooky agent type." Both helping teenagers. Duh. At least Vince wasn't gloating.

His cobalt blue eyes deepened. "It's dangerous for your father if you talk about those things."

She traced the edges of his goatee. "And for you?"

"I'm just a plain old zipper-suited sky god." He kissed the inside of her palm.

"Like my dad." She tugged the magenta duvet to ward off a fresh wash of gooseflesh.

"I know your parents had a rough time, but military members have successful relationships. You have to realize that."

Not according to what Smooth had told her.

"If so, they must be hiding from me." And she was certainly smart enough to realize they weren't just speaking in the hypothetical here. They were testing the scary waters for something that went beyond spending a week in bed together. "Maybe some people have a special connection that survives the stress." Crushing stress. "Maybe sometimes even the kids make it through. But God, Vince, we live in a world where happily ever after is growing scarcer by each statistical poll. Your career heaps on circumstances that make the odds even slimmer. Why would I want to set myself up for that kind of failure?"

"Do you have so little faith in yourself?"

She flinched outside and in. "Don't try to shrink me. I've already spent years in therapy."

His searing blue eyes immobilized her. "Because of the suicide attempt?"

"You heard that back at the center, huh?" She twisted her watch around without thinking, then noticed his attention drawn to her wrist.

"Tough to miss." He stroked the outside of her thigh, sliding gently inward over her faded scars.

Why hadn't she told him from the start? This conversation hurt so much more with her emotions as tender as her well-loved body. "I don't believe in making excuses for what I did. I spent too many years blaming other people for my unhappiness."

"Why were you unhappy?"

"For the same reasons a lot of teenagers here are unhappy. My parents were splitting. My dad was messed up from too much war time. School sucked." She'd thought she was in love with someone who didn't love her back. "Things that happen to kids every day and thankfully most of them don't cut themselves to ease the pain."

"And some do." His palm rested warm and steady over those faded scars. "What brought you back from the edge?"

"I went to counseling in college. It took a while, though. I wish I had some huge story of a lightning strike or some such, but finding peace snuck up on me in a subtler way."

"Tell me." He squeezed her leg. "I want to hear."

Could she tell him what she hadn't shared with anyone other than a grandmotherly therapist? Her only other option was running scared, hiding from relationships for another decade or so.

Time to talk. "I was having a bad day, a really bad day my senior year of college. The pressure had mounted, planning for real life on my own. I had decided to give up."

Each breath grated on its way in and out, but she pushed past it. "But I wanted to make sure I had everything in order. I was going through my mail to be sure all my bills were paid, and I came across this brochure. It was for a hiking weekend that doubled as a treasure hunt." The intensity of that moment, the soft voice inside urging her to live still overwhelmed her years later. "Suddenly I absolutely had to go on that trip."

"Ah . . ." His intense, strong features softened with understanding. "That's why you had all the hiking stuff in your trunk."

She shrugged, smiling. "I'm a nature junkie. A weekend in the wild levels me out."

"Like a road trip for me."

Wow, she hadn't expected it to be this easy. "You understand."

He gathered her against his chest, her leg sliding between his thick thighs. "Sounds like we have hobbies that could blend, biking until our butts go numb, then pitching a tent where the impulse strikes us."

Her breath hitched halfway down her throat. He painted a beautiful picture full of possibilities. She'd tackled rebuilding her life and conquered those hurdles alone. Totally alone and comfortable in that.

Being with Vince and the feelings he stirred were anything but comfortable.

* * *

Lewis stared out the hotel window overlooking Lake Erie. Such a peaceful view.

And nobody had a clue what would slide through those waters tomorrow while everyone had their eyes glued to that congressional hearing.

Excitement filled him until his perfectly pressed clothes felt too tight. He was only hours away from his first seven-figure payoff and the status that coup would bring him.

He whipped the curtains closed again, sealing himself in the room for a rare moment where he didn't have to worry about letting his roots show. He peeled back the bandage he wore to hide his own gang tattoo.

A skull stayed inked on his forearm with a snake slithering through the open eye and mouth.

Flexing muscles, he made the serpent come alive with each twitch. He should have the marking removed, and he would. Someday.

His boss actually knew about his past, had in fact hired

him because of it and the skills he brought to the table in understanding gang politics. Of course his boss had no clue he wasn't "reformed" after all. He'd merely cleaned up his appearance and educational credentials enough to exist in polite society where he had access to a gold mine of information. His boss called him a real mover and shaker.

The man had no idea.

Lewis pivoted away from the window altogether, restless for this night to pass, eager to see his twofold plan come together. Threats to the congressional hearing had the authorities in an uproar. The perfect distraction for a special shipment to glide through the Port of Cleveland: an experimental brand of compact explosives, MP-5 9 mm submachine guns, and a small cache of handheld surface-to-air missiles perfect for popping a civilian airplane during take-off or landing.

The guns would go to local gangs. The rest? Sold to terrorists in the U.S. who were having trouble outfitting their arsenals.

He dropped into a chair and watched the numbers change on the clock. Sure, he dealt with terrorists, but purely on a financial level. Through his gang connections, he provided what they could no longer smuggle into the U.S. Growing gangs from major cities to midsize towns expanded the possibilities for moving illegal goods in and out of the country.

And who said the entrepreneurial spirit was dead?

The best part of all? Webber's suicidal distraction during the hearing provided the added bonus of ridding the world of a major thorn in his side. He stared at the wall as if he could pierce through and get directly to Shay Bassett now.

As of tomorrow, there would be one less "crusader" in his way.

EIGHTEEN

"You need a spotlight to do this."

Shay's voice drifted over his shoulder as they stood in the shower with her shaving his head. Something he'd never let a woman do for him before. Something he found surprisingly erotic.

She slid the razor over his head slowly, following her other hand along to make sure of a smooth shave. Hot water sluiced off her and around to him. Steam filled the Swedish shower cubicle.

He sensed an urgency in her that gave him pause. Hopefully it was nothing more than nerves about her upcoming congressional presentation.

His instincts told him otherwise.

Reaching behind, he clasped her wrist and turned to pluck the razor from her hand. "Thank you."

"But I'm not done."

"Next time." And there would be a next time, if he had anything to say about it. He dipped to kiss her quiet.

Shay hooked a leg around his waist, and he scooped her the rest of the way up until she locked her ankles behind his back, her arms around his neck. She cupped his face and kissed him, water sliding between them and mingling with the taste of her in his mouth. He cupped her hips and raised her higher as he nuzzled his way down her neck, lingering along the curve of a breast.

Sighing, she stroked her hands over the smooth surface of his scalp, her bare thighs squeezing his waist before her lips fell to rest against the top of his head. Something hitched in his chest. He didn't know why, other than that something about the moment felt . . . intense. Control seeped from him as if riding the steam right up the vent.

He eased her away from him and set her firmly back on her feet. "I'll finish up here. You should start getting dressed. You don't want to be late for your big presentation."

The hearing wasn't scheduled to take place until the afternoon, but they had to arrive hours early for the security screening.

Smiling, she smacked him lightly on his butt. "Spoilsport."

While he finished shaving his head, he listened to her bustle in and out of the bathroom, her shape nothing but an outline on the other side of the fogged glass. He shifted the razor to his face. Time to do away with any category of relaxed grooming standards. Today, he would wear his service dress uniform for the official function.

A clean face later, he swiped his hand over his jaw and head until satisfied he hadn't missed a patch of bristle. He stepped out of the shower and into the empty bathroom.

His gut pitched, then he heard her hair dryer blowing in the other room. Still, he needed to keep her in sight every second in a professional capacity today. He tugged on his underwear and T-shirt, then slipped his uniform pants off the hanger. Routine took over like a checklist in the aircraft. Light blue button-down with long tie. Black socks and high-sheen black shoes.

His wheel cap waited in the next room with Shay. He hooked the uniform jacket over his shoulder, stepped out of the bathroom, and stopped short.

He'd seen Shay in sexy, leg-hugging jeans. He'd seen her gloriously naked. But this Shay was a new woman he hadn't met yet.

Striding closer one slow step at a time, he eyed her up and down in her pinstriped power suit. The thin skirt ending just at her knees showed off her killer legs. Simple gold at her neck and wrist shouted elegant. "Va-va-va-voom."

"Well hello to you, too, Major."

Her eyes, smoky with desire and a subtle eye shadow, slid to half-mast as she walked toward him on high-heeled pumps. Lord help him, he couldn't wait to see her in those shoes and nothing else.

He extended an arm. "We really don't have time for this."

She cocked a hand on one hip. "Not even a quickie?"

"You're too pretty to mess up."

"Thank you—I think. You sound a little surprised."

"No insult intended. I'm just discovering a new side of you. Day-to-day, you're an earthy woman, minimal makeup, a shake-and-go haircut, jeans and T-shirt type. A natural beauty." He sketched his hands over her hair, down her curves, not touching, half afraid of messing something up on this perfectly put together woman. Then his gaze hitched on something familiar. "Of course you always have something flashy on your wrist."

Her arm twitched away from him.

Oh God. His eye snapped up to her face, his gut somewhere around his polished shoes. Carefully—giving himself time to think, to process—he draped his jacket over a chair. "Is that how you tried to kill yourself?"

She nodded, a hard swallow moving her neck.

He'd assumed she took a bottle of pills. He should have known better. The signs were there with the cutting on the inside of her thighs, yet for some reason his brain had shied away from this bloody, violent conclusion.

Okay. Deal with it. He touched her gold watch, more of a wide, clamp-style bracelet. "I don't know what to say except I'm so damn glad it didn't work."

He skimmed a finger on the inside of her band.

She flinched again. "Don't. Please." She wobbled on her heels, backing away. Much farther, and she would be in the hall. "I don't know if I'm ready to show you."

Frustration kicked around inside him when he needed to think of Shay, of reassuring her. "What happened between us against that door actually was a mistake, but not in the way you think." He advanced a step. "I'm not looking for casual sex."

Her back met the wall. "I don't do that, no-strings sex, I mean. What happened between us was an . . . uh . . . anomaly."

Anomaly? Not an encouraging word to say the least. "So if you don't have casual sex, and you don't believe in marriage, are you planning to join a convent? Quite frankly, I can't see you in a penguin suit."

She toyed with her watch with fidgety fingers. "I never said I don't believe in marriage. I said happy ones are rare."

He closed the last three feet between them. "Something that rare is worth working for. So why"—he tapped her gold band—"are you holding back?"

She snatched her wrist away—no involuntary flinch this time—and whipped past him with brisk strides. "What gives you the right to demand I lay myself bare, just because you've been in my life for a few days?"

He turned to watch her restless walk. "We have a lot more history than that, and you know it. Why do you insist on putting the negative spin on things?"

She spun on her heel and snapped, "That's unfair."

"I don't think so, not when it comes to relationships." Thoughts connected for him, giving power to the notion, taking it down a path he didn't want to go. He hoped she would surprise him with a detour. "Look at how you've reacted to every good thing that's happened between us."

"I don't know what you're talking about."

"You're shutting us down again by holding back." He could see her shutting down even now.

What would it take to break through walls that high?

He yanked his uniform jacket off the back of the chair and stuffed his arms inside. "Everything your father does, you see in a negative light." Anger sending him on autopilot, he fastened the buttons, checked the rows of ribbons and silver wings above them. "Your father may have made mistakes, but he's doing everything he can to save your life now."

Uniform crisp and in place, he looked up. At her. Ah hell.

Shay stood stone still, staring at him, her lips pursed tight. "Of course you would see it that way." She waved her hand to encompass his uniform. "You spent most of your teenage life wanting to *be* my dad, right down to your save-the-world chest of awards."

"Now you're the one being unfair."

"Are you sure?" Rather than backing down this time, she stalked closer. "When I think back, every time something dangerous happened to me or I showed some vulnerability, you were all over me."

"That's total bull."

"Am I just another cause for you?" Her high heels brought her nearly nose to nose with him. "Something to save or fix?"

Defeat derailed him like an oil slick on a wet highway. "You're not going to accept what we have here, are you?"

He could already see her negative answer gathering force behind her darkening brown eyes. Her chest heaved inside her sleek suit coat. He could have kissed that pink lipstick right off her, and within two seconds flat she would be totally turned on. So would he. She would be distracted from the fight—for now.

Eventually they would be right back here.

A knock echoed through the door.

Vince hauled his focus back to where it should have been all along. Keeping Shay safe. His uniform shoes squeaked as he walked across the carpet, not as comfortable or broken in as his boots.

Or maybe they just pinched right now like everything else in his life.

He stopped at the door, peered through the peephole. Agent Wilson. He flipped the locks and opened.

Paulina Wilson filled the door in her own power suit. She glanced from him to Shay and back again. "Is everything okay here?"

"Fine." Shay picked up her black leather case containing her speech and laptop, keeping her eyes steadfastly off him. "I'm ready to go."

"Good." Paulina gave them a skeptical look but continued as if nothing were wrong. "I'll be riding in the limousine with the two of you. You also mentioned an interest in speaking with the aide that visited the community center yesterday. He works with Congressman Mooney. I thought you would appreciate the chance to speak with him one-on-one."

She gestured for Shay to precede her out the door. Vince didn't much like being dismissed by Shay, but there wasn't a thing he could do about it now, and with the way she was squeezing her watch tighter on her wrist, he feared later wouldn't be any better. He reached onto the top shelf of the closet and pulled down his uniform wheel cap. Tucking the round hat under his arm, he followed the women into the hall.

"Ah, here comes Congressman Mooney's aide now." Paulina pointed down the hall, gesturing to the young man padding down the corridor in top-of-the-line loafers and a designer suit paired with a baseball tie. "Shay Bassett, Vince Deluca"—she paused—"meet Anthony Lewis."

NINETEEN

Her "perfect" day sucked.

Sitting by Special Agent Wilson, Shay wished she could savor this accomplishment, riding in a limousine on her way to the hearing, finally bringing together a dream.

Instead, it felt like her world was falling apart.

She peered through her lashes at the source of her frustration sitting across from her in the limo, beside Mr. Lewis, neck deep in conversation. Vince filled the leather seat with his bulk and military presence. As much as she cringed at reminders of her father, she couldn't deny how flipping hot Vince looked in his service dress uniform with all those rows of ribbons topped by silver wings. Yet she couldn't deny memories of her dad in the same uniform.

Things had actually been going so well with Vince. At least they'd moved from the door to the bed. Sure, she'd shied away from thoughts about the future, but for the first time in longer than she could remember, she'd been happy. What was wrong with living in the moment?

And the icing on the cake? There had been a wreck downtown that caused a traffic jam, making them late.

A drink from the limo's minibar sure would be nice.

Limousines ahead of theirs snaked closer to Case Western Reserve University in a well-guarded procession past white stone and redbrick buildings. Mammoth modern art sculptures and fountains broke up the woodsy scenery along their way deeper into the campus. With Brody in custody, authorities weren't as worried about the threats that started with those calls, but par for the course, they were concerned about protestors.

And they still hadn't answered the question of who Brody answered to. Could he simply be an angry youth acting alone? Possible. But they couldn't be certain until he opened up more.

Vince would be attending with her while his crew buddies flew their monitors, sending info via earpieces to him and other security personnel stationed around the Case Western campus.

Lewis turned from Vince to her. "Miss Bassett, I enjoyed your presentation yesterday afternoon at the community center."

Another moment she should be reveling in—and making the most of.

"Thank you, Mr. Lewis. I'm sorry we didn't get a chance to speak before you left." She hoped he had sway with Congressman Mooney. "I'm glad you were able to stop by the center during your time here. We appreciate your willingness to see our operation up close."

"The congressman is all about these kids. He even puts his money where his mouth is. One of his scholarship funds enabled me to put my old life on the streets behind me and get a fresh start. Much as the major here changed his ways."

Shay sat up straighter in the butter-soft leather seat. She'd done her research on the congressman, and even she hadn't known this about him, or about one of his staff members. She struggled to keep from looking at Paulina Wilson to see if the agent knew either.

Vince locked his eyes on her, clouds still shifting behind the deep blue. "Miss Bassett and her father have a way of reaching these kids."

His determination to push her buttons when it came to her father left Shay digging her nails into the backs of her thighs.

"People like the Bassetts," Lewis continued, "like you, Major, and like the congressman could really put a dent in that way of life."

"Way of life?" Vince's eyebrows rose. "More like a dead-end existence."

At least she and Vince agreed on something.

The looming redbrick gymnasium ahead cut short further conversation. They'd arrived at their destination. Cars and people packed the driveway and lots, her late arrival actually increasing the amount of media exposure.

The limo slid to a stop. Her stomach lurched.

Lewis reached for his briefcase. "Well, that brings our discussion to an end for now. Good luck to you, Miss Bassett. I'll have my eye on you today."

The chauffeur opened the door, a gust of muggy summer air sweeping inside. Shay followed special Agent Wilson out onto the cement walkway leading to the stairs. Security lined the roped-off path, forming a wall between them and—

Camera flashbulbs snapped repeatedly, blinding her.

A hand palmed her back, startling her. She searched for

security, then relaxed as the feel became familiar. Vince. How could he be so comforting and infuriating at the same time?

He leaned close to her ear, his aftershave teasing her nose and her rocky emotions. "Stay vertical."

"Excuse me?"

"Biker lingo for ride safe. Good luck." He squeezed her waist lightly before ushering her toward the stairs and doors.

As much as she appreciated the encouragement, frustration knocked around inside her. Why did he have to insist on such timetables and benchmarks for revealing their emotions?

She pressed a hand to her head. God, this wasn't the time or place. She needed to find her composure and get through the afternoon. The crowd grew thicker and thicker as she pressed through the first layer of security. There would be two more checkpoints to clear.

The press of bodies made her claustrophobic.

She glanced over her shoulder, but the crowd had already sealed Vince and the agent out of sight. She'd been briefed ahead of time about going to a quiet room before the hearing. Thank goodness, because she could use a reprieve from the noise and shoving and raw emotions.

Lewis tipped his head down to hers, steering her past gold-plated awards and glass trophy cabinets. "It's a security nightmare out here. I'll escort you to the waiting room."

"I thought Agent Wilson would do that."

"That's what aides are for."

His logic made sense. She glanced back again. The crowd had thinned, and still she didn't see Vince or the agent.

Wariness crept over her the quieter the hall became. Her

intuition shouted, *Run, run, run,* but she had no logical reason to feel that way. This was a congressman's aide, for crying out loud. She needed to win him over, not totally alienate him. Sure, he'd said he used to be a gang member, but look at Vince. She'd made it her mission to believe these kids could be saved.

Sometime during her rambling thoughts they'd entered it into a deserted hall. Where were the police? She searched for security cameras along the ceiling but turned another corner before she could locate one. Could any of Vince's little bugs be flying around?

She didn't hear so much as a buzz.

"This way." Lewis tapped her elbow, nudging her left.

Forget manners and worrying about offending a congressional aide. "I want to find Vince and Agent Wilson."

"I don't think so." The soulless look in his eyes chilled her clean through.

Lewis turned her, tipping her balance. "This young man's going to take very good care of you."

She regained her balance, coming face-to-face with . . . Webber?

Even in khakis and a button down, she recognized him. His long, dark ponytail draped over one shoulder. His hand seized her arm, FEAR blaring from his knuckles.

She shivered.

"Come with me," he said softly, his lumbering body too big for his age. "Lewis has to go back before he's missed."

Lewis? What did Anthony Lewis have to do with this? Apparently nothing good.

Webber walked faster, a photo security badge clipped to his shirt flapping. No way in hell could he have gotten that badge through legal channels. Every instinct she'd honed in her job shouted that something was seriously wrong.

She opened her mouth to shout. To hell with causing a scene.

Webber's hand moved forward in a flash. The sharp tip of a knife dug into her side. Painfully.

She gasped. He pressed harder until she could feel the cool steel stabbing a tiny hole through her suit, pricking her side. Not a knife. Anything but a knife.

Oh God, she was going to be sick.

Somehow he must have palmed the blade. She couldn't even imagine how he had gotten it past security. A moot issue anyway, because somehow he had.

"Really, Miss Bassett. You need to be quiet, and everything will be okay."

Miss Bassett? He had a knife in her side and he was worried about formality? Hysteria boiled inside her.

"Webber." She stumbled alongside him, terror making her clumsy. "I don't know what this is all about, but you have to realize—"

"Shhh . . ." He dipped his head, his dark ponytail swinging over his shoulder. "I don't want you to die."

Don't want you to die.

Don't want to die.

The cadence of his voice resonated in her memory. Settled in her brain. Scared her to the core.

Webber was her caller.

* * *

Webber nudged Miss Bassett down the hall, watching for any surprises. But thanks to the information Lewis had provided him, the corridor was clear.

Lewis just hadn't known that security hole would be used against him once Webber took charge.

The breach wouldn't last long, though. Even shorter because he'd squeezed his own agenda in along with Lewis's plan. He had to make sure that no matter what happened, Shay and Amber were safe.

If only Shay understood. She'd tried to scream twice already, and he'd been forced to nick her side to shut her up. Her fear of knives was obvious. He hated to use that to his advantage, but it was better than risking her life.

"Webber, listen to me, please. I don't know what Anthony Lewis has to do with this, but you need to listen to me instead of him." Shay gasped with each hurried step away from the crowd gathered for the hearing.

"Not now. There will be time for you to talk." He had to hurry before Lewis realized the script had been changed.

Webber checked numbers above the doors. Not much farther. He was *supposed* to walk out into the lobby with Shay Bassett, the witness, as his hostage, taking her with him in the big blast. Lewis had a weakness for making his statements with too much of a big deal, like that whole bomb scare idea back at the center. By the time Lewis would see Webber had come alone, it would be too late to do anything about it.

He stopped at the janitor's closet where he was supposed to hide out if things went wrong. He unlocked the door and shoved her inside with the buckets and mops and the stink of floor cleaner. He wasted one valuable second on the thing about this he regretted most.

"Miss Bassett, I'm really sorry about that old man who died in your car."

"The guard at the center?"

"Yeah, he was a loser, but he didn't deserve to die."

She blinked fast. "Do you think I deserve to die?"

"I tried to help you." Her perfume smelled nice, but then he realized he could only smell it because she was sweating.

"By putting a bomb in my car?"

The pain in her eyes bothered him, but he could only trust her so far. He wished she could know he wasn't all bad. He'd taken her bag to try to save her life.

Maybe this was his punishment for everything else he'd done. He wouldn't be able to explain his side of things. Why hadn't those special bomb dogs found the explosives like they did in all the movies?

"Webber, why does someone want me dead?"

"I'm already risking a lot for you. Good-bye—"

"No, no, please, just stay for a couple more seconds." She blinked fast, those eyes of hers so honest, like she cared. "You don't have to talk about any of this. Let's talk about you. You have important people in your life. People who care about you. Think how they'll be hurt if you die."

She went on just like she'd done on the phone, trying to help him. It hurt to listen.

With a speed honed on the streets, he whipped a gag over her head, into her mouth, and yanked the slipknot tight. He held the knife high. "Turn around."

Her eyes went wide. She shook her head.

"Miss Bassett, look behind you."

She backed away, her eyes darting as if searching for a weapon.

"Do it," he barked.

She tensed, only half turning. Then sagging as she must have finally seen Amber.

Her pretty brown hair sliding down her shoulders, Amber sat crouched in the corner, bound and gagged. It had been the only way he could be sure she was safe as well. Lucky for him, Shay had a soft spot for Amber, too.

"Now kneel down, Miss Bassett. I'm just going to tie you up like Amber. This will all be over soon."

She knelt slowly, her eyes nowhere near trusting. He tugged out another slipknot and secured her hands. She would probably work her way free after a while, but he would be done by then. "Move over there, across from Amber."

He hunkered down beside Amber to talk to her just once more, but he had to make it fast. He was running out of time.

Webber leaned toward Amber's ear, the smell of her shampoo so much nicer than anything he could remember. "There's fifty thousand dollars in a box at the bottom of the trash can." His payoff from Lewis. Lewis thought he was stupid enough to send his mother here after the hearing. There were other ways. "If I don't come back, take it for you and the baby. Use it to go away from here, and don't come back."

He wanted to hide Amber and Shay somewhere else, but this was the only place Lewis had secured for him. If everything went according to plan, the cops would escort Lewis in the gym and he would never get a chance to return here.

So many problems to work out, but at least there was a chance Lewis wouldn't get away with this. There was a chance for Amber and Shay and his mom.

He didn't want to think about what chances he might have.

For himself, just something for *him* today, he touched Amber's hair, just a strand to see how she felt. She winced. He wanted to cry.

Webber turned away from Amber, Miss Bassett's horrified eyes slamming into him. He owed her something. He owed her the truth.

"Miss Bassett, you made me decide to live."

He wished he could have trusted her with more, maybe

even earlier, but she would have gone to the cops or to that big military boyfriend of hers. Then Lewis would have found out for sure. Amber and his mom would be murdered while he was forced to watch. He really couldn't trust anybody but himself.

Bomb strapped to his chest, Webber stepped into the hall and locked the door behind him.

★ ★ ★

"Where the hell is Shay?"

Paulina heard Vince just behind her. She wished she had the answer for him. Somehow, as they'd been going through the first security, they'd been separated from Shay and Anthony Lewis. She was concerned but not completely freaked out.

Not yet.

She scanned the audience in front of her in a C-SPAN kind of sweep, then the stage with a witness table prepped with microphones and pitchers of water. Two of the seats were already filled, and one remained empty where Shay should be. The panel of congressional committees who were interested in this testimony glad-handed the local press and university officials. Cameras were rolling, after all.

"There, Vince . . ." She pointed over the sea of heads. "I see Lewis."

The aide skirted the edge of the group, but there was no sign of Shay.

The large crowd outside the political event worried her. People were pressed into such close confines, hepped up, discontent brewing in some of the protestors.

She wished they had some of Vince Deluca's crowd control options he'd used during that Honduran election mission she read about in his file. But with everyone inside, they would have to use more standard options in conjunction with the military's nano-bug flight surveillance.

Even now, she could hear Vince in her earpiece speaking low with his crew back at the hangar, instructing them to use their intelligence technology to expand the search for Shay. Paulina breathed a little easier knowing she had backup beyond regular mounted surveillance cameras.

Her BlackBerry buzzed against her hip. Absently she lifted it and scrolled, reading . . .

Holy Shit.

"Don, Deluca," she spoke into her sleeve, "my people have a lead from the cell phone web your trackers have been building. Looks like something's up at the Port of Cleveland. Jaworski's on his way over with backup now."

She could see Don's frown from across the room. "The Port of Cleveland?" his voice softly stroked her ear over the airwaves. "What's that got to do with the threat here?"

Maybe nothing. Maybe coincidence. Or maybe—

A teenager stepped from the audience in the back of the room, a familiar teen. Not surprising, necessarily. They'd expected teens from the center, thus the three levels of security checks.

Still something about him niggled at her. The way he walked. His clothing was actually fairly appropriate—khakis and a button-down—a bit loose, but that was the norm for kids these days. He even had some kind of security tag. The kind for a student volunteer, perhaps?

She shoved the Port of Cleveland issue out of her head and focused on the here and now. She worked her way around the edges of the gymnasium toward him, angling carefully past a woman with a cane.

The teen stopped, his back to a wall.

She shouldered through harder, already calling into the mic in her sleeve. "Back left of the gym. Check the teenager with a ponytail."

He jumped up onto a chair.

Webber.

His name came to her in a flash as fast as his hands ripping open his shirt to display explosives.

Paulina stopped, the crowd around her screaming. Security drew weapons in a stadium wave of raised barrels.

"Stop," Webber said, not even shouting.

People froze like in some sick and twisted game of freeze tag.

Dead silence thrummed through her earpiece for three stunned seconds before a barrage of voices filled the airwaves. Experience on the job served her well in sifting through the chatter while keeping her focus full front.

The boy—Webber—raised his hand, thumb resting on top of what must be a plunger.

Paulina whispered into her sleeve. "Hold your fire. Hold your fire. We don't want to risk so much as a twitch from his hand on that detonator."

As much as she trusted her sharpshooters stationed throughout the building, she didn't much like the idea of bullets flying around so many people. She eyed the explosives strapped to the boy's chest. Thin metal cylinders, plenty of wires. It looked authentic.

So did the intensity on the young man's face.

"Stop running away, or I'll blow this thing and half a city block right now. I want you to listen. I need for people to listen."

Where was Shay Bassett with her suicide prevention skills?

Paulina tried to eye a path to the front of the room, but

the press of people rushing out squashed her back against a wall. The smell of fear and too much cologne rolled off their bodies. Footsteps pounded from all directions as uniformed cops and plainclothes security converged to form a semicircle around the boy.

And in the far corner of her peripheral vision she saw Don, edging along the wall toward the boy.

Bile soured in her mouth.

Webber's hand didn't so much as shake. "I see the way you're looking at me, all judgmental like. I'm just another thug to you. But this could happen to any of you. It could be someone closer to you than you think." He looked straight into the television camera, red light for Record blazing. "Anthony Lewis. He's the one to blame for all of this. He planned it. I would have gone to the cops, but nobody ever believes us or listens to us. I would have been arrested, and he would have been free to keep right on working. Well, I'm making you listen."

He paused, staring straight into the camera. "You don't know me. People like you don't want to know me. You see me and others like me every day on street corners and close your rich-ass eyes, hoping we'll go away and not rob you or your uptown friends. Maybe you even hope we'll kill each other off. But the more you close your eyes, the more we grow. The meaner the streets get. The more you turn your own backyard into a war zone."

He raised his hand higher. "Well, I'm not closing my eyes anymore. I've been pounded on, and I've seen people I care about abused. In more ways than I can—" He cleared his throat, no doubt willing away the catch in his voice. "It ends today."

The boy spoke like someone with nothing left to lose.

At least most of the room had emptied out, but oh God,

Don was still inching closer from the side while Vince kept the boy's attention on the cameraman still rolling tape.

Shooting the teen was still an option in her mind now that most of the civilians had left the building, especially if they could all put some distance between themselves and Webber. But the shot would have to be a kill, or he could still push the plunger. For that matter, a death twitch could set the thing off.

Don—God love his bleeding heart for these kids—would do everything possible to save the boy.

Her pulse hammered in her ears louder than the cacophony of frantic voices in her earpiece. Her last words to Don roared back, drowning out all the rest with the awful way they'd left things with each other.

Too late. Too late. Too late.

She ached to talk to him, to apologize for throwing away their relationship, for not trying to work things out. Even if he could hear her in his own earpiece, she couldn't risk distracting him. His lean body moved with a honed stealth that barely rippled his suit. With his handsome face, his full head of steel gray hair, he could have been an action hero, except, oh God, this was real life, and Don was seconds away from launching himself at a suicide bomber.

What a time to realize she'd fallen in love with her CIA lover.

TWENTY

Don kept his steps steady, his eyes locked on the sweating teen with a bomb strapped to his chest. His earpiece told him most of the building had been cleared, other than a few stragglers like that overeager cameraman determined to make his career or die trying.

He couldn't think about Paulina. He had to trust her to protect herself. Right now all he kept remembering was Shay, alone and hurting as a teenager who saw no other way out than taking her own life. He hadn't been there for his daughter.

But he would do his damnedest to make sure this boy, one of Shay's kids, did not commit this desperate act. He understood how she felt about them. He and Shay shared more in common than she realized. Hell, *he* hadn't realized how much alike they were until now.

Vince asked the boy a question, and Don saw his chance.

Coalescing all his training into this one split second, he launched.

His fingers locked around the kid's wrist. They slammed back. Chest to chest, he pinned the teen, praying like crazy he wouldn't set the bomb off. The boy looked him in the eyes and Don saw . . .

Gratitude?

Don couldn't afford to weaken or wonder. He kept the kid restrained. The room erupted with activity as the bomb squad rushed them. Combat boots pounded the floor, reverberating through him as he sprawled across the upended chair. Don looked at the boy again and realized.

Webber had never pushed the button in the first place. The plunger wasn't even connected. He'd taken one helluva risk that nobody would shoot him.

Don scooped up the trigger while looking at the kid, reassessing, tapping into those old mentoring skills, and he knew. The boy had felt cornered and just wanted to be heard. His teenage daughter had just wanted to be heard when she tried to kill herself.

Of course nothing excused what this young man had done. It was too late for him. He would be looking at the inside of a jail cell for a very long time, but at least he was alive.

Don just prayed it wasn't too late for him with Shay.

He shifted his hold and control to the bomb squad. Now that his vision broadened, he saw police wearing flak jackets standing in a semicircle. Paulina hovered by the exit with a vest draped over her suit but not buckled, as if someone tossed it on her, and she didn't even notice. Where was Shay? He scoured the stragglers still evacuating and didn't see her. She must already be outside, thank God.

He turned his attention back to Paulina and fast-walked

toward her. He definitely wanted her as far away from the bomb as he could convince her to move. She hadn't said a word, so he could only hope he'd read her right. After the way he'd treated her, she deserved to hear the words from him first.

He scooped her up by the waist and made a beeline out the door. Let the bomb squad handle things from here. He'd done his job.

"Don!" Paulina wriggled.

But not too much. Their martial arts workout during sex let him know loud and clear if she wanted out of his arms, she could land him on his ass in a heartbeat.

He slammed through the doors and into the harsh afternoon light. He set Paulina on her feet, grabbed her wrist, and towed her down the steps. He stopped under a sprawling tree.

Don gripped her shoulders and realized she was shaking. Special Agent Paulina Wilson was trembling.

"Ah, Lina . . ." He hauled her against his chest.

Or maybe she fell into his arms.

He only knew they held each other so firmly he almost could crawl inside her. His chest went tight again, but not in an entirely bad way. Just different. Something he would have to get used to.

"Paulina," he said, not caring who overheard, thanks to the listening devices inside their jackets, "we don't have much time to talk, but I'm not wasting another second without saying a few things. I'm far from perfect, and I'm not likely to get much better anytime soon. But I hope you'll hang in there with me, because damn it all, I'm going to try. Try to make things work with you. Try to break through whatever it is that's keeping me from being the man you seem to think I can be."

Her shaking slowed, and her hands slid up his arms. "Given the wires we're both wearing, I do believe you just outed our relationship, Agent Bassett."

A laugh rumbled up his chest, easing the ache and carrying a boatload of tension on its way up and out. "I take that to mean we still have a relationship?"

"Damn straight, we do." She cupped his face, her jacket puckering just a hint and revealing creamy white lace. "And I've got you on the record."

Light laughter rumbled through his earpiece from other agents and the air force crew flying the surveillance equipment. This conversation with Paulina was definitely worth pursuing later. For now, he simply brushed a quick kiss along her full red lips, even that minimal contact enough to set his body buzzing.

Almost as loudly as his earpiece buzzing to life. No laughter this time.

"Gun!" Smooth's voice rumbled through the earpiece from his viewing station. "Gun! We've got a clear image down a side hall. That congressional aide Anthony Lewis has a gun."

* * *

Lewis unlocked the janitor's closet. Fifty thousand dollars wouldn't last long, but it was the most he could carry in small bills, and it would get him to Central America. From there, he could hook up with more from the international gang affiliated with his home connection.

If they didn't pop a cap in his ass over the screwed-up shipment. Right about the time that kid had jumped up on the chair, Lewis's cell phone started spewing freaked-out text messages about how cops were crawling all over the Port of Cleveland. He would definitely take his chances in

Central America. His life here certainly couldn't get much worse now that all his plans had gone to dog shit.

He yanked open the door and stopped dead. "What the fuck?"

Shay Bassett and some whale of a pregnant teenager stood back to back, trying to untie each others' hands. He couldn't even begin to figure out what had gone wrong in that Webber kid's head. He only knew he had to get the hell out of here.

He slid his hand onto the top shelf and whipped down a 9 mm he'd stored there earlier when he'd stashed the cash. He'd only provided Webber with a knife to keep the balance of power firmly in his own court.

He leveled the gun. "Don't move. Either of you."

Keeping his weapon steady in one hand, he dumped out the trash can, the padded folder full of cash thudding to the floor. He tucked it inside his jacket. Now what to do with the bitches? Did he have time to tie them up more securely, or should he risk firing his weapon? He didn't have a silencer with him.

Footsteps pounded in the distance, growing louder, closer.

Shit. Questions answered.

"Well, ladies, our options have narrowed considerably." He leveled the gun at the teenager, ready to plug her between the eyes. Then he hesitated. Two hostages might be unwieldy, but there were definite advantages.

He could control them by threatening the other.

He could also kill one to intimidate the other.

Or sell them both to flesh peddlers for more start-up money once he left the country. His eyes dropped to the teenager's belly. That baby could actually bring big bucks on the black market, and the leggy do-gooder was a knockout.

He couldn't afford to leave these cash cows behind with his other plans incinerating.

Lewis waggled the gun at them. "You're both coming with me."

Shay Bassett lurched forward.

He pressed the gun between her breasts. "Do what I say, or the pregnant girl dies first."

That stopped her cold. He inched around, hooked an arm with the girl, and hauled her to his side. He shifted the gun fast and pointed it at her big stomach.

The teen sniveled.

"Stop the whining, bitch, or I'll cut you straight through to the kid and leave you to bleed out." He'd done that and worse before. He was just smart enough never to get caught. Before now.

Somehow he had to salvage this. He wouldn't be able to come back, but hopefully he could still secure a position in the Central American group tied to his here. He hadn't started there and had only made brief visits in the past, but international gang ties were strong.

Yeah, he was making this work. Thinking on his feet. His old survival instincts hadn't been dulled by the soft life, after all.

"You." He nodded at Shay. "Stay plastered to my side, or I will hurt your little friend here."

The footsteps got close. Too close. Time had run out.

"Stop," Lewis shouted through the doorway. "I have two hostages. One of them is pregnant. I will shoot to kill if you charge at us."

The teen whimpered, but Shay stayed silent. Anger radiated from her, almost overpowering the fear in her eyes. Too bad he didn't have time to enjoy her. Maybe later, to celebrate escaping.

"We hear you," that chick agent, Wilson, answered from the hall. "Don't do anything stupid. We can work something out."

His mind raced, reshaping his plans. "All I want is a plane gassed up and ready to take me out of the country." He eased out into the hall, both women in front of him, gun visible for any unbelievers.

He kept his back to the janitor's closet, protecting himself from behind until he was sure they understood he meant business. He scanned the dozen or so people in the hall. His eyes landed on the arrogant air force pilot who thought he was so squeaky clean, better than everyone else because he'd risen above it all. "And there's the man I want to fly us out of the country."

★ ★ ★

Late afternoon sun baking the flight line, Vince climbed out of the limousine for the second time. He'd had doubts about how this day would end, but he'd never expected it to finish here.

And certainly not with a gun pointed at Shay.

That bastard Lewis had chosen his hostages well, two women, one pregnant. Vince wasn't sure how they were going to get out of this alive, but he would die trying to save them. Thank God Paulina had been able to orchestrate this trip to the airport where his Pilatus waited.

Lewis had promised to release them once they reached Central America. Not that Vince believed him. This bastard wasn't letting anyone go, and Vince knew damned well he would be the first in line to die. At least they'd bought more time.

Vince had driven them to the airport in a limousine. Now he needed to prepare for takeoff.

He wanted to look at Shay, to let her know somehow that he was sorry for the way he'd left things between them, but he feared the distraction. For sure, that woman could steal his attention faster than anyone he'd ever met.

The Pilatus painted with civilian colors gleamed on the tarmac. His crew, dressed in civilian clothes, readied it for flight. Thank God for those relaxed grooming standards that allowed them to blend in.

Lewis hadn't met any of them, and so far it appeared the California congressman genuinely didn't have a clue as to what his aide had been doing. So Lewis was in the dark about their operation here. Surely he wouldn't have asked for Vince to fly him out if he'd had even an inkling of their surveillance operation.

Vince studied the bastard's face, and he appeared uninterested in the surroundings, although Lewis hadn't so much as loosened his grip on the gun as he sat beside the women in the limo.

Vince walked up to his squadron mates, pretending to ready his plane for flight.

Smooth handed Vince flight paperwork. "Sir, the tanks are full. Looks like you might want to do a center of gravity calculation, since you have four people on board." With a contoured beard, khaki pants, and a polo shirt with the airport logo, Smooth shed all hints of his military persona. "You might need to put two passengers in the rear to keep the CG far enough aft and someone on the opposite side of the cockpit from you for lateral stability."

Vince understood moving passengers aft, that happened all the time, but what the fuck was lateral stability?

Smooth winked at him, took out a slip of paper and placed it on the clipboard. "If you could sign for the fuel right here, please."

Vince snagged the pen dangling from the clipboard and looked down at the paper. Smooth had written: "No bolts in aft right seat belt."

The perfect place to put Lewis and pitch the plane.

Now *that* would sure screw up somebody's "lateral stability."

He scrawled his name on the sheet, and Smooth put it in his pocket. "Have a good flight, sir." He extended his hand. "Don't forget to do your CG calculations."

"Thanks." Vince clasped his crewdog pal's hand, this handshake the only way to say good-bye, good luck, stay vertical. "I appreciate you guys getting her ready. *See ya later.*"

And damn it, he would. Failure wasn't an option. Not with Shay's life in the balance.

Lewis approached with both women and, for the first time since they'd left the university, Vince let himself look in Shay's eyes. He would have been better off keeping his distance, because he found all the same things echoing around inside him.

Fear, regret, apology and, ah hell, a love that they'd both worked to erase for seventeen years.

Love.

Vince entered the plane first, ever aware of the gun too close to Shay, and took his place up front. He looked back at Lewis, who was making himself comfy directly behind Vince.

Time for a seat change. "We are a little heavy. I need to do a quick worksheet to make sure we can get off the ground."

Lewis snapped, "Whatever you fucking got to do. Get to it."

"Take the gags off the women. I need to ask some questions."

Lewis eyed him suspiciously. Vince kept his face blank until finally Lewis complied.

Keep eyes off Shay.

Her gasp for fresh air still sucker punched him.

Vince started filling out the sheet, going through a process he didn't need, but the bastard wouldn't know better. "What do you weigh, Lewis?"

"About two hundred pounds."

"And Amber, what do you weigh?"

"Um," she whispered, almost too soft hear, poor kid. "One hundred fifty-five at my last doctor's appointment."

"Shay, how about you?" he risked a side glance at her.

She held her composure, other than the sweat dotting her forehead. "One thirty-five."

"Yeah, we're a bit uneven," he lied. "I need two people to sit all the way in the back seats and, Lewis, you need to be on the opposite side of me."

Lewis leaned forward in his seat. "What kind of bullshit is that?"

"Sorry." Vince shrugged. "We need a stable center of gravity, or the plane won't get off the ground."

Lewis studied him through narrowed eyes for what felt like for-frickin'-ever before rising. "All right, whatever." He waved the gun at Amber. "Move up to the front, and let me switch sides. No funny stuff, asshole."

Amber moved out of the seat to the front and allowed Lewis to switch sides. "All right, bitch," he called to Shay. "Get back here and sit down."

Vince hated putting Shay so close to that bastard, but they needed the pregnant girl as far away from Lewis as possible. Shay would want that.

And Shay could help him subdue Lewis.

Vince frowned. Now wasn't that a kick-in-the-butt revelation. When had he gone from seeing her as a fragile victim to valuing her as a strong woman who could hold her own?

Maybe there'd been reason for her to hold back from him after all. He hadn't earned the right to look below that watch. He wouldn't have seen the strength it took for her to survive.

It seemed he had a copilot for this flight, after all. She just happened to be riding in a seat behind him.

He exhaled hard and pulled his focus in tight. Vince called for engine start and readied the airplane to fly, all the while keeping an eye on Lewis in the mirror overhead.

Lewis kept his gun trained on Amber, while he instructed Shay to buckle his seat belt. He sagged back in his seat. "All right, Major Deluca, let's get this plane airborne. I want the radio on broadcast. No sneaky maneuvers over a headset. One false move, and I'll throw one of our hostages out the hatch without a parachute."

Amber whimpered, pressing her hand to her swollen stomach.

Vince mumbled low, "Hang in there, kiddo."

He checked the prop, cranked the engine, rolled the plane out onto the runway. As ordered, he kept his radio contact public and minimal. The engine rumbled louder and louder, the plane gaining speed, yoke vibrating in his hand as the wheels spun along the runway.

Whoosh.

The nose tipped upward. The Pilatus soared. Hogs and planes. He was in control here in the open sky much like on the open road, he reminded himself. His crew had come through in offering an edge.

He swept out over the water. He didn't want to consider that they could die in a crash, but Lewis was a wild card with that gun. Vince couldn't risk the Pilatus diving into a subdivision.

"Miss Bassett," Amber sniffled from beside him, "please don't let anything happen to my baby."

"I'm going to do my best." Shay leaned forward in her seat.

Amber circled her hands over her belly. "I've spent so much time hating this baby for ruining my life, but I did this. The baby didn't. Do you think I brought this on myself with all those bad thoughts?"

Vince wanted to bark that the asshole with the gun was responsible for all of this. However, flying the plane and watching for a sign of weakness from Lewis seemed the better alternative.

"Of course not." Shay's gaze flickered to Vince then back to the girl. "You didn't do anything to deserve this. Your baby knows you love her."

"But I still want to give her away. Even if I live, I want her to be brought up by somebody else. Not that it even matters anymore, because I'm gonna die, aren't I? And I deserve it."

Lewis groaned. "Good Lord, you people. Do I really have to listen to this shit all the way to Central America? Hey wait. I have the gun, so that means I don't have to listen to anything."

Shay jabbed a finger at their kidnapper. "Unless you want to deal with a hysterical pregnant teenager or a totally pissed off me, you'll let us talk so I can keep her calm."

Lewis chuckled low and dark. "Damn lady, you're hot."

Vince's fists tightened around the yoke as he imagined all the ways he would pummel that piece of garbage into the ground once he got the gun out of his hands.

Shay lowered her arm. "Amber, you have to forgive yourself."

Her chin quivered. "But I slept with Caden. He's my baby's daddy. If anyone in the Mercenaries knew, they would have killed me, maybe even my little girl."

Caden? That kid from Apocalypse. The kid who'd complimented Shay's yellow kicks. The one Shay had said was banging some crack whore in a bathroom stall during the bomb threat. No wonder Amber was scared as hell for herself and her baby.

He checked Lewis in the mirror and, well, look at that, it appeared even the jerk was actually getting wrapped up in Amber's life story. Vince monitored that gun, waiting for just the right moment to pitch the plane.

Amber cradled her stomach, rocking. "Caden used to live next door. We walked home together in elementary school. I thought he was still my friend. Because of everything you were making happen for us, I thought maybe we all wouldn't have to be enemies anymore. I was wrong about so many things."

Slowly, the gun wobbled, just a hint, then more until the barrel pointed toward the deck of the airplane.

Vince rammed the yoke forward.

Everyone jerked upward in their seats, restrained by their belts. Except Lewis.

The bolts snapped loose.

Lewis slammed into the ceiling.

The gun tumbled free.

Vince pulled out of the dive and slapped on the autopilot. Amber's screams raked the air, along with Lewis's guttural curses as the kidnapper crashed to the deck.

Vince launched out of his seat and on the gun. He leveled cold steel at Lewis. The bastard tried to elbow up. Vince's hand fisted.

Shay's foot shot out, and she kicked Lewis in the jaw.

Lewis's head smacked the floor. His eyes rolled back in his head as he lost consciousness.

Vince grinned. "That's the way to bring it."

She made one helluva copilot.

Vince grabbed Lewis by the collar and rolled him onto his stomach. He opened a storage cabinet and rummaged around until he found the plastic ties used to hold wire bundles together. He restrained Lewis's feet and hands, gathered the gun, and moved back to the pilot seat.

He buckled himself back behind the yoke.

Amber screamed again.

Vince jerked, and the plane bobbled. "It's all right, kiddo. He's not going to hurt you."

He steadied the craft just as Amber screamed again.

Shay lurched from her seat to the front. "What's wrong?"

"It hurts." Amber rocked, tears streaming down her face. "It really hurts. It feels like the baby is coming."

Shay placed her hand on the girl's stomach. Her eyes went wide. "Okay, it could just be a Braxton Hicks." She glanced up. "Practice contractions. Even if they're real, this is your first baby. It takes a long time for your body to prepare itself for labor."

"But it feels like I gotta push."

Shay shushed the teen. "There will be plenty of time." She peeled off her watch and gave it to Amber. "Why don't you start timing your contractions, and we can see how far along you— Oh no."

He didn't like the sound of that. Vince's stomach took the nose dive the plane hadn't gotten to. "What's wrong?"

"Amber's water broke."

TWENTY-ONE

Amber was going to have this baby now.

Shay knew stress could bring on labor early—in Amber's case three weeks early—but it hadn't even entered her mind that this baby would be born in an airplane. Likely Amber had been in labor since back at the university. The plane going into a dive probably moved things along.

Not that she could complain. Vince's fast thinking and skill had saved their lives.

His broad shoulders in the front seat reassured her now. He watched in the mirror, steady as he radioed ahead for an ambulance to meet them when they landed back where they'd started—the closest airport, since they'd flown out over Lake Erie.

Lewis's moans as he awakened mingled with Amber's whimpers through another contraction. Shay's wrist burned from where the rope had cut into her old scar, but she couldn't let it distract her.

Only five minutes had passed since Amber's water broke, and Shay had realized the baby's head had already crowned. There was no way to keep this baby in until they landed. She'd moved the teen to a more open backseat. She would have to deliver this child in an airplane with nothing more than the first aid kit spread open beside her. Her nurse's training had covered emergency deliveries. She'd just never expected to use that part of her schooling.

This had to be one of the fastest first labors on record. Although maybe Amber had been suffering for hours and hadn't shown it. The kid had been through so much that pain was nothing new to her.

Shay knelt in front of her, using the seat like a birthing chair. To think that empty center section had contained monitors the other time she'd been on this plane to receive the briefing from Vince's crewmates a few short days ago.

Aircraft vibrating under her knees, she focused on her patient and making everything as sterile as possible with the limited supplies in the first aid kit. She'd already done a mental run-through of Amber's chart, done a verbal review as well. Vince had a doc on standby on the radio to offer advice if Amber went into distress.

With the baby fully crowned, there was nothing left to do but coach Amber through another contraction. And holy cow, this one looked painful. Amber's face contorted as her belly tightened and spasmed. The girl's fist turned white-knuckled from clutching Shay's watch.

"Hold your knees and push, Amber, push."

"I am pushing," she screamed, red-faced and panting.

"Hey," Vince called from the front. "Count with me while your nurse works her medical magic. Listen up, okay?"

His voice carried just the right blend of calm and authority, while Amber struggled with pain. "One, two, you're doing great, four, five, come on, Amber, stay with me, seven, eight, you're just about done, ten."

Amber gasped and sagged in the gap before the next contraction began. "You count too slow. Ditch the small talk."

"You got it, kiddo."

Shay dabbed the girl's forehead with tissue from the kit. "It's going to be over soon. Okay, it's time for you to hold your knees again and push."

Amber's scream built again.

Lewis groaned from his corner of the deck, his eyes flickering open. "Hey Shay, listen, I've got money here, fifty thousand dollars in an envelope in my jacket, and I'll give it all to you if you'll just pass me a parachute."

Shay held on to her calm. Barely. "Not a chance."

"Ah, of course you don't want the money for yourself"—Lewis rolled to his side with a groan—"but I'll bet this girl here could use the cash to take care of that baby. Just give me the chute."

"Go to hell," she snapped at Lewis without looking away from her job. "I hope you know how worthless you and your whining are compared to what Amber's going through. You're a destroyer, while Amber is bringing new hope into the world and creating something—someone— with the potential to be better than all of us."

Shay steadied her breathing and focused on Amber who . . . *Oh no.* "The baby's coming, Amber. Vince, are you ready to count?"

"We're," Amber gasped, "already on four. Got that, Major?"

"Fair enough." Vince nodded in front. "Five, six, seven . . ."

Shay palmed the infant's head in her gloved hands. Amber's fingernails cut into the seat belt as her face turned crimson with her efforts. Pride seared through Shay as she watched the teenager fight to bring her baby into the world.

The head inched farther into Shay's waiting hold. Turning, guiding shoulders, and the baby's body slithered free. Shay went on autopilot, tending her new tiny patient. Sweeping the mouth clear just as the baby girl let loose a healthy wail.

She cradled the squirming miracle in her hands, tiny, but whole and healthy and screaming like a champ. Tears streaked down her face. How could she not cry? She held the newborn up for Amber to see, for Vince to look at, too, in the mirror above his head.

"It's a girl," she said, "a perfect little girl."

Her eyes met and held with Vince's as they shared the moment, the victory they'd pulled through together. As she looked at him and her own reflection, she realized, her arms were bare. Her wrist was bare.

That last barrier she'd tossed up between them had come tumbling down when she hadn't been looking.

Finally, she was ready to embrace her future. Her happiness.

★ ★ ★

"Are you ready to call it a day?"

Vince looked over at Jimmy Gage in a Hawaiian shirt and with the start of a handlebar mustache. His crewdog buddies lined alongside Vince an hour after he had landed. Smooth looked preppy even in his fake airport personnel gear. Berg stood alongside the rest, not hanging back for once.

And Lieutenant Colonel Scanlon. The boss had a big, rare smile on his face.

Vince tugged at his uniform tie. "Most definitely ready."

They'd helped avert a bombing, a kidnapping, and even managed to provide the information needed to stop a major shipment of illegal munitions from being smuggled into the country. Jaworski was having a field day wrapping that one up over at the Port of Cleveland.

Vince rubbed his shoulder over the old phoenix. He was actually starting to like that opinionated cop. Maybe that came from seeing things without the crap from his past clouding his vision.

He searched the tarmac for Shay. A halo of lights shining through the dark illuminated fire trucks, police cars, and officials filling the small airport. Finally, he found her, over by the EMS truck assessing Amber and her baby. Shay jotted notes on a technician's chart.

Taking care of business the same as he was. Their time would come after.

He looked back at his crew. There would be more missions, more risks. Some wins, some losses. But today, the good guys had come out on top. "Thank you."

Scanlon clapped him on the shoulder. "It's what we do, Major, it's what we do." His boss persona slid back into place before Vince could even respond. "Come on, boys, Deluca has police reports to give, and we've got work of our own."

The crew filed behind Scanlon as the commander barked out a list of duties.

Footsteps sounded off to his right. He looked fast, his nerves still wired tight. Don walked toward him, hands in pockets.

His old mentor stopped beside him. "I owe you more than I could ever repay."

"You don't owe me anything." The man had saved his life years ago.

Although what happened with Shay today had nothing to do with Don and everything to do with being there for the woman he loved. Vince frowned, looked at Shay, then smiled. Hell yes, he loved her, and he didn't intend to give up on her so easily this go round.

Don rocked back on his heels. "Regardless, I want to thank you for saving my daughter's life."

"With all due respect, sir, she's the one who knocked out Lewis inside that plane." Now the aide was cooling his heels in a cop cruiser, already spewing the names of higher-ups in hopes of securing a deal for himself.

A fine way to end this day.

Then he saw Shay walking toward them in scrubs borrowed from the EMTs. Her killer suit had taken a serious hit when she delivered the baby—an absolutely awesome moment he would never forget.

"Sir," he said to his old mentor, "I hope you know you've got an incredible daughter there."

Vince scooped up her hand and pressed a quick kiss to her cheek. Screw worrying about arguments. They would deal with their differences soon enough. Tonight was about celebrating the victory. "Your father wants to talk to you. I'll be right over there with my crew when you're ready."

With a final squeeze to her hand, he turned away, ignoring the half-stunned, half-panicked looks on Shay's and Don's faces over being left alone to talk.

Sometimes people needed a nudge. He had every confidence Shay could hold her own.

What the hell was Vince doing? Shay wanted to take hold of his big broad shoulders and shake him for leaving her here alone with her father. She scuffed her toes along the concrete, the borrowed foot covers from the EMTs doing little to protect her feet.

"Are you okay?"

Her father's words startled her even more than his voice. Vince had filled her in about what Webber had done back at the gym. It would take time to sort through how she felt about what he'd done, but she knew without question she would be visiting him in jail. "Yeah, I am. Thank you for asking." She hesitated. "And you?"

"I'm all right." He kept his hands stuffed in the pockets of his suit pants. "We handled things back at Case Western, but I'm sorry to say they had to take the boy, Webber, into custody."

"I expected that. Vince told me what happened while I was locked in the closet." She was still dealing with the shock that Webber was in so deep and that her local gang kids had such big national ties. She was lucky to be alive. "I'm glad they were able to take Webber in unhurt."

She looked up from her toes to her father. She didn't know all that had happened, but she sensed . . . "I believe I have you to thank for that."

He shrugged but didn't deny it. "I hear he's already co-operating with the police. This may not have had the outcome you wanted for him, but you still worked a change in that boy. I'm proud of you for what you're doing with those kids, for how you held your cool today."

"Guess I'm a real chip off the old block." How many times had Vince told her that? She just had to be ready to hear it, accept it.

"That's the general consensus." His eyes darted around the airport and for a minute she thought he was looking for an excuse to leave. "How's the girl? The one who had the baby?"

"She and her baby are both doing remarkably well, considering the traumatic delivery."

Shay watched the ambulance pull away. She could learn something about strength from Amber rather than the other way around. Amber had tried to be a bridge between the gangs, seeing the humanity on both sides. What a credit to how she'd maintained a gentle sweetness despite where and how she'd grown up.

Shay knew how hard it was to protect your sense of self in that kind of rough world. She'd failed to manage it herself, even with all the opportunities she'd had with a strong father figure and parents who could afford to get her help.

Her fingers gravitated to her scar, stroking by instinct. "I'm sorry for putting you and mom through so much. I've always felt guilty for wrecking things between you two."

Her dad went still, then his shoulders slumped, his fifty-six years showing. "Ah, baby girl, don't blame yourself. You have to remember things were wrecked between your mother and me long before that. It wasn't your fault or even that lazy lout of a brother of yours."

She snorted on a laugh, a much-needed laugh. "Sean's a professional student."

"Professional moocher," he grumbled but with less force and more wry humor than she could remember hearing before.

Talking this way with her father would have unsettled her a week ago. Now? Not so much. Looking death in the eye for the second time in her life left her with an overwhelming desire to live. To let all the old worries and fears go. To claim whatever happiness she could with her father.

With Vince.

She wouldn't let old insecurities rule her again.

Shay elbowed her father in the side. "Once Sean finally pulls it all together he will be infinitely hirable with all those degrees. Maybe we'll all be able to retire while he supports us for a change."

"We can only hope."

Her smile faltered, then held. "You know, Dad, this is the longest we've talked in quite a while."

Dad.

She hadn't called him that in seventeen years.

Shay held back tears. She'd missed him. And maybe somewhere down deep he'd even missed her.

He hooked an arm around her shoulders and watched the activity on the tarmac. It wasn't some warm and fuzzy hug like she'd sometimes dreamed of having from him, but this felt good. It felt right.

"Well, baby girl," he said, his arm falling away. "I need to check in with Special Agent Wilson." He looked down at her with eyes the same color as her own. "We'll talk later?"

"You can count on it."

★ TWO WEEKS LATER

Vince waited outside on the steps while Shay finished answering questions from the press after finally giving her congressional presentation.

She stood poised and in control in another va-va-vavoom suit, a traffic-stopping red one this time. Not that she needed the bold color to steal his attention.

Shay held up her hands, signaling an end to the interviews. "Thank you for your questions, for your interest, and for your support. I look forward to celebrating with you when the legislation passes, bringing a comprehensive plan to help stem this very real threat to American youths. Thank you again, and have a wonderful afternoon."

She strode through the throng of reporters, straight to him. She'd insisted she didn't want to ride away in a limo this time. No pomp and circumstance or affectation. The real Shay had gotten her this far, and the real Shay wanted to ride off in a style that reflected who she was.

Vince waited by the Ducati that he'd purchased, her helmet tucked under his arm. "Hey, beautiful, you ready to roll?"

"Absolutely." She snagged her helmet and snapped it in place. "Where are we going?"

"Do you mind being surprised?"

"Bring it on."

He wasn't sure how she would manage straddling his bike in her pencil-thin skirt, but he had fun watching her handle it with total class. She wrapped her arms around his waist, even though they both knew she didn't need to hold on.

He settled into the ride with the perfect bike and the beyond-perfect woman behind him. At first, weaving through traffic, they attracted stares. No surprise. A woman in a red suit riding behind a man in uniform demanded attention.

Once he left the city and opened up the engine along Lake Erie, it was only about Shay and him. Them and the road, leaving behind all the bad they'd survived to make it to this point.

The past two weeks had been packed with legalities. Beyond just stopping the arms shipment, the network they'd built from linking cell phone numbers would enable the FBI to corral enough criminals to keep the justice system busy for a long, long while.

Webber was cooperating with the police with the help of his attorney. The boy couldn't walk away from what he'd done, but his age had been taken into account. Vince still could hardly believe the boy was only fourteen. Kids really did start younger.

The boy's lawyer had hopes he could get Webber tried as a juvenile, which meant he could be out of jail by twenty-one. Surprising them all, Webber had made his cooperation contingent on Amber receiving placement in the witness protection program.

Brody's fate, however, would be trickier, since he was responsible for the brutal murders of both Kevin and the young student. The terrorist-recruiting CDs in Kevin's apartment had been intended to divert their attention away from Lewis's shipment.

No question about it, Lewis would be spending the rest of his life behind bars. Sadly, the bastard would probably find plenty of protection, given his strong affiliation to Los Angeles and Central American gangs. As best they could tell, California Congressman Mooney had no knowledge of Lewis's dealings, but the politician's career was likely over, all the same. A damn shame, because Mooney had appeared to be a genuine advocate for more gang legislation.

Vince squeezed extra juice from the engine, the bike surging beneath him, putting miles between them and the mess continuing to be untangled in Cleveland. He and Shay had been neck deep in questions and aiding the investigation. Ending every day in bed together, they made love and went to sleep, too exhausted and drained to talk anymore.

Yeah, he knew it was love, even if neither of them had said it yet. Soon, though. This moment had been seventeen years coming. He intended to make it one to remember.

Two mind-clearing hours later, Vince slowed the bike at their off-road destination, a private campsite he'd set up ahead of time on the Erie shore.

Shay's squeal as she leapt off the Ducati reassured him he'd chosen well.

"Camping?" Whipping her helmet off, she shook her curls loose again. "This is so perfect." Her smile brighter than the sun streaking through the trees, she gestured toward the tent, the campfire pit, a bench with fishing poles and hiking gear propped against it. "You heard what I said about loving the outdoors. You really listened."

Somehow he was the luckiest bastard on the face of the earth to have found a woman so easy to please. "I also brought changes of clothes. They're stored in the tent."

"Perfect. The suit is fun on occasion, but I miss my jeans and tank tops." She kicked off her shoes and slipped out of her suit jacket.

He rubbed from her shoulder down her arm to link fingers. He raised her arm, displaying her bared wrist, no watch in sight.

Her scar had been covered earlier this morning with a tattoo of a phoenix. The bird's body rested along the inside of her wrist, with the wings wrapping around to the front.

He squeezed her hand. "Does the tat hurt?"

"Of course it does." She swatted his shoulder, laughing. "Only a few hours ago I had needles prick my skin in a couple of million places."

He should have thought of that before he brought her out here. "There's ice in the chest."

She shook her head and cradled her wrist to her heart. "No, I want to feel it."

"Uh, I'm not tracking here."

"What I did with the cutting . . . ?" She turned her hands to flatten her palms on his chest. "The emotional pain became so overwhelming, the physical pain somehow canceled out any pain. A twisted rationale, and so horribly wrong to do to myself, but it's there."

Understanding settled inside him. "So you're saying your wrist hurts. And that's a good thing."

"Pretty much."

He held up her arm. "This is a battle scar, without question." He blew cooling air over her new tattoo. "This says you're a survivor."

"That I am." She arched up on her toes to kiss him, her lips soft and giving and a perfect fit against his.

His uniform jacket fell to the ground before he even realized she'd unbuttoned it. Not that he cared. He helped her with his shirt, then hers.

She peeled off his T-shirt then teased her fingertips along his phoenix. "We've waited a long time for what we've found together."

"You were worth waiting for."

She slid her hand up to cup his face. "I love it when you grow in the category one grooming facial hair." Her smile turned serious, her hands stroking his face tender. "Actually, Vince, I love you. I always have, even back when I was too much of a mess to know how to tell you or show you, or even how to love myself."

He kissed each palm before resting his forehead on hers. "I know you love me, and I'm so damn glad. I look forward to spending the rest of my life showing you how very lovable you are, if you'll let me. Because, Shay, I do love you, too."

He stared down into the brown eyes he knew he would be looking at for the rest of his life. For a guy scared of commitment, afraid of being some loser like his dad, he'd sure been healed fast by the hottest nurse he'd ever met.

She tickled the base of his scalp. "I guess this means I'm relocating to Las Vegas."

And she surprised him yet again. He'd been wondering how he would persuade her. "Are you okay with that?"

"The good thing and the sad thing about my job is that there are teens who need me everywhere. And I trust that Eli and Angeline are here for these kids." Her fingers played along his neck. "So, is there good camping in Nevada?"

"Absolutely."

She eased away from him, reaching behind her to unhook her bra. "And you're in Las Vegas."

He scrambled to focus on her words rather than the scrap of red satin falling away from her beautiful breasts. "Not as often as I would like, but every single minute I can manage from now on."

"Sounds good to me." She flicked away one high heel, then the other.

"Are you ready to head into the tent and help each other change clothes?" After spending some serious naked time together.

"I was thinking"—her thumbs hooked in her waistband, and she continued to back away toward the shore—"that we could go skinny-dipping and check out each other's tattoos."

"Skinny dipping sounds great, but we've already seen each other's tattoos."

She shimmied out of her skirt, a fresh hint of color flashing on her hip and reminding him he hadn't been with her the entire time at the tattoo parlor.

Blowing him a kiss, she sprinted toward the water. "*All* of our tattoos? That's what you think, Hotshot."

Turn the page for a preview of
the next Dark Ops Novel by Catherine Mann

RENEGADE

Coming soon from Berkley Sensation!

For Tech Sergeant Mason "Smooth" Randolph a great flight
was a lot like great sex.

Both brought the same rush, sense of soaring, and driving need to make it last as long as absolutely possible. On
the flip side, a bad flight was every bit as crappy as bad sex.
Both could quickly become awkward, embarrassing, and
downright dangerous.

As Mason planted his boots on the vibrating deck of an
experimental cargo plane, his adrenaline-saturated gut told
him that today's ultra-secret mission had the potential to
rank up there with the worst sex ever.

The top-notch engines whispered a seductive tune, mingling with the blast of wind gusting through the cargo door
being cranked open. Whoever came up with the idea to

drop supplies out of the back of a fast-moving aircraft must not have stood where he was standing now. Of course for that matter, nobody had stood in his boots on this sort of flight. That was the whole purpose of his job in the air force's highly classified test squadron.

He did things no one had tried before.

On today's mission, he would offload packed pallets from a test-model hypersonic cargo jet, a jet that could go Mach 6, far outpacing the mere supersonic speed of Mach 1. The deck of this new baby gleamed, high tech and totally pristine, without the oil and musty smell that accumulated over the course of many successful missions.

The metal warmed beneath his boots as the craft ate up miles faster than the pilot up front—Vapor—could plow through a buffet. If the plane completed testing as hoped, future fliers could travel from the U.S. to any point on earth in under four hours. Entire deployments could be set up and ready to roll in the matter of a single day, rather than the weeks-long buildups of the past.

No doubt, the price tag on this sleek-winged sucker was huge, but for forward thinking strategists, it saved the expense many times over by shortening deployments. Of course, money had never meant dick to him.

However, he did care about all those marriages collapsing under the strain of long separations.

Radio talk from the two pilots up front echoed in his headset as he checked his safety belt one last time, then raised his hand to hover over the control panel. His empty ring finger itched inside his glove. Yeah, this test in particular struck a personal note for him. It was too late for him since his own marriage had already gone down the tubes, but maybe he could save some of his military brethren from suffering the same kick in the ass he'd endured six years ago.

Without slowing, the cargo door cranked the rest of the way open, settling into place with an ominous thunk. Wind swirled inside, the suction increasing with the yawning gap. No more time to consider how the drop shouldn't even be possible. Not too long ago, going to the moon hadn't seemed possible. It took test pilots, pioneers. All the same, this was going to be spotty.

Mason tightened his parachute straps just in case and keyed his microphone in his oxygen mask to speak to the pilots in the cockpit. "Doors open. Ramp clear."

"Copy." From the flight deck, pilot Vince "Vapor" Deluca acknowledged. "Thirty seconds to release."

Mason scanned the cargo pallets resting on rollers built into the floor. Everything appeared just as he'd prepped for this final run before next week's big show for select military leaders from ally nations around the world. Pallets were packed, evenly balanced, and lined up, ready to roll straight out over the Nevada desert. Muscles contracted inside him as the pilot continued the countdown over headset.

"Jester two-one," Vapor continued, "is fifteen seconds from release."

Mason focused on the bundle at the front of the pallet. A void of dark sky waited only a few feet away, ready to suck up the offload. He mentally reviewed the steps as if he could somehow secure the outcome. A small parachute would rifle forward, air speed filling it with enough power to drag out the pallet. That chute would tear away, sending the pallet into a free fall until the larger parachute deployed.

"Five," Vapor counted down, "four, three, two, one."

A green light flashed over the door.

The bundle shot its mini-chute into the air behind the door. As it caught the supersonic air, the first pallet began to move, rolling, rolling, and out. One gone. The second rattled down the tracks, picture perfect, and then the next in synchronized magnificence as the mammoth load whipped out at a blurring speed.

Mason's gut started to ease. Next week's shindig for their visiting military dignitaries could be a huge win for the home team and move this plane into the inventory. A flop, however, could mean death to their government funding, an abrupt end to the whole project. He keyed up his mic.

The last pallet bucked off the tracks.

Oh shit. The load slammed onto its side with hundreds, maybe thousands of pounds of force. The cargo net ripped, flapping and snapping through the air. Gear exploded loose, catapulting every-fucking-where. He ducked as a piece of shattered pallet flew over his head.

"Smooth?" Vapor's voice filled the headset. "Report up."

Mason grappled for the button to respond while side-stepping a loose crate cartwheeling his way. The mesh net whipped around his leg and jerked him toward the open back. His feet shot out from under him.

"Smooth, damn it, radio up—"

His mic went silent. The cord rattled useless and unplugged. His helmeted head whacked the deck, sparking a fresh batch of stars to his view of the night sky.

He slapped his hands along the metal grating, grappling for something, anything to slow the drag toward the back. Would the safety harness hooked to the wall hold? Under normal circumstances, sure. These weren't normal circumstances. Everything was a first-ever test at unheard of speed.

He vise gripped the edge of a seat. The pallet dragged at his leg. He kept his eyes focused ahead, squeezing down panic, hoping, praying Vapor or Hotwire would come back to check. His arms screamed in their sockets and his legs burned from being stretched by the weight of the pallet teetering on the edge of the back hatch.

Don't give up. Hang on.

The bulkhead opening filled with a shadow. Thank God. The copilot—Hotwire—roared into view, his mouth moving as he shouted words swallowed up by the vortex of wind.

Mason's fingers slipped. The weight, the force, the speed, it was all too much. "Oh, shit."

He pulled his arms in tight as the pallet raked him along the metal floor like a hunk of cheddar against a grater. Ah damn, what about his safety harness? The strap around his waist pulled taut. An image of his body ripped in half came to mind, a snapshot that would forever stay in safety manuals to warn others of the hazards of fucking up. Not that he knew what he'd done wrong. That would be for others to decide after they buried the two halves of him in a wooden box.

Hotwire hooked his own safety belt on the run and reached. So close. Not close enough.

Mason's harness popped free from around his waist. Whoomp. The air sucked at him like a vacuum. He flew out of the back of the plane at hypersonic speed only to stop short when he slammed against the pallet, his leg still lashed by mesh. Pain detonated throughout him. Then his stomach plummeted faster than his body.

Happy Fucking New Year.

Instincts on overdrive, he wrapped his arms around the pallet. The pressure on his body eased as the pallet continued a free fall downward into the inky night. His flight suit whipped against him. Images of his ex-wife flashed though his head along with regret. A shiver iced through his veins. Was he dying?

No. The wind and altitude caused the cold. Think, damn it. Don't surrender to the whole-life-review death march.

Either he could do nothing and pray that when the larger chute opened it didn't batter him to death against the pallet. Or he could free his leg from the netting, kick away from the pallet, and use his own parachute, provided it hadn't been damaged during the haul out the back of the plane.

His options sucked ass, but at least he was still alive to fight. Getting clear of the damaged pallet seemed wisest. Determination fueled his freezing limbs. Vertigo threatened to overtake him as he kicked to untangle his boot from the netting. He jerked, pulled, and strained until, yes, his leg came free.

"Argh!" Mason grunted, muscles burning.

He shoved away just as the large chute deployed. His body plummeted, pinwheeling. The pallet was jerked to a stall by the chute, tearing apart in a shower of wood and supplies. Good God, he would have been drawn and quartered.

He reined himself in, struggling to control the fall while gauging his surroundings but the solitary void was combined with an eerie silence. How much farther until he landed? If he pulled the cord too soon, he could float forever with no sense of direction, ending up lost deep in the desert.

Screw it. Better too early than waiting too long and shattering every bone in his body by not using his parachute soon enough. He reached down, feeling along his waist until he found the handle.

He yanked. Cords whistled past and overhead. Nylon rippled upward until . . . whoomp.

Air filled the chute and yanked him. Hard. The rapid stall knocked the wind out of him and, damn it to hell, crushed his left nut under the leg strap.

He shook his head to clear his thoughts, no time to piss and moan. He grabbed a riser and hefted into a one arm pull up to ease pressure on the strap. Ahh, better, much better. Pain eased. His brain revved.

Now, how did that "You just fucked up bad and are now floating towards the earth" checklist go?

Canopy. His eyes adjusting to the dark, he checked the canopy and no rips, no tears, not even the dreaded "Mae West" where a line looped over the chute for a double bubble effect.

Visor. Little chance of landing in a tree here so he pulled the visor up.

Mask. He stripped his oxygen mask off his face, unhooked the connectors on his chest and pitched it away into the abyss.

Seat kit. Strapped to his butt, it contained a raft. Not much call for that in the desert. He opened the connector and ditched the raft, too.

LPUs. Life preserver units. He thumbed the horse collar LPU around his neck and down his chest, pulled the inflate tabs and a high-pressure bottle inflated the floatie. It might cushion the landing and save a few broken ribs. Although there was no telling what he might have already busted back in the plane. Thank goodness for the adrenaline numbing his system.

What next? Oh yeah. Steer. Damn, he was punch drunk. He reached up for the risers and grappled until he wrapped his fingers around the steering handles.

The next step? Prepare. Yeah, he was so prepared to smack into the ground he could barely see. He scanned below as best he could, checking out the sand, sand, sand, and occasional bundle of desert scrub. Okay, dude. Final step.

Land. He put his eyes on the horizon and bent his knees slightly, ready to perform the perfect PLF, parachute landing fall. The ground roared up to meet him. He prepped for . . . the . . . impact.

Balls of the feet.

Side of the leg and butt.

Side of the arm and shoulder.

Complete.

Mason lay on the gritty sand, stunned. No harm in lying still for a few and rejoicing in the fact he would live to fly and make love again. There wasn't any need to rush out of here just yet. He wasn't in enemy territory.

Although he didn't have a clue exactly what piece of the Nevada desert he currently occupied, his tracking device would bring help. Rescue would show up in an hour or so. Maybe by then he could stand up without whimpering like a baby.

He shrugged free of his parachute and LPU one miserable groan at a time. Already he could feel the bruises rising to the surface. He would probably resemble a Smurf by morning, but at least he still had all his limbs, and no bones rattled around inside him that he could tell.

His teeth chattered, though. From the freezing cold of a winter desert night or from shock? Either way he needed to get moving. He pushed to his feet, stumbling for a second before the horizon stopped bobbling.

A siren wailed in the distance.

Already? Perhaps this flight experience wouldn't suck so much after all. Even bad sex could be rescued with a satisfying ending.

He blinked to clear his eyesight. Twin beams of light stretched ahead of a Ford F-150, blinding him as the vehicle approached. He shielded his eyes with one hand and waved his other arm. Ouch. Fuck.

A loudspeaker squeaked and crackled to life. "Get back down on the ground. Lay flat on your stomach," a tinny voice ordered. "If you move at all, you will be shot."

Shot? What the hell? Had he landed on some survivalist kook's farm?

But that wouldn't explain the siren. He must have drifted into restricted territory, not surprising since they flew many of their secret test missions in secured areas. The truck screeched to halt and someone wearing cammo stepped out. A flashlight held at shoulder level kept him from seeing the face, but he could discern an M4 carbine at hip level well enough.

He shouted, "Don't shoot. I'm not armed, and I'm not resisting."

"Stay on the ground," the voice behind the light barked.

A female voice?

Okay, so much for his PC rating today. He'd assumed the security cop was a male, not that it made any difference one way or the other. He respected the power of that M4.

Mason flattened his belly to the packed desert floor, arms extended over his head. A knee plowed deep in the small of his back. If he didn't have a bruised kidney before, he sure did now.

A cold muzzle pressed against his skull. All right, then. The knee didn't hurt so much after all.

"Hands behind your back, nice and slow." The lady cop's husky voice heated his neck. "So, flyboy, do you want to tell me what you're doing out here in Area 51?"

* * *

Jill Walczak had a secret. But she was used to keeping them in her current job as one of the highly classified civilian security forces contracted to patrol the perimeter of Area 51, anonymous guards known simply as "cammo dudes." With a serial killer on the loose trying to stir up the alien conspiracy nuts, she couldn't afford to relax her guard for even a second.

"Flyboy? Nothing to say?" Keeping her M4 against his head, she carefully set her flashlight aside so it illuminated his face. "Okay, then. We'll chitchat in a minute after we take care of business. I'm not telling you another time after this. Put your hands behind your back. Slowly. Grunt if you hear me."

"Got it," he growled, his discarded parachute ruffling and snapping in the night wind.

One broad hand in a flight glove slid along the parched earth and tucked against his lower spine. His other hand started to move, inching a little too close to the flashlight for her peace of mind.

"Touch that flashlight, and I'll shoot you in the wrist."

His fingers froze.

Then he started moving his arm again, slowly, not so much as a flinch or suspicious move. Thus far he was the perfect detainee. She hoped he would stay that way.

Quickly, she set aside her weapon, locked the handcuffs around his wrists, and regained control of her M4. She was toned and trained these days, but she knew better than to underestimate the hard-muscled man in her custody. She was alone out here in the desert tonight, and she'd driven deeper into Area 51 than was normally acceptable, all because of an anonymous tip.

Was the parachuting flyboy her "something spectacular and lethal on the horizon" that would lead her to the "Killer Alien"? Four bodies—one man and three women—had shown up around Area 51 and nearby Nellis Air Force Base, all murdered in the past year, all in a manner to make it appear extraterrestrial linked.

She shivered. Desert winter nights were damn cold and desolate. But her chill settled deeper in her bones as she thought of how her friend had died.

Jill inched off her captive and scooped up her flashlight, wind kicking sand up until it stung her face. "The time for grunts has passed. Tell me what you're doing in Dreamland."

The flyboy kept his face down, nose to the gritty ground. "I work as a loadmaster and flight engineer in the U.S. Air Force. A cargo drop went to hell, and I got sucked out the back of the plane. The heavy wind tonight must have drifted me over into the box."

The box. At least this aviator spoke the flyboy lingo for Area 51.

The man cleared his throat. "Hey, do you mind if I turn my face to the side?" His muffled voice rumbled low in the night air. "I'd rather not talk through a mouthful of sand."

"Fair enough. But just your face." She did not intend to end up like those four murdered souls, sliced like a science experiment. And around their dead bodies the killer had left an eerily undisturbed sand circle. "Slowly. Then I'll need your name."

She shifted her flashlight to his mug again. The more she kept the beam on him, the less visibility he would have in the dark to see her or attempt an escape. She swiped the piercing shaft of light over his face. The chill of darker thoughts eased.

Move over Hugh Jackman.

The flyboy blinked fast, his green eyes glinting as she studied him more closely. Recognition tickled the back of her brain. She looked closer, taking in the smoothly handsome face. A tuft of dark hair twisted by a cowlick ramped in front as if refusing to submit to the military cut.

Yeah, she'd seen him around, all right.

The people working top secret jobs in this region shared certain facilities as budget savers. It wasn't uncommon to pass someone in the mess hall multiple times and have no knowledge of the other person's job or even name . . . until now. "Who are you?"

"Tech Sergeant Mason Randolph."

She'd heard him called a number of other things from the women dining at her table who he'd winked at, smiled at, flirted with, dated. They'd called him names like Smooth, Loverboy, and lastly, That Jackass.

Would he remember her when he wasn't blinded by the flashlight? She ratcheted up her grasp on his cuffed wrists.

He winced beneath her. "Hey, aren't there police brutality rules against that hold?"

"Then don't move."

"No worries, ma'am. I'm a lucky son of a bitch, so we're going to be just fine." He flashed his killer smile her way, the first time he'd turned that power on her.

She was immune.

Jill eased her knee off his back, ready to haul him up. The wind howled, tumbleweed speeding past, the parachute whipping faster, lifting. Jill yanked at the flyboy's arm to pull him aside.

The nylon sheeted forward, toward her. She barely had time to blink before it wrapped around her and her captive.

She stumbled, her feet tangling with his. "Stay still."

He did, but she couldn't. Her feet shot out from under her. Cord and nylon binding them together, he fell with her, his muscled bulk sending them tumbling.

"Damn it all," he snapped seconds before they both slammed to the ground.

His body covered hers, his leg nestling between hers. Hot breath gusted over her cheek, sending gooseflesh prickling along her skin at the possibility she could be sharing air with a monster.

She forced herself to breathe anyway. He was cuffed so she was safe. All she had to worry about was the teasing she would take at work if this part of the arrest leaked out. They were all looking for an outlet for the stress, especially with the added pressure on finding the killer and locking down security before some big shindig at Nellis Air Force Base next week. "Roll to your side, please."

"I'll try, but it would help if you freed your left boot from that cording that's lashing our feet together."

"Sure, I'm on it." She started inching her leg away.

The ground rumbled under her with an ominous reminder that anything could happen in Area 51. What the hell? She clawed at the nylon, thrashing until finally, finally, finally the parachute swooped free of their heads.

The warning rumble in the distance increased. What if Mason Randolph wasn't what the tipster had meant after all? His muscles tensed beneath her grip.

An explosion blossomed into a hazy red cloud on the horizon.